Girl on the Brink

"Such an emotional rollercoaster that makes you really see what goes through someone's head when abuse starts out so slowly. The flow in this story is flawless and to see how it ended makes me love it even more."

— Audiobook Obsession

"Reading about Chloe and Kieran's relationship was like reliving the nightmare of what my friend experienced when we were teenagers...the manipulation, the mind control, the separation from family and friends, the intimidation, and the physical abuse. And it was scary. Christina Hoag is very effective in her storytelling as she depicts the many stages of this relationship and the aftermath of its demise."

— Actin Up with Books

"The novel is well written, the story is completely believable, characters and dialogue felt realistic, and the cycle of abuse is portrayed frightfully accurately. Unlike other domestic abuse stories I have read, this one doesn't end when Chloe "frees herself. I liked that it went further into the aftermath of it all."

— AudiobookReviewer.com

"Much like Speak by Laurie Halse Anderson, Girl on the Brink is a book people NEED to read."

— Author Rachel Barnard

"All in all, I absolutely recommend this book!!!"

— Kendra Loves Books

"*Girl on the Brink* is a must read for all teenagers. It's both light and dark, happy and sad.

— Caroline Andrus, author

"This is a book all teens and women should listen to. It really brings home just how easy it is to slip into and how hard to overcome that circle of abuse."   — Rabid Reader

Girl on the Brink

Christina Hoag

Three Jandals Press

Girl on the Brink Copyright © 2016 by Christina Hoag

Third edition published by Three Jandals Press, 2022
All rights reserved.

ISBN: 979-8987188743

Three Jandals Press
Santa Monica, California, United States of America

Also by this author

Fiction
Skin of Tattoos
Law of the Jungle

Nonfiction
I Am the Famous Carlos:
The Story of the Jackal, the World's First Celebrity Terrorist
Peace in the Hood:
Working with Gang Members to End the Violence

*To all those who have experienced an abusive relationship.
You are not alone.*

One

"Chloe! Where are you?"

My heart seizes. "Just getting water. Want some?" I try to make my voice sound as casual as possible, but it's not that easy when you're in fear for your life.

The couch creaks in the living room. Shit. I guess I didn't succeed. Kieran's getting up. His footsteps thud. He's in the hallway. It's now or never. I dash for the back door, but I fumble with the lock, forgetting in my panic which way it turns to open.

"Chloe!" He's entering the kitchen. He's right behind me.

The tumbler clicks. I fling myself through the door and fly across the dark backyard into the woods.

"Come back here! Chloe! What are you doing?" He crashes into the woods behind me. I up my pace. "You think you can run away from me? Don't bother coming back, ever. Hear me? I'm done with your shit!"

My legs pump. Branches slap my face. Twigs poke the soles of my bare feet. A stick slashes my calf.

"You're not getting away from me so easy, Chloe! I know everything about you, don't forget!"

Fear fuels me. I blunder wildly in the pitch black then a bare patch of ground shines in a lacy sliver of moonlight through the trees. The trail.

I canter down the path. It comes to me suddenly. I know where I can hide. I come to the turnoff to a narrower path and veer down it. I hear Kieran thrashing through the trees behind me. I have the advantage of living next to these woods practically my whole life, but he's taller. His legs take longer strides.

My eyes adjust to the darkness, and I spot the silhouette of the log I'm looking for a couple yards in from the path. I drop to my hands and knees next to it, scraping through the dead leaves frantically.

Kieran's footsteps are nearing. It has to be here. *Come on. Come on.* My hands detect the nylon tarp. *Thank god.* I yank it up, and feet first, I drop eight feet into the party pit, landing in a crouch that sends spears of pain up my legs.

I daren't move. I draw as shallow breaths as I can, remaining in a squat as I look up. I told him about the party pit when we first met. Will he remember? I calm myself. Even if he remembers, figures out that's where I may be hiding, he doesn't know where it is. I never showed it to him. Still, Kieran always seems to have an uncanny sixth sense of knowing what I'm thinking.

I hear him jogging along the trail. He stops right next to the log. My stomach clutches. He saw me! I wait for the tarp to be thrown back, his barking laugh at seeing me caught like a mouse in its own damn trap. But he's still tramping around, panting.

I picture him pivoting as he searches for any sign of me in the woods. It occurs to me that maybe this wasn't such a good idea. If he finds me in this hole, there'd be no way to escape except fight my way out. And I'm pretty much certain to lose.

His breaths grow silent. He's gone. Relief starts to flood my muscles, then I realize I didn't hear him walk away. I tense again, remembering that he used to hunt.

He's playing possum, watching and listening for any telltale of his quarry's location. It seems an eternity until I hear his footsteps crunch on. They grow fainter, and finally silence falls. I wait another agonizing thirty seconds just to make sure, but the quiet feels real. I unfold my stiff legs and stand. The place reeks of stale cigarettes and pot. A bunch of kids dug this giant hole last spring as their subterranean party hangout, furnishing it with lawn chairs, milk crates, carpet remnants and candles.

Right now, I can see nothing. I feel around and my hands come across a beach chair, one of those low ones you can put your legs up on. I crawl onto it. I'm trembling. I guess this is the excess adrenaline in my system I read about when we covered the nervous system in biology.

I lean my head on the seat back. Gradually, anxiety subsides, replaced by a storm of thoughts as I contemplate my situation.

What have I done to my life? I'm a seventeen-year-old A student, a reporter at a local newspaper, and I'm hiding from the guy who just a few months ago I believed was my true love, an angel sent to me by heaven. I even told him that. The same guy who held my head under the bath water until I almost passed out a couple hours ago. I suddenly realize the brutal reality of what he did.

Kieran tried to kill me.

The irony of it, the absurdity of being murdered by someone I considered an "angel," of all people, hits me. I break into a soundless laugh, spasms wracking my chest as I am overcome with sadness and tears spill from my eyes. Am I laughing or crying? I don't know. I don't even know the answer to the biggest question of all:

How the actual fuck did this happen?

Two

I feel like a fish caught in a net. I'm staring into the camera's screen at my interview subject who's jabbering away, but I have this creepy sensation that somehow, *I'm* the subject. This guy is standing on the side and drilling me with his gaze, like *he's* filming *me*.

I glance sideways. Noticing me look at him, the guy grins. He *is* watching me. A hot flush spreads under my skin. I try not to feel rattled. This is the first assignment of my summer internship as a reporter for *The Indian Valley Weekly News*. I can't screw this up.

I turn back to Mr. Yamamoto, Ed as he told me to call him.

"I have a Zen garden out back that might make a good shot," Ed's saying. "Do you want to see that?"

"Sure." I jump at the chance to get rid of the looky-loo.

We plunge into the steamy air of Ed's greenhouse and wind down a path, brushing through leaves as big as platters and fern fronds dripping from hanging baskets.

We exit through a door next to a fake rock wall with a waterfall tinkling into a pond at its base. A crooked sign next to it reads: "Summer special! Garden water feature $599, installation included!"

A square patch of pebbles raked into concentric circles lies outside. The sun's glare from the bleach-white stones is so strong, I have to shield my eyes with my hand. I quickly figure out a shot that the fierce light is not going to wash out.

"Ed, why don't you sit on this rock in the shade, then I can get the garden in the background," I say, pointing to the side.

Ed perches on a boulder under the scant shadow cast by a red-leafed maple sapling.

"Hey Ed, if I'd have known you were going to be on camera, I would've done your makeup this morning," a male voice behind me calls. I know who it has to be. I roll my eyes.

"Kieran, you can put those orchids out on the table." Ed pats his glistening bald pate with a handkerchief.

So, the guy works here. That explains why he's hanging around. I thought he was a customer.

"Seriously, your face and head are going to come out all shiny," Kieran insists, stepping forward. "You should've told me. I know about this stuff."

"I'm sure we'll figure it out," Ed says.

Kieran gives me a conspiratorial "what-can-you-do?" shrug. "Make sure you get his good side," he says as he moves off.

I squeeze out a thin smile as a safe response and turn to Ed. Raising the camera, I press "record." "So, Ed, why are you organizing Indian Valley's first multicultural fair?"

"I decided to do this after that incident when anti-Semitic graffiti appeared on the synagogue. It brought back memories of when I came to this country from Japan. I was a teenager, and I had many difficulties fitting in at high school with the language, my clothes, my look. Kids weren't used to anyone different than themselves.

"I thought things had changed, but the graffiti incident made me realize they hadn't. I decided to do something about it, and I thought the best thing was a celebration of Indian Valley's multicultural population."

I hear someone shuffling behind me, Kieran no doubt. It throws me off, and the next question disappears from my tongue. "Uh..." My mind is as blank as the front page will be if I don't get this story. The words of Marion, the editor and owner of the newspaper, crash into my brain: "Just stick to who, what, when, where, how and why, and you'll be fine."

"Who's participating?" I ask in a rush of relief.

"Soi Siam, the Thai restaurant..."

Kieran's padding back and forth in the background distracts me. I force myself to focus and get through the rest of the W's and the H.

"That'll do it. I just need a photo."

"Sure. Where do you want me?"

"How about by the bonsais?" Kieran again.

What is his deal?

It's actually not a bad suggestion. I snap a couple stills of Ed with my camera as he explains the tradition of dwarfing trees by cutting their roots.

"We're done," I say.

"That's a wrap, as we say in show biz," Kieran calls. I ignore him.

As I stow my gear in my backpack, I take out one of the newspaper's business cards that Marion gave me and give it to Ed. I'd penned in my name and cell phone number.

I walk to my car in the nursery's dusty gravel parking lot. My first interview, and it went well, at least I think it did. Now I have to edit the footage for the video story, write the print article and download and edit the photos. And deadline is five o'clock tomorrow.

I'm definitely not at the high school newspaper anymore.

"Hey! Hey, Ms. Reporter!"

It can't be. I pivot. It is. Kieran has his hands thrust in the back pockets of his dirt spattered jeans, shoulders hunched, a slightly sheepish expression on his face. "Sorry, I don't know your name. I'm Kieran, Kieran Dubrowski."

He wipes his right hand on a faded green T-shirt and extends it with a smile that widens a single freckle dotting his lower lip. His dark chocolate hair is pulled back into a messy nub of a ponytail. His weirdly formal introduction takes me aback.

I shake his hand. My palm seems lost in his.

"Chloe Quinn."

"I just wanted to tell you, you did a great job."

"Thanks." I remember I'm peeved at him.

"But no thanks to you."

His smile crumples. "What do you mean?"

"You distracted me."

"I did? I didn't mean to. I was just trying to help." He tucks a loose tassel of hair behind an ear.

"Hanging around staring doesn't help. It threw me off."

"You didn't seem thrown off at all. You acted like a real pro. I figured you were used to people watching you. I mean, that must happen all the time, right?"

"Not exactly, no." I don't want to confess that I haven't actually done this before, at least professionally. I feel the intensity of his gaze again, soaking me up in his coffee-colored eyes. I shift my feet.

"I'm really an actor. I just work here to eat, you know?"

Intrigue tugs me. "Are you in movies or TV shows?"

"I've been in a couple plays. I have an audition for a TV commercial coming up."

"Kieran!" Ed booms. "Customer carryout!"

Kieran arches his eyebrows. "Gotta go. Nice meeting you."

He hurries off, and I stroll to my car. What Kieran said to Ed about makeup makes sense now. An actor would know about that, and he'd be naturally interested in the filming. He did suggest the bonsai shot. Maybe I misjudged him.

Despite the shade from the "Yamamoto's Garden Center" sign, my car is an oven. Cranking the AC full blast, I wait for a gap in the traffic to pull into the street. I glance in the rearview mirror. Kieran's carrying a tray of pansies across the lot, but he's looking right at me. I glance away. The road clears. I press the gas and head home.

Entering the kitchen, I place my backpack on the table. "Mom?" I call. No answer.

The house is super quiet and super big in the way that houses are when you're the only one in them. I'm not actually the only one here, although it feels that way.

Mom's car is in the garage but she's no doubt lying down. She's been doing a lot of that since Dad left after spring break. I mean left left, as in moved-out-of-the-house left.

It came as a real shock. My parents never argued or yelled at each other. Neither me nor my fourteen-year-old brother, Tyler, had an inkling that anything was up.

My parents had always seemed like they were a unit, a big rock, but now the rock had a gaping crack in it. When things happen like your parents splitting up, it kind of shakes your whole world, turns it upside down. One minute everything's so normal, it's boring. The next, well, life is crumbling like a stale brownie. And you can't put crumbs back into a brownie.

I know things have changed forever.

I'm surprised to see a pepperoni pizza and a six-pack of vanilla cupcakes with strawberry frosting on the counter. This means Mom actually remembered I'm going over to Clarissa's and went out to the supermarket. A small miracle. There've been a couple times when she was so out of it that we ran out of food and I had to go get the groceries.

Encouraged by the fact that Mom got herself out of the house, I check her small studio off the living room—maybe she's sculpting again, but the room is untouched, as it has been for the past three months. Nothing new except for another layer of dust covering her tools and the sheet over the piece she was working on when Dad split.

I trot up the stairs. "Mom?" I call again.

Maybe she's sorting laundry or something. I enter her bedroom. Disappointment crushes me. She's lying on her side in bed, back facing me. She's wearing her bathrobe, her hair all mussed.

I'm so sick of seeing her night and day in that frigging bathrobe, its deep apricot color faded to a pukey yellow, the cuffs and collar fraying.

I want to wrench it off her, throw it in the garbage, yell at her to get dressed in real clothes. Instead, I say, "Thanks for the pizza and cupcakes."

She rolls onto her back. Her face is pale with charcoal-dark smudges underneath her eyes, which have a weird glassy look. People always say I look like her. I would never have pegged us as mother-daughter, but I guess you don't see yourself as others see you.

I have her auburn hair and lima-bean-green eyes, but she has a straight nose and small eyes. I have a ski-slope nose and almond eyes. I'm taller. Unfortunately, I inherited her flat butt.

She pulls her mouth into a smile as if it's a huge effort to make her facial muscles move. She's obviously taken those pills again. I sit next to her on the bed and take her hand. It's limp and clammy. She licks her sandpapery lips. The pills give her dry mouth.

"How was your first interview?"

"Great. Ed Yamamoto showed me his Zen garden, his bonsai collection. I think I got good shots to make an interesting video story."

Mom smiles wanly.

"How was your day?" I ask.

She hikes a shoulder in a semblance of a shrug. I drop that line of questioning.

"I'm going over to Clarissa's now. Can I get you anything before I go?"

"I got you pizza and cupcakes to take."

"I saw them, Mom, thanks." She's already forgotten that I thanked her for them. "Have you eaten today? You have to eat, you know."

"Some water maybe."

I fetch her a glass of cold water. How long is she going to stay like this?

She sits up to drink it and downs almost the whole thing. "Hear anything from Tyler?"

"Mom, you ask that every day. He's probably too busy playing soccer." I don't mention that he's mad at her for sending him to sleepaway camp, so why would he call her unless he had to?

I fling my arms around her shoulders and hug her. The pizza and cupcakes mean there's still a smidgen of the old Mom in there somewhere. She's not all gone. She pats my back faintly.

I refill her glass and leave it on a coaster on her bedside table. She's already zonked out again. I change into cutoffs and flip-flops, grab the food and my purse.

At the last minute, I take the tripod for the phone, too.

Clarissa's leaving tomorrow to be a counselor-in-training at the Blue Mountain camp in the Poconos in Pennsylvania. The summer looms long without her.

Home has definitely changed—Dad's physical absence hovers like a ghostly presence, and Mom's physical presence hovers like a ghostly absence. And now I won't have Clarissa's house as a refuge.

We both live in the section of Indian Valley called the Knolls. I drive through winding streets of two-story houses and yards filled with azaleas and hedges. The one perk to Dad's departure is that I get to use his car.

He moved to an apartment in Manhattan, where he works, so he doesn't need a car to commute and does all his errands on foot. When he comes out to visit us, which has happened exactly twice since he left, he rents a car to make the forty-minute drive to our New Jersey suburb, Indian Valley.

After parking on the curb in front of Clarissa's house, I head around the side to the back, where I glide open the sliding-glass door into the kitchen. No one's around.

"Helloooo. Blue Mountain mamaaa."

"Chlo, I'm up here," Clarissa calls.

Leaving the pizza and cupcakes on the kitchen island, I bound up the stairs three at a time and enter her bedroom.

"Hey Riss."

She sits cross-legged on the floor surrounded by a duffel bag and piles of clothes.

"I'm just starting to pack. I can never decide what to take."

"Check this out." Grinning, I whip out my *Indian Valley Weekly News* business card.

Her eyes widen as she studies it. "You're the only kid I know with a business card." She frowns. "Aren't you going to put your middle initial?"

"You think I should?"

"I don't know. Seems like a business card should be formal."

"Chloe A. Quinn. Or I could put my full middle name—Chloe

Ann Quinn."

"Or how about C.A. Quinn? Like J.K. Rowling or C.S. Lewis."

"Then people would call me C.A."

"You're right. Doesn't have a ring to it. Just stick with Chloe."

"Hey, I brought pizza. Let's eat. I'm starved."

"Genius idea."

"It's in the kitchen. Cupcakes, too."

Clarissa springs up. "What are we waiting for?" Our feet ripple down the stairs and land with a thud on the first floor.

Clarissa nukes slices on paper plates and hangs on to the microwave oven door waiting for the beep. "That internship is going to look so good on your college apps. I wish I knew what I wanted to be."

"The counselor-in-training will look good—leadership skills. Colleges eat that stuff up." I take out a jug of lemonade from the fridge and pour two glasses.

"Yeah, but I wish I had a real career plan. I don't want to waste my time in college studying something for nothing." The microwave beeps, and Clarissa slides out the plates. "Ow, that's hot." She sucks a fingertip.

"A lot of people don't know what their major is at first. I always liked writing, so I joined Daze of Our Lives at school and then I knew I wanted to be a reporter."

"See? That's what I mean. You love writing. Jade loves animals so she wants to be a vet. I don't have anything that I love."

"You'll figure it out. Where's your mom?"

"Went to get Hailee from gymnastics. Let's eat in my room since she's not here."

We take the pizza, lemonade, plenty of paper towels, and the cupcakes upstairs, and picnic on the floor.

"I can't believe you're going to be gone the whole summer again," I say.

"I'm gone every summer." She pinches off a string of cheese trailing like a cobweb from her mouth.

"I know, but still."

"I thought about staying at home this year, but since I got the counselor job…"

"You should do it, definitely."

"I'm just freaking that Caleb is going to forget all about me."

I roll my eyes. This is the real reason Clarissa considered staying home—her latest crush on this jerk, er, jock. They made out at a party a month ago. Clarissa's been expecting him to ask her out since then, but he's basically ignored her.

She doesn't seem to be getting the message that he's not into her, and I'm more than a little tired of hearing about every Caleb-sighting, who he was talking to, what he was wearing, etc., etc.

Clarissa has a new crush practically every month. None of them ever develop into anything, but this one's lasting longer than usual, I guess because she had actual contact with him.

"I don't know, Riss. Since he hasn't made a move by now, maybe he's not going to. Maybe it was just a one-night thing."

Clarissa drops her pizza crust onto the plate. "He was really into me that night. I think he's just shy. You've never been into a guy, so you don't know how it is."

Shy? Mr. Football Quarterback? I let it go. "Cupcake?" I nudge the box toward her.

She eyes them dubiously. "I don't really like Pantry Market cupcakes."

Meaning they're cheap supermarket cupcakes, not the gourmet kind from the Cupcakerie. Annoyance nips me. Clarissa can be such a snob sometimes.

"Fine, don't eat them then. I'll take them home."

"Promise me you'll keep an eye out for Caleb around town. Jade and Morgan are going to do that, too."

"Too bad your phone doesn't work up there."

"I know. Major bummer." She moves the picnic remains to the side. "I better pack."

I want a cupcake, but Clarissa has kind of ruined them for me now. I lie on my side on her bed, propping my head on a hand, watching her zip a small, fuschia-colored cosmetics bag and toss it in the duffle.

"You're taking makeup?"

She grabs the bag, unzips it, and displays a square packet in her fingers.

"Condoms?"

"Always better to be prepared. You never know who you'll meet."

"Is that guy, what's his name—Matt?, going to be there this year?"

She makes a face. "I hope not. I didn't like him that much. I only did it with him to say I did it."

"And because he lives on Long Island, so you won't get gossiped about."

"Exactly." She holds up an orange vee-necked, Lycra ie. tight-fitting, T-shirt. "Should I take this?"

"Don't you wear camp T-shirts every day?"

"I might need something else." She flips it into the bag.

"Clarissa! Come and get your laundry out of the dryer already." Her mom.

We look at each with scared faces. "Do you think she heard us?" Clarissa whispers.

"We weren't talking loudly."

"Coming!" Clarissa uncrosses her legs and stands.

While she's gone, I check out her collection of snow globes from all different places. I shake the globes one by one, making the flakes flutter down and turn the cheesy little plastic monuments inside into mini-wonderlands.

I've always wanted a cool collection like that. I tried stamps, but that seemed too nerdy, then I tried salt-and-pepper shakers, but that seemed dumb. I had a bunch of shells from a trip to my grandmother's in Florida, but most were chipped, and shells weren't as cool as snow globes anyway. Eventually, I gave up on the idea of collections.

I shake the last globe—San Francisco's Golden Gate bridge, and remember I brought my video camera.

I hustle as I hear Clarissa shuffling up the stairs, and I'm ready with the camera when she enters holding a pile of freshly laundered undies. I press record. She hams it up right away, as I knew she would, pretending to be a model, swishing her hips this way and that. She puts down the clothes and picks up a cupcake. She bites into it and leers into the lens.

"Simply the most scrumptious cupcakes, dahling," she says in an exaggerated British accent. She places one on top of her head and struts. "You can also use them to improve your posture."

She balances another cupcake on the ends of several fingers. "Practice finger-twirling, or both at the same time." The finger-held cupcake falls with a splat of frosting on the carpet.

She grabs another cupcake and quickly smushes it into the side of my face. I put down the video camera and get her back. We're now decorated in pink and white frosting.

"I want a selfie of us," she says.

I pick up the camera and aim it at us, cupcaked faces squeezed together as we crack up.

Clarissa's mom calls up the stairs. "Girls, what are you doing? Have you finished packing, Clarissa?"

Hailee, Clarissa's younger sister, appears in the door. "They're having a cupcake fight, Mom."

Clarissa tosses a pillow at Hailee, who dodges it with a squeal. "Mo-om!"

"Tattle-tale," Clarissa says.

The moment is over. "I better wash my face and get going," I say.

We scrub our faces in the bathroom and go downstairs. I say hi to her mom in the kitchen, and we walk outside.

"Save that video for me," Clarissa says.

"I will. I'll edit it into a little piece. I'll call it 'Frosted Faces'. We'll be seniors when you get back. Can you believe it?"

"Chloe, we're already officially seniors."

I mock-wag my finger at her. "Hey, don't do anything I wouldn't do."

"Forget that. Then I'll never have any fun."

We hug, and I get in my car, feeling a little lonely already. I have Jade and Morgan to hang out with, but they're not the same. I've been best friends with Clarissa since seventh grade.

I drive home. My phone rings as the garage door hums closed. Clarissa. I answer without checking the screen.

"You miss me that much already, Riss?"

"Er, Chloe?" a guy says.

"Yes." I frown, wondering who on earth it could be.

"It's Kieran, you know, from Yamamoto's?"

Did Ed tell him to call me?

"Listen, I feel really bad about what you said, about throwing you off today."

It's not about the story. I relax. "Don't worry about it. No big deal."

"No, really, I'd like to make it up to you. Do you want to grab a burger or something tomorrow night?"

"You don't have to do that."

"Unless your boyfriend wouldn't like it."

"No. No, I mean, I don't have a boyfriend."

"So, you'll go out with me then?"

It hits me that he's asking me on a date. This is the type of thing that only happens in movies, not to me. I suddenly feel embarrassed.

"Well, uh, yeah, I guess, okay."

"Cool. I thought of it as you were leaving today. I was willing you to turn around and come back, but I guess my mental telepathy was off."

I giggle. "How did you get my number?"

"I found your card on Ed's desk, and I said to myself 'Hey, what do you know? It's meant to be.' How 'bout I pick you up at the News office when you get off?"

"I'm off at six."

I hang up. I have a date! The timer on the garage light switches off, swamping me in darkness.

Three

It's not even nine o'clock in the morning, but the muggy heat is already making me sweat through my blouse. I walk across the parking lot to the storefront office of *The Indian Valley Weekly News*, "Your Community Source," and push on the grimy glass door. It opens with a jangle of bells.

I'm still trying to get used to the idea that I'm a real reporter now, covering real stories, not just asking kids about the band trip to Washington D.C. or the new "healthy" lunches for the school paper.

Marion's on the phone. "That's what I'm saying, Raymond. I need to be paid in cash. I can't pay my bills in dry cleaning ... All right then, I'm taking out the ad for this week."

She crashes the phone into its cradle, whipping off her glasses and tossing them onto the desk. She rubs her eyes, then looks up as I deposit my gear on my desk.

"Raymond's Cleaners. He always tries to pay for his ads in dry cleaning. What does he think I run this place on? Clean clothes? I go through this every month with him. Pain in my ass."

I nod, unsure of what to say to that.

"How'd it go with Yamamoto yesterday?"

"Good. I'm going to start editing it now."

"Write up the print story first. The paper goes to press tonight. We don't have to post the video until tomorrow."

Marion heaves to her feet, surprisingly quickly considering her rather large bulk, and waddles down the aisle flanked by three desks piled high with yellowing newspapers. The only occupied desks are Marion's and mine. We're the sole employees, besides a stringer who covers high school sports.

The water cooler gurgles in the back as I wait for my ancient computer to power up.

Marion Martinelli bought the *Weekly News* five years ago after being laid off from *The New York Times* where she'd been a reporter and editor for years. My English teacher Ms. Margolis said interns could learn a lot from her so even though the internship only pays a stipend to cover gas, I practically busted my bra strap when I shot up my hand to apply. To my surprise, I got the job after submitting several of my clips from the school paper and an interview, which I thought I'd bombed.

Marion lumbers back to the front of the office, stopping at my desk. Her upper lip is dewed with perspiration although the AC is cranked up. She takes a gulp from her paper cup of water.

"Remember, do not, on any account, ever write 'first annual' when you refer to the multicultural fair. An event cannot be annual if it's the first one. We should also get a man-on-the-street quote about the idea of such a fair and someone else—maybe some organization like B'Nai Brith—to comment.

"Aim for at least two sources in every story. Don't forget to put in the background about the graffiti on the temple. You can look up the archive online. It's on the home page. Got it?"

I gulp. "Yes, um, what's a man-on-the-street quote?"

"Joe Schmo. Just go to the Pantry Market and ask someone what they think of the idea. Get their name, age and occupation." Marion plonks into her chair and picks up the phone.

I take a deep breath and jot down what I have to do. I look up the archive on the graffiti, then call B'nai Brith. I talk to a person in "media relations," who praises the idea of a multicultural fair. I run out to the Pantry Market to get an opinion from a "Joe Schmo." I find a stay-at-home mom who thinks it's a great idea.

By lunchtime, I have all my pieces to assemble the story. I don't stop to eat the sandwich I brought from home. I plunge into writing, erasing, rewriting, re-erasing, as the hands on the clock keep moving around the dial. At four-forty-five, I have no choice but to go with what I've written. Crossing my fingers, I file the story.

"Pull up a chair and watch as I edit," Marion says over her shoulder, her fingers still clacking at the keys. "It's the best way to learn."

I watch as Marion tightens up my lede, the first paragraph, deleting extraneous words, then announces I'm missing a "nut graf." "That's where you tell the reader what your story is in a nutshell. Like this."

She writes in the paragraph and proceeds through the rest of the story. "You also don't have a kicker. Your story just breaks off. You have to have an ending. Let's take this quote from Ed and make it the kicker." She cuts and pastes, and suddenly the story has a neat ending.

"Are you going to take my name off the article?" It seems like nothing's left of what I actually wrote.

"That's what editors are for. By the way, your name is called a 'byline.' Considering this was your first story, it wasn't bad at all. How far did you get with the video?"

Crap. I haven't even started it. "Can I finish in the morning?"

"That's fine. What about the photos?"

"They're in my camera."

"Download them and be quick about it. I'll write the cutlines this time, but in the future, you'll have to write them."

Cutlines? I guess she means captions. How am I ever going to learn all this?

I literally just finish sending the photos to Marion when the doorbells jangle. I look up, and my gut constricts. Kieran! I totally forgot about our date. His eyes laser-beam on me, and he grins as he halts at my desk.

"So, this is a newsroom." Kieran sticks his hands on his hips and looks around with interest.

I glance over at Marion, worried about her reaction. She's absorbed in the "cutlines."

"Yep." I shut off the computer and stand.

"Good job today," Marion calls. "I'll show you the police blotter tomorrow."

"That your boss?" Kieran asks as the door closes behind us.

"Yeah, that's Marion. She's a media mogul in tent tops and polyester pants."

Kieran laughs. "Sounds like she likes you."

"I don't know."

"Take it from me, Chloe, she likes you."

He opens the door of a battered, navy-blue pickup truck parked in the red zone at the curb, sweeping his arm and bowing his head in an old-fashioned gallant gesture.

I suck in my lower lip. "I'm really sorry, but I got behind today. I finished the print story, but I have to do the video tonight. I should've called you, but I was so freaked by deadline and..."

"Aren't you going to eat dinner?"

"Well, yeah."

"So, what's the difference if you eat with me or eat at home?"

"Uh..."

"Have dinner with me then go home and work on the video. You're hungry, right?"

In truth, I'm famished. "As a matter of fact, I never even ate lunch."

"So, hop in." He gestures again at the truck.

I smile and slide into the front seat.

"There's always a solution," he says, getting behind the wheel. His eyes twinkle.

"By the way, I saw the meter maid give someone a ticket for parking at the curb yesterday," I say. "Maybe you ..."

I halt midsentence as Kieran reaches over and pops open the glove box. A sheaf of crumpled parking tickets tumbles out.

"That's what I think of parking tickets. People should be able to park where they want. I mean, they talk about this being a free country, right?"

He pulls out as I stuff the spilling tickets back into the glove compartment and shut it.

"So where are we going?" I ask.

"Burger-O-Rama all right with you?"

"Sure." I finger a wooden peace sign dangling from his rearview mirror. "This is cool."

"That's an old thing, my dad's."

"I like it. He was a hippie?"

"Something like that."

Burger-O-Rama is down Indian Valley Road, the main street that cuts through the center of town. I push a wayward strand of frizzed hair from my eyes. I haven't even brushed my hair, touched up my makeup, cleaned my teeth, changed my sweaty blouse. I'm royally screwing up this date. We pull into Burger-O-Rama.

"Wait!" Kieran commands as I place my hand on the door handle. He jumps out and runs around to my door, ceremoniously opening it.

I smile. "You didn't have to do that. I can open my own door."

"Chloe, cut me a break. This is our first date. I'm trying to impress you." He leans in conspiratorially. "Is it working?"

I crack up because it actually is working. I like him more than I did at Yamamoto's.

He takes my laughter as a yes and mock-wipes sweat off his brow. "Whew!"

He opens the restaurant door for me, releasing a blast of cool air, and we line up at the crowded counter.

"I'm having a veggie burger and root beer," Kieran says. "I try to avoid fatty foods. I've got to stay lean and mean for acting. The camera puts ten pounds on you."

"Shouldn't you drink diet soda then?"

"Chloe, I can't give up *every*thing. I've drunk root beer since I was a little kid. My dad always drank it. I guess it's kind of old-fashioned. Hardly any places have it, that's why I always come here."

"I've never tried veggie burgers," I confess.

His eyes spark. "Now's your chance. You gotta try new things, right?" I nod. "Now you'll remember me forever—your first veggie burger. You always remember firsts."

He's right.

Since all the tables are full, we take our tray to an outside table under an umbrella. Kieran reaches over the table and plucks loose a hair stuck on my lips, like I've known him forever.

"You have a cool job, a regular Lois Lane." He slurps his root beer.

"Well, I hope to be." I bite into my veggie burger. It's surprisingly tasty, although I'm so hungry anything would taste good to me right now.

"Good?" Kieran chin-points to my burger as he chews.

I nod as my mouth is full.

He smiles. "So, you're a...senior?" He's doing it again, studying me like a painting in a museum.

"Yep, good ol' Indian Valley High."

"I just graduated. I squeaked by. School was never my thing."

"How come?"

"Most of the crap they teach you'll never need in life. I mean, are you really going to need to know the value of pi, the periodic table of elements, or the past imperfect tense in some language? It's just not practical stuff."

"A lot of high school stuff is really dumb, like cheerleaders. Why do teams need cheerleaders? People can cheer without being led. And why aren't there boy cheerleaders for girls' teams?"

Kieran throws back his head and laughs. "Totally."

"And yearbooks. I mean, according to yearbooks, everyone's super happy. Everybody plays on a team or in the band. Everyone's got tons of friends because even people who hate you write corny stuff like 'Have a great summer' and 'See you next year' on the inside covers. Read a yearbook and you think no one wakes up with pimples, fights with their parents, gets grounded, goes high to class. That's really what high school is about. None of my friends agree with me. They think cheerleaders and yearbooks are great."

"You're just smarter than they are. You probably get all A's."

"Well, I'm in the National Honor Society."

"I figured you for the brainiac type. I like smart girls. Reporters need to be smart."

"Actually, I want to be a foreign correspondent. So where did you go to school? I never saw you at Indian Valley."

"I'm from Crystal Lake."

Crystal Lake is the next town over from Indian Valley, a town of clapboard houses with pickup trucks in the driveways, men who wear beards, baseball caps and jean jackets, and women with tattoos, too much mascara and lank hair.

"I know what you're thinking," Kieran says. "Crystal Lake sucks, but I got out of there, and I'm not going back."

How did he read my mind? "No, I wasn't thinking that at all."

"I know you were. I can tell things about people." He shrugs. "S'okay. It's all true. I cut outta there soon as I graduated. I was already working part-time for Ed, and when he hired me full-time, I moved into a camper this lady owns down by the river. It's parked in her driveway. She lets me use her washing machine and shower in the basement. I can even use her computer and Internet hookup. I do a few odd jobs for her around the place, help her out so she doesn't charge me much rent. It's a pretty good deal."

"So, you're eighteen?"

"Nineteen. And you—let me guess—seventeen?"

"Just turned seventeen. May twenty-fourth."

"Get out! I'm the twenty-fourth of April. That's so unreal!"

He gets so excited, like a little kid at his birthday party, that I have to laugh. He joins in. His laugh sounds like a seal bark, which makes me crack up even more. We're laughing so hard that other people turn to look at us.

When I stop spluttering, I become aware that Kieran is no longer laughing. He's leaning on the table, head propped on an arm, a smile of amusement dancing on his lips as he watches me, drinking me like a tall glass of cool water.

"Chloe, you are so beautiful."

No one has ever told me that. I've never thought of myself as "beautiful." My eyes lock with his, and I slip right into his smile.

"Beauty is in the eye," he says, somewhat mysteriously. "You're not used to getting compliments, I can tell. So, I'm going to give you another one—your hair looks radiant in the sun, like the halo of an angel."

I feel a blush creeping over my face. He's right, again. I'm not used to compliments. I downplay the one he's just given me. "I cut it every summer. It gets really hot. It's like wearing a cape on my head."

"Oh no, I love long hair. I'll spank you if you cut it."

"My mom never let me have long hair when I was little because she didn't want the hassle of brushing it. I looked like a boy with some of the haircuts she gave me. I guess that's why I have it extra-long now."

"My mom practically shaved my head every summer. That's why I have mine long now, too."

The crickets buzz as dusk falls. The outdoor lamps switch on, flooding us with light.

"I better get home. I have to start on this video and check on my mom."

"How come? Is she sick?"

I hesitate, then it all pours out—my parents' split and Mom's shipwreck. Kieran listens intently, his eyes grave. When I finish, I feel a little embarrassed.

"Sorry, TMI, right?"

"Why sorry? You need to talk about it. That's heavy stuff, Chloe. That's a lot for you to handle. I don't tell a lot of people this, but my dad walked out when I was a kid. We never heard from him again."

"That's awful."

He shrugs with one shoulder. "I got over it."

"You know what I'm secretly scared of, and I never told anyone this, that I'm going to come home one day and find Mom overdosed on pills."

Kieran nods. "My dad was into drugs, all kinds. I know exactly how you feel."

I look at his somber face. "You do, don't you?" I whisper. "You do know how I feel."

He gently kisses the palm of my hand. "Come on, I better get you home."

As we walk to the truck, he wraps his arm around my waist and kisses the top of my head. I lace my arm around him. It's like we've known each other for a million years.

We drive back to my car in easy silence, his hand resting on top of mine on the front seat. I point out my car to him, and he pulls up behind it.

"I had a great time, Chloe. I knew I would."

"I had a great time, too."

"You weren't sure at first, right?"

"Well ..."

"I'm like a rash. I grow on people."

I burst out laughing, and he joins in.

"You want to go out again?" He hikes his eyebrows in a question.

I bob my head up and down like a dashboard dog.

"Awesome." He kisses me on the cheek.

I get out of the truck. He waits until I start driving, then follows me out of the lot. We turn in opposite directions to go our separate ways. I keep glancing in the rearview mirror to follow his taillights until they melt into the traffic.

I float into the kitchen on the cloud of my evening, which immediately deflates when I see Mom in her bathrobe. She's heating something in the microwave. At least she's eating.

"You're working late," she says.

I wonder whether to tell her the truth or just say I was at the paper. I opt for the latter.

"I had a busy day, and I still have to get my video piece done. How are you?"

The microwave beeps. She gingerly takes out a bowl of tomato soup and places it on the table.

"Oh, you know, trying to figure out stuff."

"Has Dad called? He's supposed to be taking me on the NYU campus tour a week from Saturday."

She toys with the tail of her bathrobe sash. "I don't know what I did, Chloe. He just came out of the blue and said he wanted a divorce."

Divorce! The D-word hasn't been mentioned before. I thought

they had just separated, which of course might lead to divorce, but it also wasn't divorce. I sink into a kitchen chair as she sits at the table.

"I asked him if there was somebody else and he said no. He just wanted to make changes in his life. In other words, get rid of me. Throw twenty years away overnight. Like a piece of garbage."

Her eyes water. I feel a crack inside me. I don't remember ever seeing my mother cry.

"Don't cry, Mom. Please. We'll be all right." I kick myself for mentioning Dad. I'm never going to bring him up again. Never ever.

She sniffs and wipes her eyes with the sash. "I'm sorry. I'm not much of a mother, am I?"

The crack splinters like a broken mirror. "You're the best, Mom, the best." I hug her and her shoulders shudder under my arms.

She breaks away, tears spilling. "I better take another pill. I just can't stop crying." She gets up and crosses to a cabinet, where she takes out a pill bottle.

I want to flush those meds down the toilet. "Those pills turn you into a zombie. Why do you have to take them?"

"I just need them for a little while until I get through this. I'll be okay."

"What if you become addicted or overdose?"

She slaps her cupped palm against her mouth and gulps down the pill with a glass of water. I can't stand seeing it. I gallop up the stairs and slam my door shut.

I'm furiously brushing my teeth a few minutes later when my phone beeps. It's a text from Kieran.

I just wanted to say goodnight to a beautiful girl.

The taut rope inside me loosens.

I pirouette out of the bathroom. I hem and haw over my reply, typing and erasing a gazillion messages. I finally opt for simple.

Goodnight & sweet dreams.

I will dream of you then, he replies instantly.

I switch on my laptop to do the video, my head buzzing.

I've never been a member of that exclusive club of girls wearing halves of gold hearts around their necks, boyfriends' class rings or letter jackets. On the last Valentine's Day flower sale, Clarissa and me sent each other carnations to pretend we had admirers.

The sum total of my experience is three boys—makeout sessions with two and all-the-way with one.

Buddy Ambrosiano was the first guy I made out with—sitting on the curb in the shadow of the Corolla he was working on in his driveway. He's the older brother of a guy Jade knew.

"You're very passionate," he murmured in my ear at our first tongue break. I didn't know quite what that meant, but I took it that he liked me. So, I called him up the next week.

"This is Chloe."

A second of puzzled silence. "Who?"

"Chloe. I was with Clarissa and Jade. We met at your house last Friday? We, uh, sat on the curb?"

"Oh, yeah. I remember."

I should've got the hint then and just hung up, but I barreled on like the naïve idiot I was. "Um, you want to hang out some time?"

"Uh, okay."

"Friday maybe?"

"How 'bout I meet you in the parking lot of Dairy Cream? Seven?"

I hung up. A guy was interested in me!

That Friday night, I walked down to the DC, arriving fifteen minutes early. Buddy bounced up in his Corolla with jacked up rear suspension in a boom of heavy metal music. He greeted me with a grin. "Hop in," he yelled.

The music was too loud to talk. Since he was in the cool crowd, I figured he'd have something exciting planned, like a party.

We drove to a dark cul-de-sac in a housing development under construction. He parked and rolled down the windows. This was it? It wasn't exactly my idea of a date.

His idea involved a lot of traveling hands and wet mouths. I was willing to go along until he tried to unbuckle, unbutton and unzip. I kept pushing him away, like a dog sticking its nose between my legs.

"What's the matter?" He sat back in his seat.

I looked down at my hands twisting in my lap. "I just ... I don't want to do that." My voice sounded tiny, like it came out of a chemistry lab pipette.

He exhaled loudly and looked out the window. "Have you done this before?"

I shook my head.

"Jeez." He combed his hair with his fingers. "I thought that's why you called me."

"I thought you liked me," I squeaked.

He turned the ignition key. "Where do you live?"

I made him drop me off around the corner from the house and I shuffled home, feeling as shriveled as a raisin. I had made a total fool out of myself. How could I have been so stupid? He didn't like me at all. I was lucky he didn't rape me. If he had, I wouldn't have told anyone, absolutely no way. I was too ashamed. Fortunately, I never ran into him again.

Dan Levin, my ballet teacher's little brother with a pudding-bowl haircut, was pretty much the same. After a milkshake at the diner, we ended up making out in a thicket of trees behind the place. Dan was getting sweaty and breathing heavily, then he grasshoppered my hand onto his crotch. I snatched it back.

"Well, aren't you going to...?" He gestured south with his head. I didn't really know what he meant, but I wasn't going to find out. I got up and left. I texted him the next day that I wouldn't be seeing him again.

The message couldn't be clearer if it was announced on the football field PA. If I wanted a boyfriend, I had to put out—right away, or it was no go. Sex was what lay behind the initials in hearts scratched on bathroom walls and the doodles on binders and notebooks, but girls never talked about that. They just showed off the love notes, the hickeys, the rings, like boys were really into them. Since girls weren't supposed to be "easy," they pretended they weren't. It was all a big show.

So, when Angus Magillicuddy groped me at a party one night, I knew what I had to do to turn him into a "boyfriend." It happened in the absent parents' bedroom. In five minutes, it was done—and totally overrated in my opinion—but it worked. He plugged my number into his phone. He called me up the next day and invited me to come over and "watch TV." I was in. I had joined the club!

On the third invitation to "watch TV," I realized Angus Magillicuddy wasn't interested in being a real boyfriend and going out on dates. I was just being used. I told him I wouldn't be "watching TV" anymore.

Kieran seems different from those jerks. He took me on a real date. He listened to me. He wanted to know about me and my life. He didn't try to stick his tongue in my mouth.

Maybe I finally found a guy who liked me for me, not just to get in my pants.

I stare at the laptop screen. It's no use. I can't concentrate on the video. I decide to go to bed and wake up early to do it. I set my alarm and slip between my sheets. With Kieran buzzing in my head, I fall asleep.

I bound out of bed at five a.m. and get the video done in record time. As I enter the newsroom, a chemical odor hits my nose. A stack of fresh newspapers sits by the door. There's a box of doughnuts next to it on a desk.

I can't wait to see how my story turned out, but I have no time to check it out.

"Chloe, the paper's already gone out for delivery. I need to post that video," Marion barks.

I upload the video. "Ready, Marion."

As soon as I hear Ed Yamamoto's voice coming from her computer, I grab a paper. It's fresh off the press, still slightly damp with wet ink. My story is front page above the fold: *Multicultural Fair Aims to Celebrate Diversity by Chloe Quinn.* Excitement pings me as I flatten out the newspaper to read it.

Staticky voices clamor from the police scanner.

"We got a house fire over near the river," Marion calls. "Head over to this address. Got your video camera?" She rips off a sheet of notebook paper, sending a shower of powdered sugar from the doughnut in her other hand onto the shelf of her chest. "Call in as soon as you get something."

I seize a jelly doughnut as I fly out the door.

I don't really need the address. Billows of black smoke in the sky pinpoint the fire's location. I park beyond the barrier restricting access to the street, and ready my video camera as I stride to a small crowd watching massive orange flames engulf the house, hands over their mouths in shock.

Coughing as a breeze blows smoke my way, I aim the camera at the firefighters hosing the blaze. The roof caves in with a thunderous crack, sending up a spray of sparks. The crowd gives a collective gasp.

My phone rings. It's Marion. "Whatta ya got?"

"Not much."

"Just describe the scene."

As I tell her what I see, I hear her clacking away superhumanly fast at the keyboard. She stops.

"Good. Ask for the captain and find the homeowner and a neighbor. Call me when you've got that. And get pictures." She hangs up.

A firefighter points out the captain, who tells me the fire was caused by a short circuit. I approach one of the bystanders, who luckily is the person who spotted smoke and called 911. I get her story.

She also tells me the owner is the woman with tears running down her cheeks. I agonize about going up to her, but it's part of my job. The lady actually talks to me. She'd lived there for just six months.

By the time I finish my interviews, most of the house is reduced to a pile of smoldering, charred debris. Wisps of smoke curl into the sky. I snap a couple of pictures and call Marion to give her the information.

"Come on back and get the photos and video up."

I return to my car, wondering if every day is going to be this hectic. My phone rings. "Lois Lane? This is Clark Kent."

I chuckle. I'm getting used to Kieran's corny jokes. "Can you put on your Superman outfit? I'm staring at a house burning down by the river."

"Really?"

"Yeah, I'm covering a fire. It's actually out though. I'm on my way back to the paper."

"I just wanted to tell you the story and video look great. Ed loved it. He's sending links to the Chamber of Commerce."

"You've made my day."

"Listen, the carnival opens tomorrow night. Want to go with me?"

My heart fires a piston. "Sure." I hang up and drive back to the paper. Crap. Why did I say yes? I go with Jade and Morgan every year to the carnival's opening night, but I really want to go with Kieran. I'll tell them tonight. We're playing miniature golf.

I spend the rest of the day on the fire story. By the afternoon, I'm totally beat.

"We'll get to the police blotter tomorrow," Marion says. "I hope it's a slow news day."

"Me, too."

Four

I meet up with Jade and Morgan at the shabby miniature golf place on Route 17. Of the two, I like Jade better. She has a sweetness about her. Morgan has a bit of a sharp edge, though once you get past that, she's nice underneath. But she can be hard to take sometimes.

I give them each a copy of the newspaper. "Check out who's got a front-page story," I yell over the roar of semi-trailers hurtling north to New York State. "Above the fold."

"Front page with your first story," Jade says.

Even Morgan nods admiringly.

"And..." I can't wait for their reaction to this. "I had a date last night!"

Their eyes widen. "What? You've been holding out on us, Chlo," Morgan says.

"I've been super busy."

"Details, please," Jade says.

I fill them in as we clap the balls around the threadbare fake lawn, through the chipped and peeling doll-sized houses, bridges and windmills.

"He's nineteen, just graduated from Crystal Lake. He's going to be an actor."

"He must be cute, then," Jade says.

"Actors just starve," Morgan sneers. "That's not a real career." Her shot totally backfires, and the ball zings from wall to wall in the same stretch. "Argh!"

"You jinxed yourself," I say, with unabashed glee. "He has an audition for a TV commercial coming up. I think people should do what they want."

"Some people obviously make it in acting, so maybe he can, too," Jade says.

"That's what I think," I reply.

"He's always going to be working crap jobs that make no money," Morgan says.

"Money isn't everything." Jade whacks the ball out of the maze and into a hilly area. She raises her arms like a champion. "Jade takes the lead! So, you like him?"

"Yeah. He's funny, always joking. He seems more mature than guys our age. We went to Burger-O-Rama and talked and ate and talked. He didn't even try anything on me."

"You didn't even make out?" Morgan asks.

"Nope."

"I like that. It's kind of old fashioned," Jade says.

"All that boys our age want to do is see how far they can get so they can brag to their friends," Morgan says.

Her ball crests the hill and dribbles down the other side, right into the hole.

"Morgan leaps ahead!" She lifts her arms in the air and swivels like she's addressing a stadium of cheering spectators. "Thank you! Thank you!"

"I'll catch up." I pelt the ball too hard, and it flies into someone else's game. "Oh no!" I fetch it, excusing myself to the couple my ball interrupted. "Can I have another shot?" I call, coming back with the ball.

"No way!" Morgan says. She's already through a pipe tunnel onto the next hole.

I hit the ball too softly this time, and it doesn't make it over the summit. "

Argh!"

"So how did you leave it, Chloe?" Jade says. "Are you going out again?"

I swallow. "Well, he asked me to go to the carnival with him tomorrow night."

"Oh ho! I bet you said yes. Some guy comes along, and you dump your friends, typical," Morgan says. She's surged ahead to the next hole, a figure eight. "It's all over for Jade and Chloe now."

"Would you guys mind if I went with him?" I say in a small voice, scrunching up my face.

"It's our tradition, Chlo. I can't believe you're going to break it for the first dude who comes along." Morgan scratches her back with her putter. "But even if we do mind, you'll go with him anyway because that's who you really want to go with. I really don't even know why you bothered to ask."

"I don't want to piss you off. If it's a big deal, I'll tell him to forget it."

Jade putts her ball. "Go with him and we'll meet you there, and we can all hang together." Her ball plops into a hole. "Hey, this game ain't over til it's over."

"That's a good idea. Then we can check him out," Morgan says.

"We can go together another night," I suggest.

Morgan just humphed. I take my time lining up my shot, and I manage to get the ball over the hill, but it trickles past the hole.

"Hey, maybe Kieran's got some friends, Chloe, hint, hint," Jade says.

"We could use some fresh blood," Morgan says.

"Us vampire girls have drained all the dudes around here." Jade giggles. "They're all zombies now."

"You know what's great about summer?" Morgan says.

"What?" Jade and I chorus.

"You can do stuff like this on weeknights—no homework hanging over you. This must be what it's like when you get out of school and you're just working."

"Yeah, but it's not like you can party all the time. You still have to get up early and go to work," I say.

"I'm thinking of taking a year off before college, maybe travel the world, before getting stuck in the grind of school," Morgan says.

"My mom says once you get working, it's hard to break off and go to college. You get too used to making money, so she wants me to go straight on," Jade says.

I aim my shot so the ball can scoot around two corners of the maze. I make it. I jump up. "Woohoo!"

On Morgan's next shot, she finishes. "And the winner is...Morgan!" she shouts.

I throw down my club and kneel at her feet, raising and lowering my arms like a slave to the master. Morgan tosses back her hair.

"You're too much, Chloe, I swear."

Both Jade and I have to work early the next morning—Jade's volunteering at an animal shelter—so after the game we go straight home despite Morgan's pleas to hang at her house. She doesn't have to start her shift at a store until two in the afternoon so she can stay up late.

The house is quiet. Judging by the light snores coming from her room, Mom is zonked out on her pills. At least I don't have to hear anymore crap about Dad. Before this all happened, she always waited up for me, but now these pills send her into a slumber of the dead.

I leave a copy of the *Weekly News* on the kitchen table, and head to my room. My phone rings as I'm changing into my pjs. Kieran. Suddenly, I don't feel as tired.

"Hey, it was so cool seeing your name in the paper today. I can say 'I know her!'"

I laugh as I climb into bed, propping my pillows behind my head.

"So, the fire was the big news today?"

"Yep, plus the town's restricting lawn sprinkling to ration water."

"Hey, I'm sticking with you. I don't even have to read the paper to find out what's going on."

"I can be your own personal news channel. 'Stay tuned, same time, same place'," I say in a deep, newscaster voice. "So, who do you hang with, kids from Crystal Lakes? I don't know anyone from there."

"Nah, they blow. Bunch of no-hopers. I'm mainly friends with actors from my acting class."

"You take an acting class?"

"Yeah, it's at a playhouse. We do improv, scene study, cold reads, audition techniques, dramatic, comedic, you name it."

"Sounds really cool."

"It's good. I surround myself with people who are going places in their lives. I can't be with people who bring me down out of immature jealousy."

Morgan comes to mind. "Yeah, I know what you mean. Do you have siblings?"

"Two older sisters. One joined the Air Force, the other's in Phoenix."

"Why'd she go there?"

"Moved there with a boyfriend. Why she wants to live in the desert in one-hundred-and-ten-degree heat beats me. They're jealous of me because I was the baby and the only boy. You have any brothers or sisters?"

"Brother, he's fourteen. My mom sent him away to sleepaway soccer camp for the summer. After Dad left, he started hanging out at this party pit in the woods behind our house. He came home one night, totally stoned, and woke up Mom. He was reeking of pot and booze. She grounded him for the rest of the school year and then shipped him off to camp."

"What's the party pit?"

"It's this huge square hole these kids dug. You go down a ladder to a kind of underground living room. They put lawn chairs in it and hang out partying at weekends. During the day, they cover it with a tarp."

"Pretty ingenious."

"So, who's your favorite actor?"

"I like the old school tough guys like Steve McQueen and Charles Bronson. There were my dad's favorites. I have a bunch of their movies. We'll watch them some time."

"I've never heard of them. You like action movies?"

"Action, drama, comedy. Everything really. What do you like?"

"Well, romance."

"Like between humans and vampires or humans and humans?"

"Werewolves, actually. No, I prefer between real people."

"You can be excused, you're a girl."

"You noticed! I read a lot, too."

"Makes sense, you being a writer. What do you like to read? Besides romance."

"I like French authors. I'm taking French five next year."

"Wow, verrrry sophisticated. I liked history in school, like the ancient stuff. I really got into the Greeks, Romans, Egyptians, all that."

"In fourth grade, I wanted to be an archaeologist, but my dad said I couldn't be that because archaeologists don't make any money," I say.

"Yeah, but archaeologists discover stuff. They're in history books."

"I can write about the discoveries as a journalist."

"You can write about anything as a journalist, like actors."

I laugh. "I could be a movie critic."

"Cushy job, watching movies all day."

"Totally, but crime news is more exciting."

"And don't forget being a foreign correspondent. Well, I should let you get your beauty sleep, not that you need it. We on for the carnival?"

"Sounds like a plan."

"I can pick you up at your house."

I don't want him coming here, seeing Mom. "Why don't you just pick me up at the paper? That's easier."

"See you on the morrow."

"On the morrow, it is, fair lady."

We click off, and I snuggle under the covers, willing tomorrow night to come fast.

The next day Marion shows me how to do the police blotter—a roundup of small crimes around town, stuff like shoplifting, car and bicycle theft, drunk and disorderly, driving while intoxicated.

I'm amazed. "I never knew there was all this crime in Indian Valley."

"This penny ante stuff goes in the blotter. If it's bigger, we do a full-fledged story," Marion says. "Any time you need more information you call the PD's press relations officer. Put her cell number in your phone so you always have it handy."

PD? I'm about to ask then I figure it out—police department, dummy.

Marion shows me the police scanner on her desk. "This is how we find out stuff as it happens. You have to keep an ear on it all the time as the dispatcher sends patrol units to crime scenes and calls. But since I'll be here most of the time when you're here, you don't have to worry about it too much."

I'm relieved. It seems a daunting task to track the scanner's endless chatter and pick out what's relevant, as well as work on stories.

"Another thing—check the general email inbox for press releases. Put announcements of events in this folder to go into the weekly calendar. Anything newsworthy that deserves more of a story in this one."

"How do I know what's newsworthy?"

"Ask me if you're unsure. After a while, you'll learn what's news and what isn't."

I hope I remember all this.

"You can get going on the blotter first, then the calendar. Just follow the format in the paper," Marion says.

I finish the police blotter and spend most of the day debating which releases are newsworthy. As the afternoon wears on, hummingbird wings flutter in my stomach at the thought of seeing Kieran. I came prepared today. I brought fresh jeans, a ruffled top and heeled sandals to change into, plus makeup.

At precisely quarter to six, I put on my date outfit, touch up my face and bully my hair into a ponytail because I know it'll be muggy. I look in the mirror. Sometimes my face looks not-together, kind of disjointed, but today it's smooth, flowing. I smile at myself. I'm ready.

I wait for Kieran on the curb, so he doesn't risk a parking ticket. Despite what he says, I don't want him getting a ticket on my account. After a few minutes of swatting away mosquitoes divebombing my face, I spot a blue truck careening across the parking lot. My heart leaps. Kieran pulls up and gets out, running to open my door.

"Milady."

"Thank you, kind sir."

We brim with smiles at each other. His hair gleams wet and his face shines with that just scrubbed look. He has on a cream Western-style shirt with pearled buttons and milk-chocolate colored shoulder panels and stitching around the breast pocket.

As we head down Indian Valley Road, Kieran places his hand on top of mine on the seat and rubs my thumb with his. Zings shoot through me.

"I hope you don't mind me calling you again so soon," he says, darting his eyes at me. "I couldn't stop thinking about you, then finally I said to myself, 'To hell with it. I'm going to just call her and ask her out again'."

"I'm glad you did."

"You are? Really?" He squeezes my thumb.

"Really."

A smile stretches that freckle on his lip into an oval, and he speeds up, turning into the carnival's dirt parking lot with a showy cloud of dust.

The carnival sets up for two weeks every summer in a field outside town. Everyone goes. It's something to vary Indian Valley's monotonous diet of bowling, the single-screen movie theatre, miniature golf, and hanging out at the DQ.

Kieran grabs my hand as we stroll into the fair. It's a riot of dazzling lights, whirling rides and thumping music. I scan the crowd, hunting for Morgan and Jade, who I spot waiting for funnel cakes.

"Hey, there are my friends." I wave frantically at them with my free hand as I tug Kieran with the other. Morgan sees me, points me out to Jade and they both look my way.

Kieran yanks my hand in the opposite direction. "We'll catch up with them later."

"I want you to meet them. I told them all about you."

"I just want to play my favorite game for you first."

I can't refuse. I let myself be pulled and make an apologetic face at them. Morgan's expression hardens. She says something to Jade. The crowd swarms between us, and I lose sight of them.

Kieran steers me to a shooting-at-moving-ducks game and grabs a rifle. He's a good shot and soon wins a white teddy bear with a red satin heart sewn on its chest. He hands it to me.

"It's adorable." I proudly tuck it under my arm.

"Just like you," he says.

I smile. "Where'd you learn to shoot?"

"I used to go deer hunting with my uncle."

"You don't go anymore?"

"It gets damn cold sitting out in some blind in the woods in the middle of winter. Hungry?"

"Starving."

We make for the food concessions. "Carnival hot dogs are the best," Kieran says. "The pizza and hamburgers blow."

We buy hot dogs slathered with relish—and root beer, of course—and sit at a picnic table. Kieran straddles the bench, patting the seat in front of him. I sit astride like him. He inches closer so our knees touch.

"Open wide," he orders, looking at my mouth.

I obey. He feeds one end of the hot dog to me, then leans in and bites the other end. I crack up and almost choke.

"Don't laugh," which comes out something like "doan waf" through Kieran's mouthful of hot dog.

No hands, he chews, swallows and takes another bite. I do the same. We manage to eat the hot dog, and at the end, our lips touch. Kieran presses mine into a kiss.

"So that's why you like carnival hot dogs," I say when we break apart. "To steal kisses."

"Hey, I told you they were the best. Hold on, you have mustard on your face." He swoops in and licks the side of my mouth.

I wipe off his wetness. "Ew, Kieran!"

"Mmmm, salty."

I giggle. He swoops in again and licks all around my mouth and lips. His tongue tickles, and I laugh as I shake my head, sucking in my lips, trying to get him off me as I crack up harder, which only encourages him.

He slurps my cheeks and chin. I try to recoil out of his reach, but he pulls me to him. Finally, he backs off and dabs my face with a napkin as I recover my breath.

"You're worse than a puppy," I say.

"Ruff, ruff." He pants and holds up his hands like paws, then jumps to his feet, holding out his palm. "Come on. Time for rides."

We run like it's an emergency.

"Teatime, madame?" Kieran points to the tea cups then pushes open the just-closing gate and we leap into an empty cup.

We spin madly in the tea cups, chase, block and slam each other in the bumper cars, cling to each other in the haunted house. We finish with a ride on the Ferris wheel.

Kieran cuddles me to him. I rest my head on his shoulder as we gaze in silent togetherness at the landscape of lit up night. When we stop on the top of the wheel on the final revolution, Kieran turns my chin toward him and presses his lips to mine, cupping my cheek with one hand, diving his fingers into my hair with the other. The world dissolves. Nothing else exists except that electric kiss. Now I know what passionate is.

The clank of the metal safety bar's release brings us back to Earth. "Yo, lovebirds, haul it," the carney worker says.

"Take it easy, buddy," Kieran growls.

It's getting late, and the crowd has swollen with rowdy revelers who obviously made a pitstop at bars and liquor stores before the carnival. I scour the crowd for Morgan and Jade, but I don't see them. They must've gone by now.

"Let's go," Kieran says, after a guy, drunk or stoned, stumbles in front of us.

"I really wanted you to meet my friends."

"We've got plenty of time for that. It gets nasty this time of night, a lot of fights."

I give a last three-sixty turn in case Jade and Morgan appear. Kieran's right. Cliques of older guys and girls hang around the perimeter, drinking from paper bags. I catch a drift of the sweet smell of pot.

We swing our clasped hands as we walk to the parking lot. I wish the night would never end. When we get in the truck, Kieran blasts the air conditioning and rolls down the windows. We pull out into the street, and as the AC chills, I close my window. Using his control, Kieran buzzes it down again.

"The AC's on," I say.

"I know. Doesn't it feel great with the cold air and warm air at the same time?"

He accelerates. Bathtub-temperature air whooshes along the side of my body, while my chest is cooled by the AC. The combination feels luxurious.

"You're right. It feels awesome!"

He grins. "Told ya."

"My mom would kill me for doing this."

"That's why you're hanging with me, not with her."

He snakes an arm over and slides off the elastic holding my ponytail. I shake my hair loose and let the wind whip it.

"That's it, sweet pea, be free." Sweet pea! He smiles, and a glow expands inside me.

When we reach my car, Kieran encircles me with his arms, and we make out in the truck for what seems like forever.

I lay my head on Kieran's shoulder. "My mom told me last night that my dad wants a divorce. She says he's throwing us away like garbage. How's that for a morale booster?"

"She's trying to draw you into her drama, sweet pea. That's why you've got to live your own life. You can't worry about what your parents are doing or not doing."

"I guess."

"Take it from me. I've been through all this." We hold each other tightly, Kieran smoothing my hair.

When it's time to go, Kieran asks if I want to go out again. It's been a magical night. There's no answer but yes.

We kiss again and reluctantly I get in my car. We exit the parking lot in tandem like the other night. Kieran is totally different than anyone I've ever met.

Five

My ringtone wakes me up the next morning. Surprise, surprise. It's a phone call from Dad, remembering he has a daughter.

There's a big difference between Kieran's dad and mine. Kieran doesn't know where his father is, but I do know where mine is. Not to minimize Kieran's situation, but mine is almost worse in a way.

If you don't know where your dad is, you can think maybe he'd caught a rare disease that turned him mute, that he's being held by kidnappers, that he's marooned on a desert island. Something happened to prevent him from contacting you. But my dad is close by, in New York City. He just doesn't want to contact his own children, except when it suits him.

"I just got back from Europe. How's the summer going?" he says.

I retrieve the white teddy bear from under the covers and prop it beside me. "I didn't even know you were going to Europe."

"Just a quick trip. How's the newspaper gig?"

"The *gig* is fine. I got a front-page story this week."

"There aren't many reporters there, right?"

I know what he's driving at. I'm only on the front page because the staff is just me and Marion. Snarky comments are Dad's trademark. Like when he refused to go to my seventh-grade school play because I was "only pulling the curtain."

"A couple," I mutter. I change the subject since that one obviously isn't going anywhere. "Mom's not doing so well. She's been taking a lot of pills and kind of zonked out all the time."

He sighs. I know he's pinching the bridge of his nose as he always does when he makes that sound. "She's just doing that to get attention. The best thing is to ignore her, not give her what she wants. Then she'll see her little game isn't working."

"I don't know if it's a game, Dad. She really doesn't seem like herself."

"Believe me, I know what she's doing, and it's not going to work. Don't worry about her."

Something flares inside my chest. He's not here seeing her every day. He doesn't know how she is at all. It's his fault she's like this. I want to yell all this at him, but I don't. I swallow my anger.

"The NYU tour is at eleven next Saturday," I say instead.

"About that. I've got a meeting with the folks at Disney in LA about a project they want to hire me for. Let's make it another weekend. We've got plenty of time."

A wave of let-down crashes over me. "This is the last Saturday tour for the summer, Dad. Your meeting's on the weekend?"

"Since I'm out there, I might as well stay for the weekend, see some sights. Sorry, Chloe. This just came up, but we can go another time."

Sightseeing is more important than his daughter's future? Of course, it is. "No problem. I better go. I have stuff to do."

"Chloe, don't ..."

I click him off and head for the shower.

Dad is a pretty well-known illustrator. He started out drawing comic books, then moved into graphic novels. Now, he's getting into designing characters for animated feature films. That's what the Disney thing is about, I guess.

He's always on some deadline, going to some client meeting, traveling somewhere to check out an exhibition, a convention, an environment he might use. Soccer games, school plays, prize ceremonies—he's missed them all because he always has something bigger than us kids going on, and after all, we're always here, whether he comes to the Christmas concert or not.

He and Mom met at art college, where Mom was studying sculpture and he was majoring in illustration. They dated briefly, then ran into each other again a few years after graduation at an art gallery where Mom was exhibiting her ceramic pieces.

I came along six months after they got married. Maybe that's why it didn't work out between them. Maybe they wouldn't have got married at all if she hadn't been pregnant. They would've married other people, had other families and been happy. I was the big slipup.

My phone buzzes as I'm getting dressed. A text from Morgan. **Come over and hang by the pool? You disappeared on us last night.**

Sorry. Be over shortly, I reply.

I smell coffee, like the old days. Feeling a tweak of hope, I canter down the stairs and into the kitchen. Mom's stirring sugar into her mug, with *The Indian Valley Weekly News* that I left on the table two nights ago, unfolded on the counter. She's actually dressed, only in sweats, but at least it's not the bathrobe.

"A week on the job, and already a front-page article." She beams. "Congratulations, Chloe."

"Thanks, Mom." I pour a bowl of cereal. "Dad called. He's not taking me to NYU next Saturday. He has a business trip."

She sips her coffee and says nothing, which I appreciate. When you've got a bruise, you don't need anybody touching it.

"You look better today," I say.

"I had a doctor's appointment yesterday."

I'm about to say, *You mean the shrink who's prescribing you all these pills?* But what's the use?

"I might get back into the studio today," she says.

"Great. You have a couple pieces to finish."

"I know. Lark is bugging me for them." Lark is the SoHo gallery that sells her stuff.

"You better finish them, or they'll drop you."

As soon as the words are out of my mouth, I realize I sound like I'm the mom and she's the kid. I remember what Kieran told me. I have to life my own life.

✺———✺

"Where are the paparazzi?" Morgan calls as I swing open her backyard gate.

She and Jade are lying in bikinis on chaise-longues, their bodies sleek with suntan oil, a bag of chili-flavored chips between them.

"You never know. Kieran might win an Oscar one day. You'll be in all the magazines, 'Kieran and Chloe, they're just like us'," Jade says.

"They'll be interviewing us for all the dirt we know about you," Morgan says. "So, you better start paying us off now."

I dump my bag at an empty chair and whip off my T-shirt and shorts to reveal my pink-and-purple-striped halter bikini. "I'll get him to put us all in a movie, how 'bout that?"

"Then we can all win best supporting actress together and put our handprints in cement at that place in Hollywood. We'll be immortalized," Jade says.

"What happened to you last night?" Morgan says.

I forage in my bag for my number-sixty sunscreen.

"Nothing. He just wanted to show off at the shooting-at-ducks game. He won me a teddy bear. I looked for you guys later, but I couldn't see you. It got crowded."

"So, did you do it yet?" Morgan slides her sunglasses down her nose and studies me.

I apply sunscreen to every exposed inch of skin, so I don't end up like a piece of bacon.

"Noooo, we just met. But he's a great kisser."

"That's a good sign," Jade says.

I slide on my sunglasses and settle back in the lounge chair. "This is what I call summer vacation."

"We should take a ride down the shore to Seaside Heights," Jade says.

"Why don't we go today?" I say.

"Too late," Morgan says. "The parkway will be packed by now.

We need to leave super early."

"We'll have to plan it," Jade says.

I soon get baking hot and leap in the pool. The others follow and we bounce a beach ball from one to the other. Morgan nabs the inflatable raft and floats around with her eyes closed.

Jade signals me silently. We sneak up on Morgan and overturn the raft. She tumbles in the water with a yelp and emerges, spluttering. "You guys!"

We laugh and swim away.

"What are we going to do tonight?" I ask.

"We could go bowling," Jade suggests. She always wants to go bowling because she's really good at it.

"Movie?" I say.

"Bo-ring," Morgan says. "We can cruise around downtown, check out the arcade and stuff, see who's around to hang with. Be open to adventure."

That's how we wound up at Buddy Ambrosiano's last summer. "As long as we don't end up at Ambrosiano's," I say.

"I'm surprised Kieran didn't ask you to go out, Chloe," Jade says.

"Maybe you don't have Saturday-night-date status yet. Some guys have different girls for different days of the week," Morgan says.

"That's really gross," Jade says.

"We just went out last night," I say. "It might be kind of weird to do dates two consecutive nights."

"Yeah, you're probably right," Jade says.

Morgan's phone chimes with an incoming text. She picks it up. "Hey, what do you know? Cindy Hertzberger's having a party tonight, open house. That settles that then." Morgan types away a response.

We hang out until dusk descends with mosquitoes. Jade and I go home to get ready for the party. We plan to reassemble outside Cindy's in an hour.

I hear TV laughter as I enter the house. I check the living room. Mom's curled up on the couch, a nearly empty bottle of red wine on the floor. Fantastic. Now I have to deal with an alcoholic, too. I seize the bottle and pour what's left into the kitchen sink. It glugs out. I toss the bottle into the recycling bin and head upstairs to shower and change. I wonder if Kieran has a Saturday-night girl.

Cindy Hertzberger lives about six blocks from me in a large Tudor-style house, so I walk. She hangs with the fashion-plate crowd. We're not exactly friends, but we're not enemies either.

The house is ablaze in lights, the beat of techno dance music booming into the street. Jade and Morgan are leaning against a car at the curb.

"What took you so long?" Morgan says. "We're dying to go in. We almost went in without you."

With Morgan leading the way, we delve in the crowded backyard.

"Babe alert!" a guy yells and leers at Morgan. "Where have you been hiding all night?"

"We just got here," she says with a coy smile. Two other guys cluster around us, the wild look of drunkenness in their eyes.

"A new arrival! You've got a lot of catching up to do."

"Where are you from?" one of the guys asks me.

"Indian Valley." I suddenly don't want anything to do with these idiots. A thought flashes across my mind. Could Kieran be here? "Excuse me. I have to look for someone."

I move off, scanning faces as I filter through the throng. No Kieran. Despite being surrounded by all these people, I feel lonely. I think of Mom on the couch. What if she throws up and chokes on her vomit or falls and hits her head? I circle back to Jade and Morgan, who are still flirting with the guys.

I grab Jade's elbow. "Hey, I'm getting out of here."

"What? Don't go."

"Chloe, what are you doing?" Morgan says.

"I'll explain later."

"Okay, be that way." Morgan turns with a flip of her hair.

"What's up with your friend?" one of the guys says.

I hurry off before I hear the answer.

Mom's still asleep on the couch. I turn off the TV, rouse her and get her into bed. I check my phone a last time before I turn out the light. Nothing from Kieran.

Maybe Jade's right—I'm not special enough for a Saturday night date.

My favorite thing to do Sunday morning is laze around the house in my jammies and read until noon. I'm ensconced in "The Great Gatsby" on the couch when my phone buzzes.

It's probably Morgan or Jade calling to tell me I missed a great party. I reach for the phone without taking my eyes off the page, and thumb-punch answer.

"Wakey, wakey, rise and shine," Kieran sings. "Feel like going on a picnic?"

I drop my book. "You mean today?"

"Pick you up in an hour?"

"I'm not even showered yet."

"What's a shower—ten minutes? You can make it."

"I'll meet you outside the paper."

"Bring your video camera."

I scramble off the couch in a burst of energy.

The sky is a vault of deep celestial blue and the sunshine is golden as Kieran drives up a curving road. A huge feeling engulfs me. It's more than happiness. It's like a sense that everything in the world at that very moment is perfect. Joy, I think, this must be joy.

It's suddenly urgent that I connect physically with Kieran, share this moment with him with some gesture that says I am the only one in his life allowed to be so intimate.

I lace my hand across his shoulders and let my fingers dip below the neckline of his T-shirt and linger on his back. It's our first touch of skin under our clothes. He turns his head toward me and his eyes smile gently at me. I know he knows what I'm feeling and that he feels it too.

The road leads into a mountain range behind the town with a state park at its foot. On the other side of the range lies New York State. "Let me guess, are we going to the reserve?" I ask.

"And the grand prize goes to Chloe Quinn!"

I play-punch his arm. He laughs.

"What did you do last night?" he asks.

"I hung out with my friends Jade and Morgan. We went to a party, but I left right away. I wasn't into it."

"That's a relief. I was afraid you might've had a date. I was kicking myself for not asking you out."

Wait until I tell that to Jade! "I thought *you* might have a date. What did you do?"

"Just stayed in. I worked all day, and it was busy. I was really beat. I wouldn't have been good company anyway. Oh, I got you something. The bag's on the floor by your feet."

"You got me something?" I feel that pinch of warmth that comes with a totally unexpected gift.

"Just something small."

I pick up the bag and take out a baseball cap with "Yamamoto's Garden Center" across it, like the one Kieran's wearing. I put it on.

"Suits you. I knew it would." He yanks the rearview mirror so I can see myself. "Now we really look like we belong together." He grabs my hand and kisses my fingertips, swerving as the car ahead of us brakes to turn into a horse farm. An oncoming car honks as it veers onto the gravel side to avoid Kieran.

"Kieran! You're going to get us killed." I twist back the rearview mirror.

"Hey, if we die, at least we die together, sweet pea."

I shake my head, as if to say, "I can't believe you said that." He laughs.

We arrive at the reserve. Kieran gathers a blanket and small cooler from the truck bed. "Got the camera?"

"Yep. Are we going to film something?"

"You'll see."

Wondering what he has planned, I sling the bag onto my shoulder and grab his outstretched hand. We make our way down a trail to a grassy area beside a pond.

Cicadas buzz as the early afternoon heat intensifies. A mother duck glides across the pond, followed by a ruler-straight row of ducklings, like a kiddie toy on a string.

Kieran spreads the blanket and draws me into an embrace. Our arms and legs entwine. He puts his nose to my cheek, and inhales deeply. "I just want to breathe you, the smell of your skin."

"What does it smell like?"

"I don't know how to describe it. I just know I can't get enough of it."

"Let me smell you." I smush my nose against his face. "Kind of musky. I like it." I close my eyes and breathe in Kieran. All the cracks inside me fill up. We fall into a trance-like state of inhaling each other.

Kieran ends it by kissing the tip of my nose. "Lunch?"

We sit up and he takes a brown paper bag out of the cooler. "Peanut butter and pickle sandwiches."

"Peanut butter and pickle?"

"You'll love it. Adds a spicy crunch."

I chuckle. "You're a spicy crunch."

"I like that description. I'm going to put that on my résumé— 'spicy crunch'."

Kieran hands me a sandwich. I bite into it and nod.

"This *is* good."

"See?"

"Hey, we should get one of those food trucks and sell peanut butter and pickle sandwiches," I say.

"We could start a whole new fast-food trend and be multi-millionaires."

"We'd have to patent the recipe in case someone stole the idea."

Kieran laughs. We munch through the sandwiches and wash them down with water.

"What, no root beer?"

"You're getting to know me, Chloe." I can tell by his smile that it pleases him.

"I want you to help me with something. We're doing

commercials in my acting class. I thought you could video me and then I can watch myself. That's really valuable feedback for an actor."

He takes a wad of paper out of his back pocket and unfolds it. "This is the script. Let's just do a line read first." He thrusts the pages at me.

"What's that?"

"We just read our lines to memorize them. You read the coach and the mom parts. I'm the football player. Then we'll switch it around."

The commercial's for Spank detergent: A football coach tells the team their dirty jerseys need to look like new for the big game on Sunday. A player goes to the laundromat and washes his jersey with a cheapo detergent, but it still looks dirty, so he drives two hundred miles to his mom, who washes it with Spank. The final shot is of the team lining up with the player's dazzling white jersey standing out against his teammates who didn't use Spank.

"This is like a real commercial," I say.

"It is a real commercial. Dorian, my acting coach, gets real scripts. Okay, let's do it. You start with the coach."

We run through the lines several times. Kieran increases the speed every time until he can recite them by heart.

"I think I've got it down. Let's do it for real now." He pulls me to my feet and acts out the part as I say the other lines and film him.

"How was that? Did you believe I was the football player?"

"Totally."

"Really? I need the truth."

"Really."

"Let's do it again."

We go through it a couple times, then switch so Kieran plays the coach, then change up again, and he plays the mom.

"The mom too?" I ask.

"Dorian always changes things on us. He says you never know what they're going to ask you to do in an audition, so you have to expect the unexpected."

Bugs are attacking us in droves, so we end the filming session and retreat to the truck, where we huddle on the front seat to play back the video on the camera's tiny screen. Kieran watches his performance critically.

"I blink too much. I pause too long between lines."

"You're good, Kieran."

"Do you really think I can make it?"

"Definitely."

"I want to be famous, Chloe. You might laugh at me when I tell you this, but I want to star in a hit TV show. That's my dream."

"I think that's cool."

He clutches my thigh. "You're the only person who hasn't rolled their eyes or made some stupid comment about how I'll end up starving."

"Why couldn't you make it?" I tuck loose shanks of hair behind his ears.

"Exactly. That's what I tell everyone, but they just laugh at me." Kieran looks out the window. "I want to tell you something, something I don't tell anyone." He pauses. "I want to be famous so my dad will see me, to show him I never needed him. He'll see me on TV and then he'll want to contact me, and then I can dump him like he did to me."

My parent problems suddenly seem like pebbles compared to his boulder.

I tell him about Dad breaking his promise to take me to NYU next Saturday. I surprise myself by choking on the words.

"The thing is he always does this. When I was in eighth grade, I won two honor prizes, and the governor came to present them because his granddaughter was a student at the school. But Dad couldn't go because he had a business trip. I don't know why I believe him every time he says he's going to do something. I'm just an idiot."

"Know what? You don't need him, just like I don't need my old man. I'll take you to see NYU. I'll call in sick."

"Kieran, you can't do that. I don't want you to do that for me."

"No. This is more important. You have to show your dad you don't need him just like I have to show mine."

"We can wait until you have a day off and go on a regular tour."

"That's not the point, Chloe. I want to do this because you deserve to be treated better than your parents are treating you."

Hot bristles sting the back of my eyes. "You would do that for me?" My voice grows teeny-weeny as I start to dissolve.

"Of course."

His words move me like nothing ever has before. I fall into the solid wall of his chest, my tears wetting his T-shirt. Cupping my cheeks in his hands, he raises my face and kisses me so deeply that I can feel him in my toes.

As we drive back into town, I check my phone and see a text conversation between Jade and Morgan that included me, but I had obviously missed it. I scroll through and smile.

"Ha! Guess what?" I say to Kieran. "That party I went to last night—the cops busted it."

"You have to watch who you hang out with, Chloe. Friends can really steer you wrong."

I'm a little taken aback by Kieran's serious tone, then I think of Jade and Morgan flirting with those drunk morons.

"You can't be a sheep. You have to be your own person, promise me that."

"I promise."

"Good." He squeezes my hand.

I have to smother my laughter as I write up the police blotter the following day.

Seven people were arrested for underage drinking at a party in the Knolls after neighbors called the police.

I'm so glad I didn't go along with my friends, like Kieran said.

My day's assignment is to cover the ribbon-cutting ceremony for the new Indian Valley Boys & Girls Club.

I video the officials in suits and hard-hats as they pose with shovels and make speeches. Kieran calls as I'm writing up the story back in the office.

"I just wanted to say thanks for helping me with my scene. I'm gonna kill in class tonight, I know it."

"I wish I could see you doing it."

"You're my muse, Chloe. I'm so glad to have someone who's into what I'm doing. You have no idea. What are you working on?"

"The opening of the new Boys & Girls Club." I lower my voice. "Totally boring."

"I guess you're not going to get cool stories like fires every day."

"Guess what? I had to write a brief on seven people getting arrested at that party."

"That's pretty funny. You could've been one of them, you know. If you had, you would've kissed your internship goodbye, and for what? Your friends? A stupid party? A beer?"

"Yeah, you're totally right."

"Anyway, I just called to hear your voice. Now I feel better."

"I like hearing your voice, too."

"See? Good thing I called. Now we both feel better. You want to get together tomorrow night?"

"Of course."

I settle back at my computer. I do feel better. I have someone who's by my side and on my side, who's protecting me and guiding me, instead of having to go through everything alone and fending for myself all the time. No one's ever been there for me like Kieran. I feel filled to the brim, complete.

"Chloe." Marion jolts me out of my reverie. "Scoot over here, and I'll go over writing heds with you."

I assume she means headlines.

⚬⚬⚬———⚬⚬⚬

The following day drags until six o'clock, when Kieran's picking me up. I keep one eye on the time as I write headlines for the sports section, wracking my brain for alternative verbs for "win" and "lose."

As soon as I see Kieran's truck pull up, I call goodbye to Marion and dash outside. He gives me a massive hug.

"You look gorgeous, sweet pea. I was thinking we should go to the movies because there's air-conditioning."

"What do you want to see?"

"I'll let you pick."

"I kind of wanted to see 'All Juiced Up,' it's a romantic comedy." I scrunch up my nose, knowing that Kieran may not want to see a chick flick.

He laughs. "I figured. I guess I'll sacrifice."

"How was your acting class?"

"Dorian says I made a huge leap from last week to this week. It's because of rehearsing with you, sweet pea."

"I doubt that," I say but I'm secretly pleased. I check the movie schedule on my phone. "It's starting in fifteen minutes."

Kieran swings into a drive-through window of a burger place.

"What're you doing? We're not going to have time to eat."

"We'll take it in with us."

"But they don't allow outside food."

Kieran waves his hand. "Not if they don't know we have it."

We stuff hamburgers into my purse. You can smell the food a mile away, but the usher doesn't seem to notice. He tears our tickets, and we walk in.

"See?" Kieran beams.

We sit in the back row and eat our burgers as the movie starts. I'm totally paranoid we're going to get thrown out, so I wolf mine down.

After we finish eating, Kieran's hand guides my face to his. We make out through the entire movie, enveloped in the cool darkness. The movie seems to be over too fast.

"Now that's what I call a romance movie," Kieran says as we emerge into the lobby.

"We starred in our own."

"The best I've ever seen."

When he drops me off in the parking lot, we stand next to my car to say goodbye. I turn to get in my car, but he grabs my waist and wheels me around to kiss me again.

"I have to go." I break away and open my car door. He doesn't budge, just stares at me, and I rush back to him, flinging my arms around his neck. We kiss again.

"I know I have to let you go even though I don't want to," he says.

"Yeah, I guess." We drop our embrace, look in each other's eyes for a second, then reach for each other yet again.

"I really have to get going," I say when our kiss trails off.

We stretch out our interlaced arms as we step backward, holding each other's eyes, until just our fingertips are touching. We run to each other for another quick kiss. Then I jump in the car and slam the door.

"I have to leave fast or I'll be here all night," I say through the window.

"So? Then you'll be early for work."

"Kieran, you always have an answer for everything."

"It's my genius."

I wait as he gets in his truck, and we caravan out of the lot. I love that we now have a routine.

I stifle a yawn as Marion slaps a press release on my desk. I'm paying for staying out later than I should've with Kieran. He's working the late shift at Yamamoto's, so he got to sleep in late, but not me.

"Cover this kiddie beauty pageant this afternoon. It'll make good video. People love cute kids, and the parents will send around the links, so we'll get tons of clicks. The story can be short, just get good video and a few stills."

I finish the police blotter—two shoplifters caught at the Dollar Shop—then head over to the Elks Lodge, where a gaggle of pint-sized girls frolic and squeal in tiaras and princess dresses, their faces painted with eyeshadow, blush and mascara. I'm sure glad Mom never caught that bug.

I return to the paper, post the video and a short story. I'm looking forward to an early night. When Morgan texts to ask if I want to hang out, I beg off, saying I'm tired.

When I get home, Mom's car is gone. I figure it's a good sign that she went out.

I nuke the last frozen burrito. I can't remember the last time I had a meal with all the food groups. I settle in front of the TV to watch some mindless sitcom. I must've dropped off to sleep. A crash in the kitchen wakes me up in a fright. My heart pounding, I go to investigate and find Mom sweeping up shards of a broken glass on the floor with her hands.

"Mom, what're you doing? You'll cut yourself. Leave it, I'll clean it up."

She gets to her feet swaying a little. I smell booze. "I'm fine."

"You're drunk. Just go to bed."

"I'm sorry, Chloe."

For what? Breaking the glass or being drunk? "You're pathetic, Mom." Then I can't help it. I erupt with rage. "Pathetic! You sent Tyler away for drinking and look at you!" I yell.

She mumbles something and lurches off. I gather the broom and dustpan.

As I back out of the driveway the next morning, I notice the mailbox listing to the side. Mom must've hit it when she came in last night. Now I have to worry about her driving drunk, too. I can't wait to get to the newspaper. Like a robot, I go through the inbox, sorting out press releases, letters to the editor and assorted junk. I write the police blotter.

"Anything wrong, Chloe?" Marion asks.

"I didn't sleep well."

She lumbers to my desk and hands me a chocolate bar. "This is the best antidote."

"Thanks." I'm touched. Under her gruff exterior, Marion's a really nice person.

Kieran calls midafternoon. "How's it going, sweet pea?"

"Not so hot."

"What's the matter?"

"Home stuff."

We agree to meet at the park after work.

As soon as I see him, I clutch him and bury my face in his chest. He encircles me with his arms. As long as I have Kieran, I think, I can get through this.

We stroll into the park, arms threaded around each other. The air smells sweet with freshly mown grass. We don't talk until we sit down on the lawn under a tree.

He strokes my hair. "What's got you down, sweet pea?"

I tell him about Mom.

"She's going to hurt herself. I just know it. Something bad is going to happen, then I'll have no parents."

"You should've called me last night."

"But you were working late."

"Doesn't matter. You're more important. Next time, call me right away. Anyway, I know how you feel. I went through the same stuff with my old man."

"How did you deal with it?"

He plucks a blade of grass. "You've got to show them their own truth."

"What do you mean?"

"Like you shouldn't have cleaned up the glass. She probably won't even remember dropping it. But if you left the pieces on the floor, it would force her to remember."

"What if she steps on it and gets cut?"

"Then it's her own fault, isn't it?"

"Yeah, but..."

"One time, my old man puked then passed out on the floor. Me and my mom always cleaned him up. He never remembered anything he did. Finally, Mom said, 'Know what? Let's just leave him to wake up smelling his own vomit.' So, we did. The next day, he apologized. He didn't stop getting shitfaced, though. Not long after that, he left. The good part was the living room stayed clean."

He gives a sour chuckle. "Like I said, you gotta live your own life. You can't let them hold you back, detour you from your goals. If it means you have to forget them, you have to forget them. Leave them in the dust."

"Sounds kind of cruel."

"It's the only way, or they'll just bring you down and never let you get back up."

We hold each other in somber silence and watch the sun set in a palette of pastel pinks and oranges.

Later at home, I march upstairs. Mom's in bed. I shake her shoulder roughly, forcing her to pay attention to me.

"Do you remember coming home really drunk last night? Do you realize you crashed into the mailbox and left it crooked? Do you know you dropped a glass, and it smashed on the kitchen floor? Do you remember trying to pick up the glass with your hands? Do you know who picked it up?"

She looks aghast. "No, what? I don't remember any of that."

"Well, you should. Not remembering is not an excuse."

Her face falls. "It won't happen again, I promise. I'm sorry."

"I'm not cleaning up any more of your crap, Mom."

I pivot on my heel and slam her bedroom door as hard as I can. I call Kieran from my room.

"You were right. She didn't remember, then she apologized."

"Good going. I'm proud you took a stand, sweet pea."

"I feel better now."

"Told you."

"I'm so glad I have you."

"Me too, sweet pea."

I hang up. Five minutes later, Jade calls. "I just saw Caleb with some girl in his car driving down Indian Valley Road. Clarissa's going to freak."

My mother is turning into an alcoholic and she's worried about Clarissa's stupid crush? "I can't talk right now. I'll call you later."

"I guess you're with Kieran." Her tone is sarcastic.

"I'm not. I...just have stuff to do."

"Go do your stuff then."

Now Jade is pissed off at me. What did Kieran say? I just have to live my life.

Six

Marion sends me to what she calls "a presser at the cop shop," which turns out to be a press conference at the police station. When I see two TV vans there as I park, I gulp. This is major league stuff.

The TV guys are setting up their camera tripods and microphones at a podium in the lobby. I sit next to a couple reporters holding thin, long reporter notebooks. I take out mine to look the part. A minute later, the barrel-chested police chief enters and stands at the podium. I roll my video camera feeling amateurish against the big shoulder-held TV cameras.

The man clears his throat. "Good morning, everyone. I'm Chief Arnold Pettigrew. We're happy to announce that last night we smashed a burglary ring that burglarized eleven houses in Indian Valley since the fall, stealing thousands of dollars' worth of property. Four arrests were made and more may be forthcoming as we pursue the investigation. We have mug shots of the suspects."

He gestures at a row of easels displaying blown up photos of guys who look like they were zapped by a cattle prod.

"We believe Timothy Higginbotham, age twenty-two, of Indian Valley, was the ringleader. He worked as a burglar alarm installer, which allowed him to case the homes that were later broken into."

He details the other three guys. Two were the actual burglars, and one was the fence, the guy who bought the stolen goods.

The reporters ask a bunch of questions, most of which the chief says he can't answer due to the ongoing investigation, and the press conference ends.

I dash back to the paper, get the video online, write the story, put up the photos—all without having to ask Marion anything. It earned me a "good job today" from her.

I head home, exhausted but happy.

I don't remember we're out of food until I walk in the door. Grumpiness takes over my upbeat mood. I check the fridge anyway. Maybe there's something I can cobble together for dinner. To my surprise, the shelves are full—bread, cold cuts, mayo, milk, eggs, fruit, vegetables. Telling Mom "her truth" last night actually worked. My bad mood evaporates. I take out the fixings for a salad, which I'm eating when Kieran calls on FaceTime.

"How's my sweet pea?"

"It worked, Kieran. Mom went out and bought groceries today. I'm still in shock." His face is drawn. "You look tired."

"I had to unload a truckload of trees today by myself."

"I covered my first press conference today, at the police station. They arrested four suspects in a burglary ring. TV was there."

"What channel?"

"Two and four."

"Hold on, the news is on now." I hear him switching channels. I run into the living room and turn on the TV.

"I've got four on," Kieran says.

"I'll put on two." I settle onto the couch as the news anchor drones on.

We lapse into silence, just staring at each other on the phone screen. "You know, we don't even have to talk," he says. "I just like knowing you're there, that we're connected."

"Me too."

"Call me crazy, but I feel like we've been together a long time already."

"It *does* seem like that."

"Don't forget tomorrow. We're going..."

The chief's face appears. "It's on." I punch up the volume.

"I'm switching to two," Kieran says.

The chief blabs on. The camera shows the mugshots, then pans the audience. "There's you, Chloe!"

"Oh my god, I'm on TV!" It was a split-second, then a car commercial was on.

"Check four, quick."

The story was on channel four, but they only showed the suspect photos and the chief. We turn down the volume.

"That's amazing, sweet pea. Your first press conference, and you're on TV. The whole world knows you're a reporter now."

"Well, my mom didn't see it—I think she's upstairs sleeping—I bet my dad didn't. He probably wouldn't even recognize me anyway. My friends don't watch the news."

"I saw it, sweet pea, that's all that counts. So ready for NYU tomorrow? I'll pick you up at your house at ten."

"I'll text you my address."

"I know it already."

"You do?"

"I took a little detour the other night and followed you. I wanted to see where you lived."

"Oh."

A slight discomfort ripples through me, but it was my fault for being so guarded about where I live. Of course, he'd want to know.

He blows me a kiss. I pretend-catch it and put it in my pocket.

"What? You're turning down my kiss?"

"I'm saving it for later, when I'm in bed."

"I like that. Can I have one, too?"

I blow him a long, noisy smooch.

"A big wet one. I like that kind."

We laugh and purse our lips in a joint kiss. "Tomorrow it'll be the real thing," Kieran says.

"I can't wait."

"Me neither. Sweet dreams, sweet pea."

I go upstairs to plan my outfit.

I hear the phone ring downstairs as I'm putting on my mascara the next morning.

"Tyler! How's camp, sweetie?" Mom's practically yelling with joy. I'm glad he finally called her.

When I come down several minutes later, I'm surprised to find her hunched over the counter, next to an open bottle of pills.

"What happened?" I ask.

"Tyler says Dad's going to visit him on parents' weekend, which means I can't go."

"You can still go."

She shakes her head. "I don't want to see your father. I guess Tyler wants to see him more than me."

I open my mouth to yell "Get a grip for once in your life!" but then I decide to do what Kieran says and not get drawn into her drama. "By the way, I'm going to see NYU today with a friend," I say instead.

No answer as she swallows a pill. She couldn't care less if I said I was going to shoot up heroin. I pour a bowl of cereal and take it upstairs.

I eat a couple spoonfuls, but my appetite vanishes. I brush my hair and sit at my bedroom window to wait for Kieran. The numbers tick over on the clock. Maybe he's forgotten, or he can't call in sick.

I curse myself for getting sucked into false promises all the time. If he doesn't show up, I'll take a bus and go by myself. Suddenly, Kieran's truck bounds into the driveway. I grab my purse and run out, not bothering to say goodbye to Mom. It doesn't matter to her if I'm home or not.

I clamber into the truck. "I didn't think you were coming."

"How could you think that?" He kisses me. "I just had a few errands to run."

"I hope we're not going to miss the campus tour now."

"Don't be a worrywart, Chloe." There's a slight edge in his

voice, so I drop the subject.

We head down the highway to Manhattan. I leave the crappy start to the morning behind me as the day unfurls like a red carpet exclusively for us—the AC's blasting, the windows yawn wide open, a seventies disco tune blares from the stereo.

"You always play this old music," I say.

"Don't you like it?"

I nod to the lively beat.

"How's the pillhead this morning?"

I glance at him sharply. "You mean my mom?"

"Let's call a spade a spade, Chloe."

I stare at the woods blurring by the highway.

"Chloe, right?"

I nod. He is, of course, right—she *is* a pillhead. I tell him about Tyler's call. "I guess she feels Tyler's choosing Dad over her."

"She pop a pill?"

I give him a "what else?" look from under my eyebrows.

"Live your life, sweet pea. You're doing what you should be doing."

"I can't help feeling bad. She's my mom."

"I know, sweet pea, I know," he says softly. I tilt my head onto his shoulder.

We merge onto Route Four, which is store-after-store-after-store all the way to the Hudson River.

"So, NYU's your first choice, huh?"

"It's where Mom and Dad want me to go. I really want to go to California, like Berkeley, or something."

"What's wrong with New York?"

"I just want to go somewhere different. I've lived next to New York my whole life."

"But that's not the same as living in the city. New York is where I'm planning to go. We could be there together, forget Jersey even exists. How 'bout that?"

I smile. "Yeah, why not?"

An SUV passes us with a golden retriever craning its head out of a rear window, tongue lolling.

"Don't you love how dogs do that?" I say. "They always look so happy, so overjoyed just to feel the rush of the wind. I wish I could be like that."

"So, do it." A gleam shines in Kieran's eye. Gripping the steering wheel with his right hand, he thrusts his shoulders and head out of his window. He whoops and bangs the side of the truck.

"Woowee! I'm going to New York with my bay-bee!" He whoops again and shakes his hair in the wind. "Yeah!" He ducks his head back in.

"I can't believe you did that!"

It's dangerous, but funny and crazy at the same time. I want to both laugh and scold him.

"Do it, Chloe."

"I can't do that."

"Take a chance and be that dog." He's dead serious.

I edge over to the window and stick my head out. My hair whips around my head. The wind shear assaults my face. I yell into the air. The wind pushes the sounds back into my mouth. I hold up my hand. The air rushes like a force against it.

Kieran pokes his head out and yells. People in passing cars stare like we're lunatics. I wave at them, grinning. We sit back inside.

"Whoa! That felt great!" Kieran shakes himself.

My skin sparks with an electric current.

"You see, sweet pea, you can't sit around wishing for things to happen. You gotta make them happen."

"Let's do it again," I say.

"Now you're talking."

I stretch out of the window to my waist and bang the car roof. Cars honk. An old lady yells at me. Kieran gives her the finger.

We crack up as we settle in our seats. My troubles are gone, literally thrown to the wind. I turn up the music and sing to the words I can pick out: "Do you remember...la-la-la...dancin' in September." Kieran joins in.

We groove in our seats, Kieran playing drums on the steering wheel and me on the dashboard. We put our heads together to belt out the chorus, "Dancing the clouds awaaaaayyyy!"

We cross the George Washington Bridge—the toll collector smiles at our antics—and bounce down the Henry Hudson Parkway along the west side of Manhattan.

New York seems almost like a foreign place when you live in the suburbs. A jagged, boxy skyline of buildings as high as the clouds, people of all colors playing basketball on the courts next to the highway, trees growing out of asphalt.

"Maybe this isn't too close to go to college after all," I say.

"Told ya. There's no place like New York City."

We dive into the narrow streets of Greenwich Village, growing serious as we scour the curbs for a parking spot. We circle the neighborhood a dozen times. The clock ticks on. I start to get anxious.

"We're never going to make the tour, Kieran, and I've made reservations. Let's just park in a lot. I'll pay."

"No way, I never pay for parking. We'll find something."

"But *I'll* pay."

"I said we'll find something, okay?" His tone is basically telling me to shut up, so I do.

He maneuvers the truck into a space that isn't really a space on a grungy street in the far East Village, a long way from the NYU building near Washington Square where the campus tour starts.

We power-walk. "I need a root beer," Kieran says.

"We're already late."

"It'll take one minute. Let's try the store on the next corner." He strides ahead of me. There's nothing I can do. We find root beer in the third store we try and arrive at the NYU building thirty-five minutes late. I hope the tour might be delayed for some reason, but I know it's a lost cause when we enter an empty lobby.

"The tour left ages ago," the woman at the desk confirms.

"Is there another tour today?" Kieran asks but I know the answer.

"We only have one on Saturdays."

"We'll catch up to them. Where would the tour be now?" he says.

"You've missed half of it already," the lady says. "It's hardly worth it."

"Listen, I took the day off work to bring her." Kieran's voice is drum-tight. "We drove three hours and we had a flat tire on the way. She has her heart set on NYU. She really, really wants to go on this tour."

I listen dumbfounded to Kieran's dramatic embellishments, the way he refers to me as *she, her*, like I'm not even there.

But Kieran's urgency works. She glances at me, then the clock on the wall.

"They're probably over at the arts building." She circles a location on a campus map with a pen. "We're here, and arts is over here. Run, and you might be able to catch them."

Kieran snatches the map and grabs my hand. "Let's fly, sweet pea."

We race like we're in a five-hundred-yard dash. "Kieran, you lied to her," I say, panting.

"It worked, didn't it? Sometimes you gotta do whatever it takes to get what you want."

A likely group of parents and kids shuffle out of a building. "Is this the campus tour?" Kieran asks.

A man nods. Kieran breaks into a broad smile at me.

As the group makes its way to the next building, Kieran pulls my hand. "Let's get up front."

He pushes through the throng to the docent leading the tour, who's answering a mom's question about dorms.

"Is there a listing of auditions for student films somewhere?" he says.

The question pops up in my mind: Is this the real reason he offered to take me on the tour?

The docent ignores him.

Kieran turns to me, as if detecting what I'm thinking. "Just figured while we're here? Take advantage of the trip."

He's right. Why not?

"Are we going to the film school?" Kieran asks the docent when he finishes with the mom.

"We already went there," the guy says.

"Can you take us afterward maybe? She really wants to see that."
What? He wants to see it, not me!

"Sorry, you should've showed up on time."

"Listen, I drove three hours to get here, and we had a flat tire. It's not my fault we got here late!" Kieran's voice tightens again.

The whole tour stares at us. I'm mortified. I tug Kieran's arm. "Just forget it."

"I can show you how to get there, and you can go on your own, if you like," the docent says, walking ahead to end the exchange.

"Asshole," Kieran mutters to me. One of the dads gives Kieran a dirty look.

The tour doesn't last much longer. We check out the film school. Kieran looks for student film audition announcements, but we don't see any.

We stroll through Washington Square Park, aiming for the big archway that faces Fifth Avenue. I decide to come back for a tour another day—by myself.

"What do you think?" Kieran asks.

"I like it. If my parents weren't in New Jersey... Actually, my dad now lives in the city."

"New York's ginormous. It's not that easy to run into people."

"Yeah, I guess. He's on the Upper Westside."

"You'd be down here in the Village. You'd never run into him."

Kieran's probably right. A flock of grey pigeons pecking the ground for food scatters as we plow through them.

"You're so lucky, Chloe. You have a lot of advantages I don't have in life. Life's always going to be a lot easier for you than me."

Guilt twangs me. "My parents worked really hard," I say rather lamely.

"So did mine, but they didn't get anywhere."

It doesn't sound as if Kieran's dad worked much at all, and he hasn't told me about his mom, but I don't say anything. Kieran plonks down on a bench and stares at the pigeons, which have resumed their hunt for crumbs.

I sit next to him and he leans his head on my shoulder. Maybe the campus visit hammered home the sore nail that he's not going to college. My fingers trace the waves in his hair. I have to bolster his spirits.

"You've got a lot going for you, Kieran. You're a really talented actor and you work really hard."

He wraps his fist around a shank of my hair. I hold him closer, feeling warm puffs of his breath on my neck. I sense that he needs me to keep talking.

"You can't help where you come from. You shouldn't feel bad about that. You can rise above it." I rub my hand down the pebbles of his backbone.

The brassy beat of tropical music punches through our trance. Some kids are performing fancy skateboard moves to music from a boom box. Kieran perks. "Let's dance." He yanks me to my feet.

"Here?" People are rollerblading, walking dogs, foraging in the trash.

He pulls me to him and starts twirling and shimmying, his eyes demanding mine. I fall in with his steps, returning his gaze. That feeling of the world dropping away comes over me. When we finish, people applaud. Kieran takes a deep bow and holds his hand out to me like we're on a stage. Laughing, I bow, too.

"Let's go," Kieran says when the applause dies down.

"Where?"

"Sweet pea, this is New York. We just walk."

We spy through the windows into luxuriously furnished living rooms of brownstones, joke about the rude shapes of cakes in the erotic bakery on Christopher Street.

We feed each other cannolis in a Little Italy café where everyone shouts in Italian over the gurgles and hisses of an espresso machine. Kieran snaps tons of photos, making me pose in an Army surplus store wearing a gas mask, or takes selfies of us both, our cheeks or mouths or heads pressed together.

We stroll by a funky art gallery in SoHo where people dressed in sports jackets and torn jeans mill around with wine glasses in hand.

I peer in. "My mother's gallery is around here somewhere."

Kieran stops. "Let's go in and get some free food."

"We can't go in there!"

"Just act like you belong. If anyone asks, use your mother's name."

He marches in. I have no choice but to follow. We grab a bunch of fancy finger-food from passing waiters—coconut shrimp, toothpicks loaded with cubes of tangy cheese, stuffed mushrooms—and pretend to be interested in this crazy art.

Old TVs are piled higgledy-piggledy like a trash heap, showing pictures of body parts on their screens while a machine in the ceiling blows feathers over them. An ominous voice recites the names of countries. People study it as they sit on benches, fingers pressed seriously against their noses and lips.

We snicker and snag some more appetizers. Kieran nudges me toward the door. I'm relieved to leave before we get caught.

"Whoa, weird stuff," he says.

"I like weird stuff," I say.

"That's why you like me." Kieran sticks out his chest and juts his thumb at it.

Something about the way he does that makes him look about five years old. I crack up and can't stop. It's the kind of all-out, intense laughter where you go into a total soundless spasm.

I double over, tears gushing out of my eyes, and collapse against the side of the building. Kieran cracks up at my cracking up, barking loudly.

We laugh helplessly, sliding down the wall, until we're leaning on each other on the sidewalk. Eventually, the laughing fit subsides, and we recoup our breath.

"Oh my god," Kieran says. "My ribs hurt."

"So do mine." I wipe my eyes.

"What were we actually laughing at?"

"It was just the way you said, 'That's why you like me'."

I break into a fresh chortle. We laugh again, but not as intensely. Kieran hauls me to my feet. We walk on, arms braided around each other's hips.

"I haven't laughed like that since forever," he says.

"Me, neither."

He kisses my hair. "Oh, sweet pea."

We walk along Canal Street in Chinatown. It's full of bustling shops selling all kinds of knick-knacks and food I haven't seen before like some kind of fruit covered with long hair.

"I'm hungry," Kieran says. "I want to take you to this place on Second Avenue. They have great pierogis."

"I'd eat anything right now," I say.

We head north, trudging along block after endless block.

I'm getting hungrier and hungrier, and my legs are killing me.

"Kieran, where is this place?"

"It's right around here."

"You said that several blocks ago. We can go someplace else."

"I want to take you to the Varsovia. You gotta try Polish soul food."

"I'll be dead before we get there. Look, there's a Chinese place."

"I don't want Chinese."

"I don't even know what pierogis are. I might not even like them."

"Chloe, don't be such a baby. Wait, this is it!"

Thank god. Kieran rockets across the street into a corner restaurant. I limp behind and collapse into an empty red vinyl booth that's luckily near the door.

A waitress comes over, pad and pen poised. Kieran orders a loaf of challah bread and pierogis. They don't have root beer, so he settles on lemonade.

"They make everything fresh here. You'll love it," he says.

"I really don't know what you ordered, but I could eat shoe leather right now," I say.

The waitress delivers a braided challah loaf on a wooden cutting board.

Kieran tears off two chunks of the saffron yellow bread and slathers them with butter. We chew in silence, too tired and hungry to talk. The bread is warm and pillowy. As I eat, I think I better call Mom.

The pierogis arrive. They turn out to be little dumplings filled with meat. We dig in.

"I've never eaten this kind of bread before, or pierogis," I say once I feel revived.

"Look at all the things you're learning with me."

"You're better than Wikipedia."

Kieran guffaws then bores my eyes with his, like he can see right inside me. "Chloe, I swear I have never felt so connected to anyone before."

Something burns inside my chest. "Me, too."

"The day you came to interview Ed, I was supposed to be out delivering sod. But a customer came so Ed didn't finish the invoice and then you arrived. Think about all that's happened because of those five minutes Ed was delayed."

I tick items off my fingers. "Pierogis, challah bread, peanut butter and pickle sandwiches, dancing in the park ..."

He laughs. "I really like that you're not one of those girls who's always texting their friends, or worse, calling Mommy or Daddy. You're more mature than most girls your age."

I stop chewing for a second. Did he know I was thinking of calling Mom?

"Your parents have put you through a lot," he continues through a mouthful of pierogi. "That's why it was destiny that you met me now, so I could be there for you, and you for me."

I forget about calling Mom.

"There's a reason for everything," I say.

We polish off the pierogis, pay and slide out of the booth. My legs feel like they've rusted.

"I feel like I'm ninety years old. We're going to have to take it slowly back to the truck."

"What? We're going out clubbing!" Kieran says.

I glower at his stupid joke.

He cracks up, barking madly, continuing as we reach the sidewalk.

"You should see the look on your face!"

"I'm too tired for jokes, Kieran."

He keeps laughing. "Oh my god, that was a riot. Your face. I wish I had a mirror. I should've taken a picture."

"Kieran, it wasn't that funny."

"It really was. You just should've seen your face."

"Enough already, all right? Joke's over."

"Oooo. Can't take a joke at your own expense."

"Just leave it, okay?"

He pulls me to him. I don't respond. He kisses my forehead. I melt a little, but I'm still mad.

We drive back to Jersey with the music blasting. I sense he's miffed at me for getting mad at his dumb joke. When we get to my house, I decide to pretend it didn't happen. I don't want to end the day on a sour note.

"Here we are. I got you back safe and sound," Kieran says soberly.

"Thanks for taking me. It was a great day." I reach for him. He hugs me so hard I can barely breathe.

"I thought you were mad at me," he says.

"I thought *you* were mad at *me*."

Everything's okay between us. As I enter the house, my head throbs like I've been on a rollercoaster all day long.

Seven

Pool hangout day with Jade & me? Remember us?

It's Morgan.

Ignoring the snark, I text her back that I'll be over. It beats hanging around my ghost-house.

I'm gathering my beach bag when Kieran calls. "Did you dream of me last night, sweet pea?"

I laugh. "Who else would I dream of?"

"I woke up with the urge to go for a hike. Wanna go?"

"I'm going over to Morgan's."

"I really wanted to see you today. We won't see each other tomorrow because of my acting class."

"I already promised Morgan..."

"You want to see me more than her, right? Maybe you could rehearse my scene with me. It really, really helped me last week. I was the best in the class."

Kieran is more fun to hang out with, and he needs me. Plus I'm sure Jade will be going to Morgan's so it's not like Morgan is relying on me for company.

I have a brainwave. I can see them tomorrow night when Kieran's at acting. Perfect.

"I can get out of it."

"I knew you'd come through for me. Pick you up in thirty?"

I text Morgan.

Turns out I've got stuff to do. How about hanging out tomorrow night?

Let me guess—Kieran? Call me tomorrow.

Crap. Am I that transparent?

Kieran beeps his horn a half-hour later. Mom's still in bed. I leave without telling her since she never asks where I'm going or what I'm doing.

I slam the front door extra hard, hoping it'll wake her up so maybe she'll realize I'm gone and that she has no idea where I am.

"I'm rethinking the plan. It's too hot for a hike," Kieran says.

Here's my chance. "How about we go swimming? We could go to Morgan's."

"I'm kind of hungry. Valley Pizza has AC."

I push again. "We could take a pizza to Morgan's."

"I don't want to hang with a bunch of yapping girls."

"You could swim."

"Chloe..."

I see his point. It would hardly be fun for him, but I can't help but feel a little disappointed.

My friends have every right to be mad at me because I keep blowing them off. I'd be mad too.

At Valley Pizza, we order slices and take them to a booth in the back. As we eat, Kieran pulls out his scripts.

"We're doing scene study in the first half of class. I have to be off book with these sides or Dorian will have a fit."

The words blow by me. "That sentence made absolutely no sense to me."

He laughs. "Actor talk. Off book means memorized, sides are your pages."

"And scene study?"

"That's the part of the class where we act out scenes from plays and movies."

"Acting is amazingly cool."

"It's hard work—memorizing lines, getting in character, showing emotion so it looks real not fake."

"What are the scenes you're doing?"

"A comedic role as a crazy person and a dramatic role of a prison inmate going to death row."

"That sounds like a lot."

"Dorian says we have to be versatile, but it means getting into totally different head spaces in the same class."

"By the way, what happened to that audition for the TV commercial you told me about when we met?"

"That didn't pan out."

"What happened?"

"Chloe, I don't want to talk about it."

I guess he didn't get it and didn't want to be reminded about it.

"Let's run the lines. You read Ginny." He hands me a page and sees my baffled face. "It means just read the lines to get them down, like we did with the commercial, then I'll put the emotion into them."

We drill the lines until I have them memorized, too. Then Kieran reads them with more emotion, changing character from one scene to the next. When he feels he's got both scenes down, he leans back.

"You should come to class and watch me perform. I'll ask Dorian if you can sit in."

"No, don't ask him."

"Don't you want to watch me?"

"Of course, but I'll feel embarrassed if I'm the only one watching."

"It's not a big deal." Kieran grips my hand. "This is such a help, Chloe. You have no idea how much it means to me to have you with me in this."

"I want to support you."

He presses my palm to his lips, and his eyes mist. I seize his other hand and kiss it.

We stay like that for a while. People stare at us, but I don't care.

❧————☙

Kieran calls me at work the following day.

"Hey sweet pea. I told Dorian you wanted to sit in on the class tonight, but he said he doesn't allow an audience. You have to be a paying student. Sorry to disappoint you. I know you really wanted to come."

Huh? It was his idea for me to go to the acting class. "Kieran, I didn't want you to ask Dorian," I whisper.

"But you said you did want me to ask him."

Did I? "It doesn't matter."

"Why are you whispering?"

"Marion might get mad I'm spending time on a personal call."

"You have a life, Chloe. What are you working on?"

Marion was getting off the phone. "I gotta go. See you tomorrow?" I say in a Little Bo-Peep voice.

I hang up, puzzled. What did I actually say about going to the acting class?

Marion calls over to me. "Just finish that obit and you can go."

I wrap up the obituary of a former mayor who died and drive home.

As I pull into the driveway, I notice the door on the mailbox, which is still listing to one side after Mom crashed into it, hanging open. The box is crammed with mail. Mom obviously hasn't been picking it up. I stop and take out a pile of envelopes and circulars and drive into the garage.

A wall of foul odor hits me in the kitchen. I check the garbage. Full. I pull out the bag and holding it at arm's length, deposit it in the trash outside the back door. Those cans are brimming and smelly, too.

I come back inside and survey the kitchen, jughandling my hands on my hips. The sink is full of dirty plates. The counter is littered with jars, boxes, crumbs, glasses. I take a deep breath and begin loading the dishwasher.

"You're home early tonight," Mom says behind me.

I continue filling the dishwasher. "I'm surprised you even noticed, Mom. The house is filthy, by the way."

I slam the dishwasher shut, punch the on button and set about sponging down the counter.

"Who was that who picked you up this weekend, in the truck?"

You mean you actually noticed something besides yourself?

"Kieran."

"Is he a boyfriend?"

"Yep."

"Am I going to meet him?"

I turn slowly. She's wearing that crappy robe, which is newly decorated with stains that look like coffee. Her hair's a jungle. Her mouth is smeared with some white filmy substance around it. She reeks of that beddy, unwashed odor.

"Mom, you really think I'm going to bring him into this pigsty and introduce him to my mother who looks like something out of 'The Walking Dead'? The place stinks of garbage, the mail's piled up, there's nothing in the fridge. What the hell is wrong with you? Yeah, Dad left, but you know what, life goes on!"

She winces like I shot her with an arrow and leaves.

"Just walk out and leave other people to clean up your mess!" I yell.

I hurl the sponge in the sink and go through the mail. We're late on the electricity. A credit card bill is due in two days. I lay them all out on the counter. I straighten up the living room, which includes scrubbing a hardened pool of melted ice cream off the floor, and then I do several loads of laundry heaped in the basement. I scrub and polish the bathrooms, wheel the trash cans to the curb.

When I crawl into bed, I find a string of texts from Jade and Morgan on my phone.

Where are you? Are you coming over?

Answer! Are you blowing us off for Kieran again?

You know what, Chloe, don't even bother with us anymore.

We're sick of playing runner up.

I totally forgot I was supposed to hang with them tonight. I'm too exhausted to deal with it. I turn off the phone and the light.

"I was amazing in class last night, thanks to you."

"That's great, Kieran, but I can't breathe!" He's squeezing me super-tight in the front seat of the truck after work.

"Sorry." He releases me and starts driving. "I told Dorian I now have a secret weapon at my disposal."

"A celebration with Dom Pérignon and caviar is in order," I say in a mock regal tone.

"Certainly, milady. In fact, I have a special spicy, crunchy caviar that's just the ticket," Kieran says in an English butler voice and holds up a forefinger.

We bounce down a potholed street to the Flats side of town by the river. The houses look they were nice a million years ago.

"Where might we be going, James?" I play along in the fake British voice.

"Dinner at Buckingham Palace, milady." He pulls into the driveway of a weather-beaten, blue split-level house with a fungus-spotted tree in the front yard. "We have arrived."

Sitting by the fence is a shabby camper with flat tires and a rusted hitch. This must be where he lives. It's basically a dump. I'm taken aback—for some reason I thought it would be nicer—but I try not to show it.

He unlocks the camper door, and I follow him into a box of hot, musty air.

"Home sweet home. Not much, but it's mine."

"It's cool."

"Tonight's menu is spicy crunchy or crunchy spicy."

He reaches in the small fridge and takes out peanut butter, pickles and bread. The fridge also contains an apple, pear and peach, all partially eaten and browning, and several yogurt containers with plastic spoons sticking out of them, half consumed as well.

"Don't you ever eat the whole fruit or yogurt?"

"I get tired of one flavor, so I go on to the next."

It seems very Kieran.

"I'll stock up on extra food next time I stop at the drug store," he says.

"You buy groceries at the drug store?"

"Or the gas station."

"You should go to a supermarket."

"Food is food wherever you buy it."

We slap together peanut butter and pickle sandwiches on paper plates. "Wait." Kieran opens a cupboard. "Since you're my special guest."

He takes out a can of peanuts and sprinkles them inside the sandwiches. "For extra crunch."

I crack up. "Spicy, crunchy crunch. Another menu item for the food truck."

"I'm out of root beer. A hydrogen and oxygen cocktail?"

"Certainly, sir."

He fills two paper cups with tepid tap water, and we carry our meal to the little table and eat.

"This is really good with the peanuts," I say.

"Told ya."

"Hey, we could make other nut butter and pickle sandwiches for the food truck, like almond butter, macadamia nut butter, even different kinds of pickles."

"Totally." Kieran wags his sandwich crust. "Seriously, that's a good idea. It's doable."

"I wonder how much it would cost."

"We'd have to find investors. Rich people. You give them a percentage of the business. That's how it's done."

"How do we find rich people?"

"You have to hang where rich people hang—country clubs and stuff."

"Hmmm." I mull over the possibilities as I finish the sandwich.

"It's fun playing house with you, Chloe. There's just one thing missing." He smiles slyly.

A thrill ripples up and down my spine like a piano scale. Kieran hasn't made any move on me so far. This is it.

"I've been waiting for the right time." He takes my hand and leads me to his bed, where he lays me down gently. "I wanted to make sure of my feelings for you. I guess I'm kind of old fashioned that way.”

“I like old fashioned,” I murmur.

“Wait. I’m forgetting something.”

He jumps up and crosses to the kitchen, where he takes out two fat white candles from a cabinet and lights them with matches. The flickering flames make glowing spots in the creeping darkness as he carries them to the bedside.

“It’s lovely, Kieran.”

He kisses me and slowly peels off my clothes. It’s not anything like it was with that jerk, Angus Magillicuddy. Kieran makes it all about me, not him. He lavishes me with caresses and tells me how beautiful I am.

We nestle in each other afterward, Kieran’s fingers feathering every millimeter of my body. “I want to have the image of you in my fingertips so I can shape you out of the darkness when I’m alone at night.”

“I just love the things you say,” I murmur.

“I’m falling in love with you, Chloe. Correction, I’ve fallen in love with you.”

My heart skips a beat. I gaze at him in the candle glow. “But we haven’t been together very long.”

“So? I know what I feel. I wasn’t going to tell you so soon, but I have to. I knew there was something as soon as I saw you. You don’t have to say it back. I just want you to know.”

I cup my cheek with his hand. “I think I’m falling in love with you, too.”

His eyes glisten as he kisses me. “We’re meant for each other, Chloe, I just feel that we are.”

“I feel that, too.”

We lie there until it’s late and I have to go home.

It’s Fourth of July, and I’m covering the town parade.

I bound downstairs. Mom is dressed and putting on an apron. Flour, eggs and butter are out on the counter.

I give her a quizzical look.

"I'm going to the Hertzbergers' barbecue. Thought I'd take an apple pie." She gives me a fragile smile. "You're invited, too. You could come after work."

The bills I left on the counter are gone. The lights still work so she must've paid the electricity. The kitchen has remained tidy since I cleaned it. The fridge is stocked. Maybe my blowing up at her blew her out of her funk.

"I'm going to see fireworks with Kieran, but I'm glad you're going, Mom."

I head to the paper, a starburst of happiness inside me at Mom's turnaround.

I unlock the door with the key Marion gave me, switch on the lights and power up my computer. The door jingles, and I look up. To my surprise, Kieran lopes in, grinning.

"Happy Fourth of July, sweet pea."

"What are you doing here?"

"I thought I'd be a reporter's assistant today."

"What do you mean?"

"I'm going to the parade with you."

I blink. "I have to work, interview people, and stuff."

"I won't get in your way. I thought it would be cool."

I'm not sure I really want him there, but I don't know how to say that. "All right, well, I just have to get my notebook then we'll walk over."

The curb is already jammed with people in lawn chairs. Little kids scamper around waving mini flags. We stroll to the grandstand where the mayor and town council members sit. "I have to get a quote from an official," I say.

"Go ahead. I want to see you in action."

Trying to ignore my unwanted audience, I introduce myself to the mayor. He agrees to an interview, straightening his tie as I ready the video camera. Kieran hovers next to me.

The red light goes on, and the mayor blathers about what a wonderful Indian Valley tradition the parade is and how people come from surrounding towns to see it.

"The parade's starting, Chloe," Kieran shouts, totally drowning out the mayor. I cringe and ask the mayor to repeat what he just said. Luckily, he doesn't seem to mind.

The parade moves off with the high school marching band. "Shoot this, Chloe," Kieran points to the band. I turn my camera in that direction. Kieran races off.

"Over here, get a close up of the cops on horses!" he yells. I run into the street, causing a horse to buck slightly.

"Slow down," the mounted officer snarls. I'm totally embarrassed.

"Hey, this Cub Scout is a cute shot. Come down here!" Kieran yells.

I scoot down to the scouts, walking backwards to film a red-haired, freckle-faced kid marching. I trip over someone's legs stretched out from the curb and land on my backside. Pain thuds through me. People gather round. Kieran pushes through and helps me up.

"You all right?" he says.

"Kieran, can you stop ordering me about? Just let me do my job, okay? I know how to do it."

"I'm just trying to help. It's not my fault you tripped."

"Just...you're not helping, okay?" He melts into the crowd. I feel relieved.

"Chloe!" Jade shoves through the crowd. "What's up?"

"Sorry. I've been super busy. I'm covering the parade, and my mom..."

"Chloe, there you are." Kieran appears out of nowhere and pulls me to him by the waist, like he's making sure she knows he's my boyfriend.

I make the introductions.

"You guys want to come by Morgan's later and go swimming?" Jade says. "Her parents are having a barbecue, but she's allowed to invite friends. She really wants to see you, Chlo."

"That'd be awesome. We'll stop by after I finish work."

"Awesome. I've got to find my little brother. He's here somewhere. Catch you later."

As soon as she leaves, Kieran turns to me. "She's jealous of you."

I look at him in disbelief. "What do you mean?"

"You have an important job at the newspaper, a serious boyfriend. You're way beyond her."

"She and Morgan are pissed at me. I blew them off a couple times for you."

"Believe me, I can tell things about people. You shouldn't hang out with jealous people. They'll just find a way to bring you down."

I shrug, not knowing what to say.

"I found some people for you to interview." He points to a giggling gaggle of leggy middle-school girls.

"I don't need them. I've got enough crowd interviews."

"Come on, Chloe. I promised them."

I know he won't give up until I do it. I plod over, ask them what they like best about the parade and turn on the camera.

"The cute boys," one says, looking at Kieran. I feel a twinge—jealousy? The others giggle.

I switch off the camera. "Let's go. I have work to do."

We walk back to the office.

"It would've been nice if you'd introduced me to the mayor," Kieran says. "I wanted to take a selfie with him."

"Kieran, I'm working. It would be unprofessional to introduce my boyfriend." Is that why he shouted while the mayor was talking?

"Next time, I'll introduce myself."

"Yeah, you do that."

We enter the office. I put gear down and stride to the water cooler.

"I have to download and edit this video, write a story then do police checks." I gulp down three cups of water.

"I won't bother you. I'll be a fly on the wall."

"You don't have to stay."

"You shouldn't be all alone here."

"I can lock the door."

"You want me to leave?" A razor edge in his voice and eyes makes me backpedal a little.

"It's just I can't talk while I'm working."

"I know. I'm not an idiot." He grabs a newspaper and sits at a desk.

I get the story and still photos online and work on the video. The AC hum is the only noise. I forget about Kieran.

As I'm waiting for the video to upload onto the website, I suddenly spot him rifling through Marion's desk drawers.

"What are you doing?"

"I could use some office supplies."

"You can't take stuff from here."

He straightens and closes the drawer. "Any food around this place?"

I don't want him raiding Marion's stash in the fridge. "I'll see what there is." I walk to the kitchenette and find a couple leftover doughnuts that Marion won't mind me taking. When I return, Kieran's sitting on my desk.

I hand him a doughnut and bite into one myself. "It's a little stale."

"Hits the spot." Kieran demolishes it in three bites.

"I have to do police checks then I'm done."

He moves off my desk. "I'm going to wash my hands."

I go to grab my cell phone, which has the police spokeswoman's number programmed into it, but it's not where I always leave it—on the right side of my keyboard. I spot it on the left side. Did Kieran move it while I was in the kitchen?

I call the officer. "Nothing to report," she says to my relief. I just want to get Kieran out of here.

"I'm done," I sing out as Kieran returns from the bathroom. "Let's go to Morgan's before the fireworks."

His face drops. "Sweet pea, I was planning on a romantic evening, just us two."

"We wouldn't have to stay long. I haven't seen my friends in ages. Why don't you want me to see them?"

"It's not that. I have a special place I want to take you to see the fireworks. You can see your friends any day, but there aren't fireworks every night."

I feel exhausted from battling with him all day. I realize that he never gives in.

"Let's go to your place then," I say in defeat.

We go back to the camper and make peanut butter and pickle sandwiches. I can't help thinking of the barbecue chicken and corn on the cob I could be eating.

"Isn't this great, sweet pea, sharing our lives?" Kieran slurps a root beer. "I can't stand being alone. I get so lonely."

"I don't mind being by myself."

"You're lucky. You don't know what it's like to need people."

"That's why I love reading. You can lose yourself in books, and then you don't feel alone."

"Books aren't the same. I'm so happy I have you. You're the best thing that's ever happened to me, Chloe. I'm serious." He winds a strand of my hair around a forefinger. I feel guilty for being irritated with him.

Dusk settles in. "We better go, sweet pea. It takes a little while to get to my special fireworks viewing spot. I don't want to miss anything."

We head to Crystal Lake and wind up a dark, twisting road to a ridge. We drive until we come to a break in the tree line and turn into a lookout point. A carpet of amber and white lights spreads before us, ending in the soaring New York skyline.

"This is incredible. You can see all the way to Manhattan," I say.

"Told you. We'll be able to see fireworks all over North Jersey." He snaps open a can of root beer, hands it to me, then opens another for himself and points it at New York.

"That's the place for us, sweet pea. That's where it all happens."

"Maybe we'll get there one day."

"What 'maybe.' Here's to your byline in *The New York Times* and my name on a TV dressing room door with a big star."

We clink cans. He takes a hank of my hair and sweeps his face with it. We pose for a selfie with my hair wrapped around his neck like a feather boa.

"I'm going to call this picture 'wrapped up in you'." He dips the tip of the lock in his soda and sucks it.

I crack up. "I totally love these crazy, unexpected things you do. Who would ever think of doing that?"

Kieran puts his head into my lap, his face staring up at me. "Dorian says actors have to be memorable. They have to stand out from the competition, so they'll get cast."

"You're memorable, all right." I laugh.

"Chloe, I need to know you're committed to me because I'm committed to you."

Something twangs inside me. "Do you have to even ask me that?"

"I want you to promise you'll never have any contact with any guy you were ever involved with. We can't have exes interfering in our relationship."

"Why are you even bringing this up? I really don't have any 'exes'."

"I want to know your whole boyfriend history. How far did you go with each guy?"

"It's not very long." I tell him about my three misadventures.

"How many times did you do it with this Angus dude?"

"Just a few."

"What an asshole. I'd like to take a baseball bat to him for using you like that. That really pisses me off."

"Just forget it." I regret telling him. I don't need to hear I was "used."

"It kills me to think of you with someone else."

"What about you? What's your girlfriend history?"

"Girls just don't know how to appreciate me. I've been involved with selfish girls, up until now, that is."

"I appreciate you, Kieran."

"What about Instagram? Or Facebook? Are you friends with any of those guys?"

I take out my phone. "I'll show you if it makes you feel better." I scroll through my forty-six friends on Facebook and my couple dozen followers on Instagram. "See? Nothing to worry about."

"I just get scared that one of these guys might come back and take you away from me."

"That's totally crazy."

"I can't help it. It's my low self-esteem."

"Kieran, you're the only person who's ever been really interested in me, who's really wanted to know me, the real me. I can't even tell you how much that means."

A boom sounds in the distance. "Look!" I point to shooting streaks of red, white and blue in the sky.

"Over there, too." Kieran signals a cascade of glittery silver and amber. "And way over there."

Fireworks explode against the black silky night everywhere we look. We ooh and ah as they whistle and burst.

"Isn't this the best, sweet pea?"

I have to agree.

When the last grand finale ends, we wind down the mountain, Kieran clutching my thigh and me leaning on his shoulder.

I realize Kieran never told me anything about his past girlfriends. My phone chimes with an incoming text. It's Jade.

Thanks for letting us know you weren't coming to the BBQ.

Crap. Sorry, work was busy.

Or busy with Kieran. I shouldn't have even bothered inviting you.

I don't answer. Maybe Kieran's right. Maybe she's just jealous I have a serious boyfriend.

Eight

We're lying in a tangled heap of limbs on a blanket at the park, sharing a mango-passionfruit yogurt, a flavor I introduced Kieran to that's now his favorite. He eats a spoonful then feeds me one as I dig out lint from his belly button and flick it away. He scrapes the bottom of the yogurt container and gives me the last spoonful.

"It's your turn," I say.

"You take it."

"I insist." I open my mouth and receive the last spoonful.

He peers at me. "You have a zit on your forehead."

"I know. It's gross."

"Hold still." Before I can say anything, he squeezes it and wipes it with a napkin.

"I can't believe you just did that," I say in shock.

"Why not? Your zits are my zits."

Shaking my head, I cuddle up to him. "I'm so glad I have my very own pimple-squeezer."

"And I have my own belly-button cleaner."

"We're in our very own world of us," I say. "Our Kingdom of Coupledom."

"Kingdom of Coupledom. I like that. We should have a blended name like celebrity couples," he says.

"How 'bout 'Chloran'?" I suggest. "Or 'Kierle'."

"Neither has much of a ring to it. Let's forget that. Hey, I almost forgot. This guy from my acting class is having a party tomorrow night. Wanna go?"

"I'd love to meet your acting class—and Dorian."

"I want to meet your mother, Chloe. It's time."

"You mean, like make it official?"

"Like be part of each other's family."

He has a point, and Mom's actually been looking more presentable lately, so I don't feel so embarrassed.

"Why don't you meet my mom when you pick me up for the party?" I say.

I change outfits a million times. What do you wear to a party of actors? I settle on a pair of nice jeans with heeled black sandals and a dark purple top with ruffles bordering a deep scoop neck that always fetches a lot of compliments. I apply my makeup with extra care and curl my hair into bouncy waves. After a last glance in Mom's full-length mirror, I go downstairs.

"You look gorgeous, Chloe," Mom says. "You need an evening bag, though. Wait here."

"He's coming any second, Mom." She's already heading up the stairs. She returns with a petite black satin purse with a braided rope strap.

"Thanks, Mom." I transfer my wallet, lip gloss and keys into it and snap it shut just as Kieran's truck swings into the driveway with a horn honk.

I open the front door as he strides up the walk. He's wearing a brown corduroy sports jacket over a dress shirt and jeans and carrying a large bouquet of yellow, pink and white lilies and chrysanthemums.

He kisses me on the lips. "I clean up well, don't I?"

I laugh as he steps into the hall.

Mom comes out of the kitchen.

"These are for you, Mrs. Quinn." He thrusts the flowers at her.

She looks sheepish but pleased. "You didn't have to do that."

"You guys have been through some rough times lately. You deserve something nice."

"That is nice, thank you. So, Chloe says you want to be an actor."

"I have an audition for a TV commercial next week. Fingers crossed."

What? I shoot him a frown. His eyes dart at me. It's a lie. Mom raises her eyebrows, impressed, which I assume was the point of the fib.

"That sounds promising. Good luck," Mom says.

Kieran pulls me to him, like he did when he met Jade at the parade. "Chloe's a great girl. I'm really lucky I found her."

I wish the ground would swallow me up. Not in front of my mother!

"You're certainly spending a lot of time together, so I guess that means you get along well."

"We're meant for each other, right, sweet pea?"

I'm mortified that he's saying this stuff to my mother. I manage to smile. "We should get going, Kieran, or we'll be late."

We say goodbye and walk down the path to the truck. "I think that went well," Kieran says.

"Kieran, you gushed too much about me."

"What do you mean 'too much'? That's how I feel."

"It's just, you know, my mother."

"You get embarrassed too easily. Just say what you feel."

We get in the truck, and he reverses out of the drive.

"The TV commercial thing isn't true, is it?" I say.

"Chloe, I don't have anything to offer you. Look where you come from—your house, your parents. I need something to make me look good, and besides, it'll be true soon."

"You don't have to make up stuff. You have a lot more to offer than you give yourself credit for."

He pecks the top of my head. "Thanks, sweet pea. I know you're trying to make me feel better."

"It's true."

"You look beautiful. I can't wait to show you off."

"Where's this party?"

"Riverton. The guy's name is Joe Favola. His parents are out of town, that's why he's having this party. They're rich lawyers in the city. They're not too crazy about the idea of him being an actor."

We enter a neighborhood of humongous houses and park in front of a lit-up plantation-style mansion with columns fronting a porch. "What did I tell you?" Kieran says.

The front door is open, so we walk in, following the chatter and music onto a back patio lit by tiki torches. A swimming pool glows turquoise with the underwater light.

"This is really nice," I say.

"They can afford nice," Kieran mutters.

A bunch of people stand around with drinks in their hands. A guy wearing a loud Hawaiian shirt with black and orange flowers barrels over to us. He's super handsome, with one of those GQ-model square jaw lines.

"Dubrowski, you made it." He slaps Kieran on the back.

"Richie Rich, you didn't think I'd miss out on this, did you? This is my girlfriend, Chloe."

Joe stares at me. "What are *you* doing with Dubrowski? You're way too good for this schlub." He seems to be only half-joking. I smile uneasily.

"Fuck you, Favola." Kieran is not joking.

Joe just grins. "Food's over there, drinks are over there, and swimming pool's there if you feel like plunging in, clothes on or off. Help yourselves." He goes to greet someone else.

"Don't take any notice of that asshole. He's jealous, that's all," Kieran says.

"He was just joking around. I didn't think anything of it."

"Might as well fill up while we're here."

We saunter over to the food table. Kieran piles ham on his plate, pushing aside the slices of pineapple on top of it.

"Who eats ham with pineapple?"

"That's common. It's like eating pork with apple sauce, or

turkey with cranberry." I spear a slice of ham with pineapple and place it on my plate.

"Well, aren't you Miss La-di-da?"

I flinch at the bitterness in Kieran's voice. "I'm just saying, that's all."

Kieran leans into my ear and signals a cluster of people by the pool with his fork.

"See the guy with grey hair? That's Adrian Gould. He's the director at the playhouse. I need to meet him. Don't tell anyone you're in high school. Just say you're a reporter at the *Weekly News*."

Kieran inserts himself into the circle, forcing people to shuffle around. A couple of them look annoyed at the interruption. There isn't really room for me, so I hang back.

Kieran focuses on the conversation about "union scale rates" and "residuals." I have no idea what they're talking about. I finish my food and search for a table to dispose of my plate.

Joe sidles up to me. "Your hand's empty. Can I get you a drink?"

I nod and follow him to the drinks table. "What would you like?" he says.

"Coke's fine."

He pours a Coke, tosses a wedge of lime in it, and hands it to me.

"Are you an actor?" Joe asks.

"I'm a reporter at *The Indian Valley Weekly News*. You're an actor, right?"

"Yeah. It's tough, but I'm making progress. I was an extra in an episode of 'Lawyers, Guns and Money'. It'll be airing next month."

"I'll watch out for it."

"I'm in the courtroom audience. I was hoping to get a role as a juror. That would've meant more on-camera exposure. But what can you do?"

Kieran's arm suddenly snakes around my waist, startling me. "Chloe, we have to go now. You've got an early start tomorrow, remember?"

I look at him in disbelief.

"You just got here," Joe says. "Stay a while."

Kieran's pupils turn into bullets aimed at me. "You're drinking too much, and I have to get you home." He turns to Joe. "She's still in high school. She probably didn't tell you that," he says in this confidential tone as if I'm not there.

I'm flabbergasted. He specifically instructed me not to tell anyone I was in high school, and I'm not even drinking alcohol. "This is a soda!" I say.

"Keep your voice down." Kieran raises his eyebrows conspiratorially at Joe as if to say "See?"

"Dude, take it easy," Joe says. "It's Coke with lime. She's fine."

"Let's go, Chloe."

"I don't want to leave yet."

Kieran drops his arm from my waist. "You win. I was just looking out for you."

He stalks off. Joe shakes his head. "What was all that about?" he says.

We chitchat for a few more minutes, but I'm queasy about Kieran. I excuse myself and go look for him. He's not in the bathroom or living room, then I spot him in the kitchen, talking to a girl, super skinny with high cheekbones and cocoa-colored skin smooth as mousse.

His arm is stretched out, propped against a cabinet, with her under it, backed against the counter. Very cozy. He's smiling and talking, she's giggling. A sourness creeps up the back of my throat.

I debate whether to slink off, pretending not to have seen them, or interrupt them. But since Kieran interrupted Joe and me, I decide to do the same to him.

I march in and wind my arm around Kieran's hips, like he does to me in front of other people. He circles my waist loosely with his free arm without looking at me and keeps talking—something about sex scenes, how they're totally choreographed and not very sexy at all for the actors.

My head throbs. His words breeze by me like fall leaves, and I can't catch them. The girl keeps looking at me and finally prances off. I bury my face in Kieran's chest.

"I shouldn't have come," he says in a morose tone. "Adrian Gould blew me off in front of everyone like I was a fly. You want to get going?"

He seems to have calmed down from whatever was bugging him before. I nod, and we head toward the front door. I halt.

"We should say goodbye to Joe."

Kieran's nostrils flare. "You're really hot for him, aren't you?"

I'm baffled. "It's just good manners to say goodbye to the host and thank them."

He shunts me through the door.

As soon as he slides into the truck, Kieran wheels toward me, his face braided with rage.

"Don't you ever embarrass me in front of my friends like that again! You're nothing but a lowlife, flirting with my friends! You made a fool of me in front of the whole party. I should never have brought you!"

He jabs his finger about two inches from my face.I reel back against the door, shocked and terrified.

"I was just talking to Joe. I was standing there, and he came up to me. You were talking to Adrian."

He drives along the street, roaring. "You were practically undoing his pants, shaking your boobs at him in that blouse!"

"That's ridiculous! We were just talking, like people do at parties."

He slows the truck to a crawl and lowers his voice into a sneaky tone.

"You were with him in the bathroom, weren't you? Somebody told me they saw you with him in the hallway outside the bathroom. Did you make plans with him? Is that why you wanted to leave all of a sudden? So, you could get rid of me and go back later by yourself? You liked him, didn't you? I saw you looking at him."

Where is he getting this nonsense? His eyeballs bulge, making him look scary, as he leans into me. I huddle against the door, my head spinning with his accusations.

I grope to defend myself. "Who saw me with Joe in the hall

outside the bathroom? That's a total lie. I wasn't with anyone in the bathroom!"

"I turned around after that asshole blew me off, and you were gone. I look around and you're all cozy with Joe. I told you how beautiful you are, and it's gone to your head—going around strutting your stuff! My friends warned me about you."

"What friends? Kieran, stop it! Just stop it!" I scream, clenching my fists in frustration.

To my surprise, he quiets down and steps on the gas. Thank god. I grip the door handle, breathing deeply in relief. I push back the wellspring of tears in my eyes.

What happened? How could he say these things? Did I do something wrong? I don't think I did, but I go over the sequence of events in my mind to see if I missed something.

"And what about all that shit on the Fourth of July?" he says suddenly.

I'm on edge again. Fourth of July? "What on earth are you talking about?"

"You didn't want me along so you could talk to dudes. You think I didn't notice that you only interviewed guys? When I found girls for you to interview, you dissed them."

"Kieran, they were middle school teenyboppers. All they did was giggle. They were useless."

"You didn't even introduce me to the mayor. Little Ms. Important Reporter!"

"I was working. You don't introduce boyfriends when you're at work. You weren't even supposed to be there. And what about you? You told me not to tell people I was in high school then you went and told Joe just to make me look bad! How do you think that made me feel?"

"I was protecting you. He's on probation for a meth conviction, but he's still using. I've given him baggies of my pee to use for his piss tests for probation. He hides it in his underwear. If you hear him on the phone ordering 'script pages,' he's really buying crystal meth. He keeps it in a sock. I know all about Joe Favola, believe me."

Is this true or one of Kieran's lies to serve his own purposes? I have no way of really knowing so I ignore it.

"I don't need your protection. I want to go home. I want you to take me home." My voice is quaking, but I try to hold strong.

"Don't worry, I brought you here, I'll take you home." He guns the truck faster. A sharp curve is coming up. I hang onto the door handle as he rounds it too fast, the tires squeal. The truck tilts slightly.

Panic grips me. "Kieran! Slow down!"

He doesn't reply. We fly over the crest of a hill, the truck landing on the down slope with such a hard bounce that my butt actually lifts off the seat. Then he careens into the oncoming lane to overtake a slowpoke. Another car is coming straight at us. As I watch its headlights close in on us, I push my back hard into the seat to brace for the inevitable head-on collision.

"Kierannnn! Nooo!"

The oncoming driver leans on the horn, but Kieran keeps going straight. My heart pounds like a jackhammer. I'm gripping the door handle with one hand and the side of the seat with the other. I can't believe this is happening. Then Kieran abruptly wrenches the steering wheel to swing hard back into our lane just in time to avoid the vehicle.

I gulp air. Who the hell does such a thing?

I say nothing, but I don't let go of the door or the seat. I keep my eyes on the road to be ready for his next crazy move. All I can think is that I need to get out of this car. Kieran is going to kill me. I need to get away from him as soon as possible.

Kieran continues driving like a maniac, but at least he doesn't try to kill us again. I'm relieved when he turns into my street. He speeds up then screeches to a stop in front of my house. I jump out. The smell of burnt rubber tinges the air.

"Chloe, wait!" His voice sounds normal, but I'm done.

I slam the truck door and take a step, but I'm pulled back.

The thought that he's holding onto me rushes across my mind, but I see the purse strap is caught in the door. I yank it hard and sprint up the path. I'm trembling, scared he's coming after me, so it takes a few seconds to get the key in. The door finally opens, and I tumble inside, closing it fast behind me. I'm jittery but I'm safe. My heartbeat starts to slow.

I look at the purse. It's ruined. The side panel ripped off when I pulled it. Shit. I run upstairs, afraid she might wake up. I toss the purse under my bed and change into my nightgown.

I'm about to get into bed when the doorbell rings, startling me. It can't be. I look out the window. Kieran's truck is in the driveway. *Go away, just go away.* The doorbell rings again.

"Chloe! I just want to talk to you. Please!" He raps on the door. "I'm sorry, please. I really need to talk to you."

For once, I'm glad Mom is zonked out on pills, but she could still wake up, not to mention the whole neighborhood. I gallop downstairs, ready to tell him to get lost or I'll scream for help. He knows my mom is here. I open the door. Kieran seizes me in his arms. Words flood out of him.

"I was a jerk, sweet pea. I was wrong. Please forgive me. I'm no good at this relationship stuff. Sometimes I don't know what happens to me. Something just takes over me. I can't control it." He hugs me so hard I can scarcely breathe. "I was an asshole. I can't live without you, Chloe, I can't."

My fear and anger evaporate. I wrap my arms around him. The Kieran I know is back.

"You scared me. You were saying all kinds of crazy things, and I don't even know what I did. What got into you?"

"I couldn't help it. It just came out of me. I'm just so afraid of losing you. You're the best thing that's ever happened to me. I mean it."

"You're not going to lose me. Just because I talked to some other guy doesn't mean that I'm leaving you for him. That's crazy."

"I know. I get too jealous. I can't help it. I guess I'm selfish. I want you all to myself."

"You really think I'm going to run off with some guy I meet for five seconds at a party, or do something with him in the bathroom? You have that low an opinion of me? Kieran, how could you even think that?"

"You don't know how much you mean to me. If you didn't mean anything to me, I wouldn't get jealous."

"I don't want Mom to wake up." I lead him into the kitchen and close the door. Kieran sits at the table, pulling me onto his lap and nestling his head on my chest. We stay like that for a minute, just inhaling each other.

Kieran picks up his head. "You were getting a little jealous yourself, weren't you?"

"You were really flirting with that girl."

"Now I know you're really into me. If you weren't jealous, it would mean you didn't care."

"Did you do that on purpose, to see if I would get jealous?"

"I just had to see how you felt about me."

I feel relieved that he wasn't really into her, but then the underlying truth pierces me.

"Kieran, don't play games with me like that. It's not right. I wouldn't do that kind of stuff to you."

"I'm messed up I know I am. I...I have a lot of pain inside me." His voice trails off in whisper.

"What do you mean, pain?"

"It's like a black hole inside me." His voice breaks. He grabs a lock of my hair and wraps it around his fist, tucking his head under my chin. I can't imagine what he's talking about, so I say nothing, just rock him like a baby. The faint bark of the neighbor's dog sounds outside.

"I had a dog once, but it ran away. The dog could run away, but I couldn't."

"What do you mean?" His words prick me out of our lull. I sense something is coming, something I need to know.

"My stepdad," he whispers. "My stepdad beat the dog. And he beat me."

I hold him tighter.

"He beat me ever since I can remember. Until he left, that is. It was my mother that drove him away. She did it. She just couldn't cut him a break. Like with my real dad. He was messed up, but he was a good guy. He wasn't a bad person."

"Did your real dad beat you?"

"Just my stepdad. He said life was a long boxing match and I had to learn to be tough, to fight and defend myself. I deserved it though, I was a bad kid. I would've been really bad if he didn't discipline me. Kids need discipline.

"One time he pounded my head against the pavement. I had such bad headaches the next day, he took me to the hospital. He said I fell off my bike. Teachers noticed my bruises all the time, but I just lied. My mom told them I was accident prone. She was afraid to say anything. He beat her, too.

"The neighbors would call the cops, but my mom and me would lie so he wouldn't be arrested, and social services wouldn't take me away. But then he left anyway, and I didn't have any dad at all. Two dads left me."

My heart wrenches. I can't even imagine growing up like that. What torture he must have gone through.

"Kieran, I wish I could just crawl inside you, pick up all your broken pieces and fill your black hole." Emotion thickens my voice.

"I used to wish my real dad would come and get me and take me away. But he never came." Kieran looks up at me, tears pearling down his cheeks. "You're the first person I ever told this to. I'm glad. I'm glad you know it."

"I'm glad you told me." My eyes brim over, too.

"Just love me, Chloe, I need you to love me so bad."

"I do, Kieran, I love you. Never think I don't love you."

We press our faces together. I feel so incredibly bad for Kieran—and angry. No child deserves to be abandoned, beaten. What kind of parents were they?

"I can't leave, Chloe. I can't be alone right now."

"You can stay here." We tiptoe upstairs to my bedroom. Kieran takes off his shoes. We fall asleep in each other's arms.

I wake when dawn's first light filters through the window. I'd forgotten to pull down the blind, which was just as well. I kiss Kieran's face and nudge his shoulder to rouse him.

"You better go, sleepyhead, before Mom gets up."

He rubs his eyes. His face creases into a slow smile. "Hey, we slept together, sweet pea."

"We did." I smile back.

"It wasn't quite what I had in mind, but that's okay."

He puts on his shoes, and we sneak downstairs. He kisses me and leaves. I go back to bed, but all I can think about is Kieran.

I must have eventually dropped back to sleep. It's close to noon when I get up. Mom's drinking coffee in the kitchen when I go downstairs.

"How was the party?"

"Good." I take the OJ out of the fridge and avoid her eyes.

"How did the evening purse work out?"

I pour a glass of juice. "Great. Thanks."

"I'm glad it's getting some use."

I drain the glass, shooting a glance at her over the rim. She doesn't seem to have heard anything last night.

She floats out of the kitchen on her fluffy cloud of pill haze. She'll forget about the purse.

nine

I go down to the basement and stuff a load of clothes and detergent into the washing machine. I haven't been able to stop thinking about what Kieran told me. You always hear about child abuse, but I never actually met someone who went through that. Two dads walked out on him. One beat him. Life is so unfair. Why was he born into that family, and I was born into mine?

I switch on the machine, and it grinds to life. I wish I could help him. He told me he just wanted me to love him. Love. Wholehearted, pure, simple. "All you need is love," like the old Beatles song goes. That's all I can do—love Kieran.

He texts me later on, apologizing again and asking me to come by the camper. He has something "special" for me.

I finish my chores and head out. As soon as I pull into the driveway, he hurries down the camper steps as if he were waiting for me and presents me a dozen red roses and a heart-shaped gold pendant with a little diamond in it as I get out of the car.

"I'm so sorry for how I acted, Chloe. It won't happen again."

He looks like a forlorn puppy. I bury my nose in the bouquet's sweet fragrance. It won't happen again because Kieran poured out his soul to me.

"It's not your fault. We're in this together now."

He kisses me fiercely. "Sweet pea, you're the best. Let me put the necklace on you."

He clasps the chain around my neck, and we walk inside the camper, arms laced around each other's waists. I fill an old peanut butter jar with water and place the flowers in it.

"You know something? We're like a Venn diagram," I say as I arrange the roses.

"A Venn diagram? I gotta hear this."

"We're like overlapping circles, and the overlap keeps getting bigger."

"Until we're one circle together. I get it. You're deep, Chloe. I never met anyone like you."

"I never met anyone like *you.*"

"Let's go out on the river in Claudette's boat," he says.

"A Venn diagram," he repeats as we walk to the backyard. "Only you would compare us to something out of a math textbook." He chuckles.

A dinghy, tied to a rickety jetty, bobs on the water. Squatting, Kieran reels it in, and holds it as I step in. I shriek as the boat rocks.

"I've got you, sweet pea, don't worry."

I sit on a bench as Kieran unties the rope and pushes us into the river. He rows with giant pulls, the oars slicing the water. We reach midstream, and he pulls up the oars into their locks.

We arrange ourselves so I'm lying on his chest in the vee of his legs. We let the current carry us lazily as twilight drops its gauze curtain. The only sound is the lapping water.

I trail a hand in the cool river. "What if I was kidnapped and taken off to the deepest jungle in the Congo, what would you do?"

"I'd call every senator, congressman, the president, whatever, then I'd fly there and hire trackers to find you. I wouldn't rest until I got you back."

I believe him. "You would totally do that, wouldn't you?"

"You're the most important thing in my life, Chloe. I'd never give up until I found you."

I twist my head to look up at him. "I've never felt so protected before. My parents never stood up for me. In fourth grade, these girls were bullying and teasing me on my way to school every day. I told my mom. She never did anything. I had to find a new way to school on my own."

"Nothing like that will happen to you while I'm around. I got your back, Chloe, one hundred percent."

I kiss the palm of his hand. He is so utterly, completely and absolutely there for me, and it's the most awesome, perfect feeling in the world.

We float a little while longer, but mosquitoes start descending on us in swarms.

"Let's go back." Kieran picks up the oars.

"Yeah, or we won't have any blood soon."

"I should row more often. It's good exercise for my biceps."

"You already have good biceps."

"I have to stay in shape. At auditions, they make guys take off their shirts to check out their abs and pecs."

"What does that have to do with talent?"

"You have to have six-pack abs and talent. When you really want something in life, you've just got to go for it and not give up til you get it."

We reach the jetty and clamber out of the boat, which Kieran ties to a hitch. He smiles. "I've got something to show you. It came yesterday."

"What is it?"

"Race you."

He sprints off, and I run behind him into the camper.

"Sit and close your eyes."

I do as he tells me, then something cool and smooth slides into my hands. I open my eyes. It's a photo book, the kind people have printed with pictures of their vacation or wedding.

The title "Kieran & Chloe" is in flowing script over a picture of us on the cover. I look at him questioningly as my heart pitter-patters.

"Go on, open it."

It's full of me and him—the photos we took in New York, in his camper, in the park, everywhere we've been.

"This is beautiful."

"I call it 'The Chronicle of Kieran and Chloe' although I thought of it too late to put on the cover. They wouldn't let me change it."

"I can't believe you did this." I stare at him in amazement. "I think this is the nicest thing anyone's ever done for me."

His eyes gloss over with tears, which makes mine do the same. He sniffs. "Peanut butter and pickle sandwich?"

I laugh as I wipe my eyes. "Sounds awesome."

"That you, Chloe?"

Mom's disembodied voice echoes from upstairs. I'm home early since it's Kieran's acting night.

"*C'est moi*," I sing out.

Feet pad down the stairs then she appears in the kitchen, a pinched look on her face.

"What's up?"

"Oh, Chloe." She clings onto a chair back as if she's going to keel over.

"What?"

"I found out the truth."

"What truth?"

She eases herself into the chair. "It's another woman, that's why your father left."

I feel a jolt. "How do you know?"

"Last week I was going through his suits he left in the closet, and I found two ticket stubs from a Broadway play from last December. I had a weird feeling about it. I didn't go with him and he never mentioned any play, so I went to a private investigator. Your dad's been having an affair for the last year. He's living with her."

Now *I* have to sit down. "Jesus. I can't believe it."

"I knew there was something more to it. He told me there was no one else. The investigator told me it was probably so I wouldn't sue him for adultery and get a sympathy settlement."

My paunchy, stinky-farting father with another woman?

"Maybe there's another explanation."

"The investigator videotaped them walking down the sidewalk holding hands."

"Dad never holds hands."

"He does now."

"How does this guy know it's been going on for so long?" I'm groping to give Dad a way out, for me to rescue and keep the father I know, for him not to be a cheat and a liar.

"He talked to the doorman in the building."

I sit in stunned silence, trying to make sense of it, but I can't. I never thought my dad would do something so underhanded, so totally shitty.

"All these lies, the bald deceit of it. How many people knew all this time? And me, taking his suits to the cleaner, making his dinner. A servant, that's all I was to him. Why was he still having sex with me all this time?"

Major TMI! I stand, but my legs feel cardboard-flimsy. "I'll make some tea."

I make tea, then Mom takes a sleeping pill and I watch TV, or try to, until Kieran's class is over, and I can call him. I catch him as he's walking to his truck.

"I'm sorry, sweet pea. This really, really sucks. But like I said before, there's nothing you can do. It's between them. You just gotta keep living your own life."

"But now I'm really worried about her. She was doing so well. This is a big setback."

"Your dad's a scumbag. I would never cheat on someone. I just want you to know that, Chloe. That's really, really low, going behind someone's back like that."

I now have a whole new picture of my father, one hundred and eighty degrees different from what I believed about him my whole life. I feel shattered.

"I'm coming over," he says.

"No, I'm all right."

"You're not all right. I can tell."

Tears bubble out. "Okay."

A half hour later, we lie clothed on my bed, not saying anything, Kieran just stroking my hair. I don't care if Mom sees us. We fall asleep.

When we wake up, it's morning. He kisses my lips. "Wakey, wakey, sweet pea."

"Kieran?" My mind is foggy then I remember last night.

"I'm going to do something to cheer you guys up tonight."

"What?"

"You'll see. I better get going. I have to be at work in an hour."

We sneak downstairs. "Thanks for being there for me, Kieran."

"Me for you, and you for me, sweet pea." He drives off before Mom even stirs.

When I get to the newspaper, Marion's waiting for me with a stern face.

"Jeannine Oglesby called. You misspelled her first and last names and got her age wrong in that story about the dressmaking camp for low-income kids. We have to run a correction."

"Shit. I know I asked her to spell it." I grab the paper and look at the story, which has "Janine Oglesbee, 63." I check my notebook and my stomach plummets—"Jeannine Oglesby, 36"—is clearly written. No wonder she's mad. I aged her by thirty years.

"How did that happen?" Marion barks.

"I forgot to double-check it." It's true, but I forgot because I was rushing to meet Kieran, although I'm not going to tell Marion that. "I'm sorry."

"Write the correction. Check the archive for the format. And be extra careful next time. We have to be accurate, or it affects our credibility and people won't read us."

I call Kieran at lunchtime from the parking lot and tell him what happened. "I feel like a total jerk."

"It's only a name and number, sweet pea. I'm sure all reporters make mistakes from time to time. Think of all the things you've gotten right. Don't worry about it. I'll be over later with something for you and your mom."

I smile. "You love surprises, don't you?"

"Gotta make life interesting somehow, sweet pea."

Kieran arrives a little while after I get home. "Special delivery of good cheer." He shakes a large bag he's holding and steps inside the front door. "Let's go into the living room. It makes a better stage."

We troop into the living room where Mom's watching "Jeopardy!" and sniffling into a tissue.

"Hey, Mrs. Quinn. I've come to cheer you and Chloe up."

"We could sure use it."

"Take a seat next to your Mom, Chloe, and if you wouldn't mind switching off the TV." I do as he tells me. Mom gives me a "what's all this about?" look. I shrug.

Kieran stands in the middle of the room. "Good evening, ladies, and welcome to tonight's show. I'm your host Kieran Dubrowski." He sweeps his arms out to the sides like he's on a stage. I giggle. "The first part of tonight's program will be an interactive experience. Charades!"

We applaud. Mom actually smiles. "I haven't played that in years."

"I'll go first." Kieran mimes a rolling camera.

"Movie." Mom shouts.

Kieran nods, holds up two fingers.

"Two words," I say.

He points to his back and holds up a finger like it's an "1."

"Back," I yell.

"One back, a back?" Mom screws up her face as she thinks.

Kieran looks around, spots a black book and points to it.

"Book?" I say.

He shakes his head and smooths the cover, then points to his back.

"Hardback," Mom guesses. "Hunchback. Wait, black!"

Kieran points at her and nods wildly. He holds up two fingers. "Second word," I say.

He nods and flaps his arms.

"Bird. Blackbird!" I say.

He shakes his head and mimes swimming.

"A water bird," Mom says.

He puts his hand around his neck and mimes lengthening it.

"Long neck, bird with a long neck, swimming," I say. "Ostrich?"

Kieran does a ballet pirouette.

"I know, swan!" Mom shouts. "'Black Swan'."

Kieran claps, and Mom jumps to her feet. She mimes "Hunger Games" and I do "Star Wars."

We play charades for a while then Kieran takes the stage again. "Now ladies, it's time for the second part of our show."

He turns around, grabbing the bag. When he swivels back, he's got a fake mustache and glasses on. He does an impersonation, and we have to guess who it is. His first is Groucho Marx.

He does more impersonations using props in his bag, tells some jokes and performs some comedy sketches like the ancient Abbott & Costello "Who's on First?" routine.

Mom and I crack up. "This is like a one-man, off-off-Broadway show," Mom says between laughs.

Kieran takes a bow. "Ladies, I hope you've enjoyed tonight's show. Tune in next week—same time, same station." He throws his arms in the air triumphantly.

We clap. Mom yells "Bravo," and I whistle. He bows.

Kieran flops on the couch next to me.

"You should do comedy," Mom says.

"Blues recovery business at your service, ma'am. I used to do this for my mom and sisters."

"How 'bout some ice cream?" She gets up. "I think there's chocolate chip mint."

She heads to the kitchen, and I study Kieran.

"What?" he says.

"You're like a marble. Every time you roll, I see a different color."

He laughs his seal-bark. "Sweet pea, you're such a poet. I just adore that about you."

As he hugs me, I wonder what else there is to discover about him.

Ten

The summer days blur by in a humid haze. I haven't heard from Jade and Morgan, not that I've contacted them either. Nor have I heard from Dad. But who cares? I have Kieran and the newspaper and Mom.

"This is the best summer I've ever had," I say as Kieran pulls into his driveway after picking me up from the paper.

"Yeah?" He seems off today, tired from work maybe.

"Thanks to you." I peck his cheek before I get out of the truck. The late afternoon sun makes everything seem painted with melted butter. "Hey, there's a note stuck in your door."

Kieran whips it out and crushes it in his fist as he unlocks the trailer.

"Aren't you going to read it?"

"I don't have to."

We step into a sauna. "It might be important."

"It's from Claudette, okay? I'm behind with the rent." He tosses the paper into the trash bag on the floor and goes to the fridge.

I don't know how much Kieran makes, but he always buys whatever he wants. Maybe that's the problem.

"You should go on a budget, so you have enough to cover expenses every month," I say.

He wheels around, eyes glinting. "You cost me a lot. That's why

I'm in this hole." He picks up a used paper plate from the counter and flings it at me. I recoil, but spits of ketchup land on my face. "How much do you think I've spent on you? Taking you out, buying you presents."

My stomach flip-flops. His face is contorted, his eyes bulge. It's happening again, the Jekyll-and-Hyde rage.

"Kieran, I didn't ask you..."

"Come on. Don't tell me you don't like all that? You like me to spend money on you. Girls expect it. If you don't spend money on them, you're dirt. That's all they want!"

I steel myself. "You bought me that frigging stuff because *you* wanted to! I don't care about presents."

"So now it's frigging stuff! That's the gratitude I get for doing something nice, for going out of my way for you, for trying to please you, and even your mom, the flowers, the show props. You're nothing but a selfish, spoiled brat!"

He stabs his finger in the air. I flinch, afraid he's going to poke my eye. My head spins. Maybe I am selfish and spoiled. I should be grateful for his gifts.

Wait. I try to stop the spin, to get back to where I know I'm right.

"I didn't know you bought those props especially. I thought you had them. I don't need presents when you don't have the money."

"I can't help it if I'm generous. That's how I am. I like to give, to make people happy. Is that so bad?"

"No, but ..." It's not bad, but it is? I grope to find the answer and then I have it. "Yes! When you can't pay the rent, that *is* bad." That makes sense.

"I thought you understood me. But you're just like all the rest!" Bitterness embroiders his voice.

"I do understand you. What's got into you?"

"I made a big mistake with you. My friends warned me."

"What friends? Why are you always bringing up other people?"

"What about Joe Favola?" he snarls.

"This has nothing to do with Joe frigging Favola!"

I can't think straight. He's lobbing my words like tennis balls.

When I have an answer that makes sense, he whacks it to the other side of the court, making me run to hit it straight again. I can't keep up with his tornado of twisted logic.

Frustration overwhelms me. I seize the first thing I see—a glass and hurl it onto the floor as I yell my frustration.

"Argggh!"

I stare at the smithereens. I've never done anything like that in my life.

Kieran's face turns serene. "You've got a lot of anger in you, Chloe. You pretend to be so steady, so mature, but now the real you is coming out. I knew you were unstable underneath. You put up a good front, I'll say that."

He's calling *me* unstable? I quiver with anger. "Stop it, Kieran!"

"Stop it, Kieran," he mimicks in a baby voice. "I'll stop it all right. You want to see me stop it?"

Is he going to do something? I have to get out of there. I flee out the door. I'm on the second step when something slams the middle of my back, pushing me off balance.

I fly headlong onto the driveway, landing on my chin and hands. Lightning bolts of pain shoot through me. Garbage litters the ground. The trash bag. That's what he threw at me.

"You can't take it, can you? Can't take the truth about yourself!" he yells.

I scramble to my feet, clenched with fear he's going to do something else to me. He's holding the sides of the doorway, chest leaning out, face twisted.

"Bitch! Traitor! Go ahead, run away!"

He pitches something at me so fast I can't tell what it is. It pelts me on the shoulder. I reel and see my purse on the ground. My wallet, phone, pens spill out.

I sweep up my stuff as fast as I can. I have to get away from him. I lurch into a run, heading back to town to my car. I hear a car behind me. Is it him? I run harder. The car passes by. It's not him. I keep running. My throat feels like I swallowed gravel. Every so often, I check behind me to see if he's following, but so far no one.

I keep going. It's like my legs are on automatic pilot. They don't stop pumping until I reach the safety of my car. I flop into the driver's seat, make sure all the doors are locked and drive home.

Pulling into the garage, I press the remote to close the door and then tears flood out of my eyes. For the first time, I feel the sting on my chin and hands. I look at them. They're mats of torn skin, blood and grit.

I realize I must've have run a mile and a half or more. I have no idea how I physically did that. I hate running, and I've never been good at it. But I did it. It must've been fear that fuelled me.

When the garage light timer switches off, I gather myself. I can't sit in the darkness. I want light. I want four walls. I want safety. I enter the kitchen. It's empty. Of course.

I wash my chin and hands under the faucet as I sob. I want Mom to walk in and ask me what's wrong. I want to show someone what he did to me, to tell me it wasn't my fault. But she doesn't come. I dab my chin and hands with antiseptic, gritting my teeth at the sting, and wrap a gauze bandage around them.

Thoughts and questions pelt me like hail. What happened? Everything was going so perfectly and then he went ballistic again—over nothing. What did I do? Why does he do this? Doesn't he know I love him? Hadn't I proved that time and again? Does he think I don't love him enough?

I can find no answers.

In the morning, Mom comes downstairs in her tatty bathrobe as I eat my corn flakes holding the spoon tenderly. She heads straight to the fridge, takes out the OJ, swallows a pill, and goes back upstairs. I can't eat any more. I dump out the cereal in the garbage and bail out of the house.

Marion assigns me to write a short feature on the Rotary Club scholarship winner who's going to study biochemistry at Stanford.

"She's going to be at the club luncheon today, so you can get a free lunch."

I barely nod.

"You okay? What happened to your hands?"

"I tripped on one of those cement bars in the parking lot last night." I'm surprised at how readily the lie flows out.

"Those things are dangerous. You've really come a long way this summer, Chloe. I'm going to be sorry to see you go in a couple weeks."

I try to smile but I just can't.

"You better get to that luncheon. We need the story this afternoon. I hope the rubber chicken isn't too bad." Marion turns back to her computer.

I trudge off to Tudor Square, Indian Valley's banquet hall. Unlike the last rage, Kieran hasn't called to apologize.

I sit at the table with a place reserved for the *Weekly News*. It doesn't matter if the chicken's rubbery. I have no appetite. I prod the meat and vegetables around my plate, ask the scholarship winner some routine questions, take her photo. An official drones on in a speech. A plate with a slice of carrot cake appears in front of me.

My phone buzzes. A text. My stomach somersaults. It's Clarissa.

I just got home! Dying to see you. Come over and hang?

Relief floods me. She's just what I need.

Be there asap.

I race back to the newspaper and ask Marion if I can go home as soon as I file the story. She says it's fine.

I bang out the story, download the photos.

When Marion gives me the thumbs up after the edit, I make a beeline for Clarissa's.

Her mom answers the door. "They're out on the deck, Chloe. How's your summer been?"

"It's been good, really busy." *They.* I'm dismayed. That means Jade and/or Morgan are here, too. I really want to talk to Clarissa alone.

"Lemonade's on the counter. Help yourself."

I pour myself a glass from a pitcher and step through the sliding door into a cloud of coconut scent. Clarissa, Jade and Morgan sit at a patio table in swimsuits, their hair piled in messy knots on top of their heads. A bag of peanuts and a pile of shells lie in the middle of the table, along with a bottle of coconut oil. This is heavy-duty suntanning work.

Clarissa leaps up and hugs me. "Chloe!" Her skin is slippery.

"Rissa, you're like a 116rench fry with all that oil. Ick."

"Is this a mirage I see before me?" Morgan pushes her sunglasses on to her forehead as if she can't see me with them on.

"A ghost from the past, more like it," Jade says.

I sit next to Clarissa. "Sorry guys. I know I've…"

"What happened to your face and your hands?" Clarissa interrupts.

"I fell."

"Who's this guy that's swept you off your feet?" Clarissa says. "Jade and Morgan say they haven't seen you all summer."

"I think we're broken up."

"What do you mean you 'think'?" Morgan asks.

"We had a fight. He got a letter from his landlady about being behind in the rent, and I told him that he should go on a budget. He didn't take it well. I guess money is kind of a sensitive issue." I don't bother with the gory details.

"All couples have fights. That doesn't mean you've broken up. He's probably letting things cool off," Jade says, cracking open a peanut shell.

"I don't know."

"He'll call you soon, Chlo," Clarissa says.

"He goes into these weird temper tantrums over nothing, I mean they're really scary. And he gets really jealous if I even look at a guy." I didn't plan on saying all that, it just came out. "I don't know what to do."

"Guys always get jealous," Jade says.

"He had a rough childhood. His dad was a druggie. He walked out, and Kieran never saw him again, then his stepdad beat him."

"A girl at camp was seeing a therapist because of problems with her parents. Maybe that's what Kieran needs," Clarissa says.

A spark of an idea burns a tiny hole in my fog of depression. That's exactly what Kieran needs.

"There was another girl who was on some kind of antidepressant," Clarissa continues. "She had to go to the nurse's office every day to take it. Maybe something like that would help him."

"Clarissa's still hung up on Caleb." Morgan replaces her sunglasses on her nose. "We think she should call him and ask him out, see if he's really interested in her."

Clarissa groans and slumps her shoulders. "No way."

"You have to do something. I am not going to spend my senior year listening to Caleb, Caleb, Caleb," Jade says. "You need a definite plan of action."

"Yeah, time to move on, girl," Morgan says.

They chatter on, their interest in my life drifting away like the scent of their tanning oil on the breeze. I don't care. I'm thinking about what Clarissa said. Kieran needs professional help. That's the answer to his problems, our problems.

I'm refilling my glass in the kitchen when Jade calls, "Chloe, your phone's ringing!"

I leave the lemonade, dash out and fish in my purse for the phone. It's Kieran.

"Loverboy?" Clarissa asks.

All three of them exchange an amused look. I nod as I move to the side of the house for privacy and press answer.

"Sweet pea, are you all right? I've been worried about you." Kieran's voice oozes concern.

"Kieran, you threw the trash bag at me and made me trip down the steps. My hands and chin are all banged up."

"I've tripped down those steps a million times. They can be tricky."

"Why did you do that to me?"

"Let's talk in person. Where are you? I went by the paper and your house, but I didn't see your car."

"I'm at Clarissa's. She just came home from camp."

"I miss you, sweet pea. I need to talk to you."

"What are you going to throw at me this time?"

"I'm sorry, I shouldn't have done that. Meet me at the park?"

"When? Now?"

"This is more important than your friends."

I want to show him my scrapes—what he did to me—and convince him to get help, which is way more important than tans and gossip. I tell him I'll meet him in fifteen minutes and return to my friends.

"Everything all right?" Clarissa asks.

"He wants to meet and talk about it."

"Look at you, a happy camper now," Morgan says.

"What did I tell you?" Jade says.

"You're going to go, aren't you?" Morgan says. "You haven't seen Clarissa all summer, but Kieran's the priority?"

"I just have to figure this out." I give Clarissa an apologetic look. "Do you mind?"

"Don't sweat it. Do what you gotta do. I'll walk you out." We stroll to my car. "I guess they're kind of pissed you blew them off this summer."

"It wasn't intentional, Riss. It's a long story."

"Let's get together soon, just us two, and you can fill me in."

"I'd like that." I get in my car. "Thanks for understanding."

She waves as I drive off.

Kieran is pacing in the parking lot when I arrive. As soon as I get out, he seizes me by the waist and twirls me around.

"Sweet pea! You came. I was so afraid you wouldn't."

I stay frosty. "I said I would, didn't I?"

When he puts me down, he sees my hands. He takes them gently and brushes them with his lips. He does the same to my chin.

"Careful, they hurt."

"You shouldn't have gone rushing out of the camper like that. You could've really hurt yourself."

I stare at him in astonishment. His face alters. "I'm sorry, okay? I'm really sorry. I was wrong. It was my fault," he says.

His apology frays my bitterness. "You scared me, Kieran. You don't know how scary you get."

He kisses me. "Please forgive me. I don't want to lose you."

"You don't know your own strength. You threw that bag hard."

"You're right." We saunter to a bench and sit, the golden light bathing our backs. My hand lies limply in his as he rubs it.

Kieran twists to face me. "Hit me, Chloe. I want you to hit me."

"What? Don't be crazy."

"You won't hurt me. I deserve it. Just slap me, punch me, kick me."

Something echoes in my memory. What did he tell me—that he deserved to be hit by his stepdad?

"I've never hit anyone in my life, and I'm not hitting you."

He takes my wrist and slaps his face with my hand. I wrest it away.

"Stop it!"

"You won't hurt me, and you'll feel better if you hit me."

"No, I won't feel better. Cut it out!"

"Just once, slap me."

I sigh at his persistence. I brush my fingers across his face. "Satisfied?"

He buries his head in his hands. "I'm such a loser. Why are you with me, Chloe? Why don't you leave me? You can find someone better than me."

"I'm with you, okay? I'm not leaving you."

"I screw everything up. I told you, I'm no good at this." He pounds his knee with his fist.

"Why don't you see a therapist?"

"I tried once, but it was too hard. I couldn't go there. There was just too much pain."

"But if you don't deal with this stuff, you'll never get better. Maybe there's some medication that might help you."

"You're right. But I don't have insurance. I can't even pay the damn rent. I'm such a loser."

"A lot of people go to therapists. It's really not a big deal. Clarissa said two girls at her camp…"

Kieran's head jerks up. "Clarissa? You were talking to her about us? About me? What did you tell her?"

"Nothing. She just mentioned these two girls at camp and that gave me the idea that maybe counseling could help you."

"Don't go telling our private stuff to people, Chloe. They won't understand. We have to keep it to ourselves. People just get in the way."

What about all these "friends" he's always throwing in my face? "The same goes for you, too. Don't talk to your friends about me, about us."

"You're right."

"If I find a free counseling place you could go to, would you go?"

He rests his forehead on my shoulder. "I'll see a shrink, whatever you want. You're the only one who's cared enough to help me. I love you so much. You just don't know what you mean to me." He winds a shock of my hair tightly around his fist, like he always does.

"I love you, too. Things could be perfect for us if you could stop these random rages."

We stay silent then Kieran sits up.

"I want to take you to meet my mother."

"Now?"

"I don't introduce every girl I go out with to her."

We walk to his truck, our hands finding their way into each other's back pockets.

We drive into Crystal Lake and turn off at a sign for Mount Airy trailer park. The road is dark. The only light comes from the shoebox-shaped houses lined up in rows among the pine trees.

Kieran parks beside a shabby white trailer with an aluminum awning of faded green stripes. A breeze rustles tree branches stirring the scent of pine. We walk up to the trailer, our feet crunching on a thick carpet of fir needles.

Kieran swings open a battered screen door. "Hey Ma! I brought someone to meet you."

Hearing the canned applause of a game show, I follow Kieran in. A woman is asleep in a recliner, her head thrown back with her jaw agape. Her legs are extended on the footrest, one foot wears a fuzzy slipper with a hole in the sole. The other slipper lies askew on the floor. She stirs.

"Kieran, that you?"

"Who else would it be? Wake up. I brought a guest." He wags her foot.

"Who?" She sits up and looks around. Her eyes rest on me.

"This is my girlfriend, Chloe."

I smile and reel off the required "nice to meet you."

She doesn't answer, just flips the recliner to an upright position and springs forward. "What time is it? I musta just dozed off. You guys want some coffee?"

"We're just dropping by, Ma. Don't trouble yourself. Just wanted to say hi, that's all."

"Whenever he says that, he stays at least an hour," she says to me. "He says he's not staying then he sits in the kitchen and starts talking a mile a minute. So, I'm gonna put the coffee on anyway."

Kieran shoots me a sheepish look. I smile back at him.

"Sit down," she says to me, motioning at an ottoman as she heaves herself out of the chair.

She's a big woman, five-ten maybe, with a beach-ball stomach that juts out further than her chest. She wears a stretchy headband around her grey hair, which is mussed at the back from the headrest.

I perch on the ottoman to be polite and look around. The upholstery on the couch and armchair is faded, and the coffee table has a few nicks in it, but the place is neat and clean. I notice a photo of a young man with Kieran's eyes and jawline on a shelf.

Kieran follows my eyes. "That's my dad. I won't let her take that picture down just in case he comes home one day. He'll get mad if his picture isn't up there."

"You mean *you* get mad if his picture isn't up there," his mother calls from the kitchen. "I keep telling him to take the damn picture. I don't want to see it."

"It belongs right where it's at. You been all right, Ma?"

"Yeah. Rheumatism kicking in a little, but that's to be expected."

"You heard from the girls?"

"Not lately, so that means everything's going good. They only call if they want money. I got some of them hard candies you like."

She tosses a bag at him. "They were on special this week. Alf gave me some venison steaks. You can have a couple of them, too."

She opens the freezer and takes out a foil-wrapped packet, offering it to him from the threshold of the kitchen.

"You keep 'em, Ma. I don't eat meat anymore."

"I shouldna said it was Alf that shot it." She returns the package to the freezer.

"Who's Alf?" I mouth to Kieran.

"Boyfriend." He rolls his eyes.

She turns to the kettle and mixes powdered creamer and instant coffee with steaming water in a mug.

"You want some?" she asks me.

"No, thanks."

"She's got real thick hair like you," Kieran says.

She studies my hair as she sips. "She does. Mine had some red in it, too, before it went grey."

I guess this is where Kieran gets his habit of talking about people as if they aren't there.

"We gotta get going," Kieran says. "Some people are expecting us."

It's my cue to stand. We walk to the door with his mother following us. "Glad you found yourself a nice girl, Kieran."

I wave to her from the bottom of the wooden steps. The only answer is the bang of the screen door. I guess that's also where he picked up the habit of leaving without goodbyes.

"You didn't stay long," I say when we're in the truck.

"The best way to do family is cameo appearances. Keep it short then they'll always want to see you."

"She loves you, Kieran. I could see that."

"Not enough to stop one dad from whaling on me or make another one stay."

"I don't think it was her fault."

"He would've stopped anyway. I was getting old enough to fight back."

I rub his cheek with the back of my fingers. He twists his mouth to kiss them.

Mom's watching some soap-opera family drama on TV when I get home. Doesn't she have enough of her own?

"How was your day?" she asks.

"Clarissa's home from camp. I went over to her house for a while."

"That's nice." She gloms her eyes back on the TV.

I go to my room, where I crank up the laptop, and type "Indian Valley mental health" into the search field.

I find a clinic in town that takes low-income patients and several others nearby. I print out the list and crawl into bed. The problem solved, I suddenly yearn to be with Kieran. I call him.

"Can we go to sleep on the phone together? Like not even talk, just hold the phone and listen to each other breathing until we fall asleep."

"I adore you, Chloe."

"I love you, Kieran."

My eyelids slide closed, and as his breathing grows deep and rhythmic, my lungs move in unison with his.

Eleven

My step has a definite spring in it the next day, even Marion notices.

"You look a lot better, Chloe. Let's get going on the story about the plan for a new library annex. Call the director and get a video interview with her, B-roll of the library, and don't forget a photo of the plan itself. And call this guy Andrelli. He's one of these watchdogs always complaining about the town spending too much taxpayer money. He'll be good for a negative quote."

I finish the library story just in time for Kieran to pick me up. I check my purse—I've got the list of counseling places. Hope fills me as I dash to the truck.

"What do you feel like doing?" he asks after we greet each other with a kiss.

"How about veggie burgers at Burger-O-Rama? My treat. That's where we had our first date, remember?"

I snuggle up to him as we drive. He pecks the crown of my head. "How could I forget? So, what did you write about today?"

"The library announced an expansion of the children's wing to put in space for events. How was your day?"

"I had to load sod onto a contractor's truck then unload a bunch of new shrubs. I'm wiped out."

"You're exercising your biceps like you wanted to."

"Yeah, and sweating in the hot sun and dust, too."

"So I can smell." I laugh.

Kieran lifts his arm. "Don't you like my perfume?"

"Ew!" I recoil, laughing. I'm happy he's in an upbeat mood.

We park and enter. I order our veggie burgers and root beer. "See, you've converted me to your diet."

"Told ya."

We take our tray to a plastic booth where Kieran wolfs down the food in three large bites.

"That hit just the right spot." He wipes his mouth with a napkin, screws it up in a ball and tosses it on the tray.

Now seems a good time to bring up the therapist. I push aside the remaining third of my burger and take out the printout.

I take a deep breath. "I did some research last night, and I found some counseling places that charge patients according to income or even free. There's one right here in Indian Valley. It would be perfect for you."

Kieran stops slurping his root beer and flickers his eyes around. "Not so loud. You're practically broadcasting to the world that I'm crazy."

I lower my voice. "Sorry. Take a look." I unfold the paper and slide it across the table. He glances at it, folds it and sticks it in the back pocket of his jeans. It's not quite the reaction I was expecting. "So, what do you think?"

"You're trying to make me out to be a sicko, and I'm not."

"I'm not trying to make you out to be anything. I think everybody could use some help. Yesterday you seemed all in favor of the idea."

"That was yesterday."

"You said you would see someone, do whatever I wanted. Now you won't?" Irritation colors my voice. I have to rein it in, stay calm.

"What if someone sees me going into one of these places?"

"A lot of people go into these buildings. Nobody's going to pay any attention to you. Why don't you just try it and see what it's like?"

He tightens his lips.

"Kieran ..."

"I'll think about it." He stands. "I'm getting a strawberry shake. Want one?"

I shake my head. As he orders at the counter, I kick myself for bringing up the subject in a public place. I should've waited until we were in his camper. He's ashamed. That's why he's acting like this.

He returns to the table with the shake, rubbing his cheek. "You really scratched me yesterday."

What is he talking about? "I didn't scratch you."

"You did. Right here." He points to his cheek. It's smooth.

"There's nothing there."

"I can feel it."

"I didn't scratch you. I just brushed you with my fingers because you bugged me to hit you."

"No, you scratched me, Chloe."

I drop the subject to avoid a fight. "Let's go." He's doing it again, twisting things.

"Sweet pea, could you help me rehearse for class?"

We go to the park and practice Kieran's scene, but my heart's not in it. When I say I want to go home, Kieran doesn't object.

The days blur by. I keep waiting for Kieran to mention the therapist. Maybe he just wants to do this on his own. Maybe he's made an appointment, or even gone already, but he's too embarrassed to tell me. I want to ask him about it, but I don't want him to get mad. I try to forget about it.

Kieran is changing out of his work clothes in the bathroom of his camper a week later. "Can you toss me the jeans in the laundry basket, sweet pea?"

As I pick them up, I detect a lump in a back pocket and fish it out. It's a wad of paper that went through the wash with the pants. I unfold it as much as I can: "dian Valley Men."

The sharp spike of realization stabs me. The therapist list. I suddenly feel suffocated. I chuck the jeans on the bed, throw the paper in the trash bag and dash outside. I stand in the driveway, my back to the camper, my chest heaving. He's not going to go to counseling. Ever. I was a fool to believe him, just like I was a fool to believe that Dad would take me to NYU.

"You okay, Chloe?" Kieran calls from the door.

"Just needed some fresh air. It's stuffy in there."

I take a deep breath and go back inside. I sit stonily at the table as Kieran putters about. He glances at me.

"What's up?"

"Nothing. Well, just my parents and all that." It's a handy cover.

"Let's go to the playground."

"What playground?"

"There's a park down the street."

We stroll down the block. I didn't know there was a park since I never went further along the street than Kieran's place.

The playground's full of little kids running around and parents talking or typing on their phones. Kieran pulls me to the swings and sits me down on one.

"What are you...?"

"Hold tight." He draws back the swing as far as it can go and releases it. My butt rises slightly off the swing seat as I feel the rush of soaring into the air. I swing back and Kieran, grunting with effort, pushes me higher, then higher again and again. My problems break loose and jettison into the sky.

After a bit, he yanks me to a stop. We run to the slide and whoosh down together, his legs around me, whooping.

We head to the merry-go-round. Kieran gets it going superfast before hopping aboard. I lean my head back and let myself get dizzy as we spin. We climb on top of the jungle gym and jump off holding hands, then race each other doing the hand-over-hand overhead ladder.

I'm breathless with smiles. Kieran catches me around the waist. "See? I made you happy again."

"What am I going to do with you?"

"Love me, Chloe, just love me."

"I do love you."

I'm not going to give up on the therapist idea.

It's just going to take a little more time for him to get used to it than I thought.

It's Kieran's acting night, and I make plans to get together with Clarissa. I really want to talk to her, tell her what happened with the therapist and get her advice.

I'm walking across the parking lot of the Indian Valley Chamber of Commerce that afternoon when Kieran calls.

"What's going on, sweet pea?"

"I'm going to interview the new Chamber of Commerce president for a profile piece."

"You really get to hang with all the honchos."

"They just want their names in the paper. Hey, I'm going over to Clarissa's tonight."

"Are you going somewhere with her?"

"Just hanging out. I've only seen her once since she got back."

"I guess that's okay."

Like I had to ask his permission? Annoyance nips me. "You've got acting tonight anyway, and she's my best friend."

"I thought I was your best friend."

"She's my best girlfriend."

"I want to meet her. Why don't I pick you up and take you over there?"

My heart sinks. Why can't I be with my friend just one night? I rally.

"Then I won't have my car to go home."

"I'll pick you up. Just call me when you're ready."

Why did I ever mention going to Clarissa's? Now I'm stuck. If I insist on driving myself, Kieran will think I'm hiding something, and it'll lead to a fight. I have to agree.

"Hey, you're getting the best of both worlds," he says.

I'm not really sure about that. "I gotta go, I'm late." I hang up and slouch into the Chamber of Commerce, where the receptionist greets me icily.

"Since you're late, you'll only have ten minutes with Mr. Davis now. He has a very busy schedule."

Great. Thanks, Kieran.

I'm still mad when he picks me up to go to Clarissa's. "Your phone call made me late for my interview. I hardly had time to get the information I needed for my story."

"So what? Nobody cares about the Chamber of Commerce president."

I stare at him. "For your information, a lot of people care. Besides, I don't say things about your job."

He conveniently ignores me. "Where does Clarissa live?"

I give him directions and remain sullen.

"Don't take your bad day out on me," he says.

I bite the pad of my thumb and stare out the window.

When we arrive at Clarissa's, I ring the doorbell. As we hear the door opening, he holds me possessively as he always does in front of people. I make the introductions.

"Do you want to come in for a minute, Kieran?" Clarissa says.

Say no, say no, I plead in my head.

"I gotta get to my class. I'll leave you two to your girl talk. Don't believe a thing she tells you about me." I can tell he's only half joking. "I'll text you when I'm on my way to pick you up." He kisses me and waves airily.

Clarissa closes the door and arches her eyebrows at me. "Wow, he is so into you."

"Yeah."

"You don't seem overjoyed by it. Mom's grilling chicken for dinner, by the way."

I detect the aroma of spicy sauce and perk up. "I could practically eat that smell. Let's go."

We head to the kitchen and slide open the glass door leading to the deck.

I say hi to Mrs. Coluccio.

"Looking forward to school starting?" she says.

I groan.

"I second that," Clarissa says.

"It's a big year for you girls. College applications and everything." Her mom points a fork at a plate of chicken on the table.

"Go ahead and eat. There's corn on the cob and salad."

We sit and fill our plates.

"He's cute," Clarissa says. "So, it's more than a summer romance?"

"You could say that. We see each other basically every day."

"True love." She gives a dramatic sigh.

"I've got stuff to tell you." I give a sideways glance at her mom, who's patting her forehead with her apron at the grill.

Clarissa gives me a knowing nod. "Hurry up and eat. I'm dying to hear."

We chow down with minimal chitchat and take our plates into the kitchen. "There's brownies for dessert," her mom calls.

"We'll get them later," Clarissa says.

We race up to Clarissa's room and shut the door. Clarissa sprawls on the bed. "So, guess what?"

"What?"

"Caleb is going out with a sophomore, some girl named Melody. I knew it."

"How did you find out?"

"Jade and Morgan saw them at the mall the other day, all lovey-dovey. Then Jade saw them at the movies."

She stretches out her legs, resting her feet on the wall above the headboard. I grab a snow globe of London and join her.

"It might be just a summer fling."

"I should be so lucky. I'm so pissed. I lost my chance after that party. I should have made a move then."

"He's not the only guy in the world, Riss."

"That's all very well for you to say. You've got a guy totally wrapped around your little finger."

"Was there anyone at camp?"

"No one interesting. So, what happened with Kieran and the counseling thing?"

"Nada. He said he'd go see a therapist, and I looked up a bunch of places that charge low fees, but then when I gave him the list, he got all pissy about it and said I was trying to say he was crazy."

"So, he totally turned around from what he said?"

"Yeah. I reminded him of that, and he said he'd think about it. Then I found the list in his jeans after it had gone through the wash. He never even took it out of his pocket."

"He's probably scared. Maybe you should make the appointment and offer to go with him."

"I don't know. He's..." I shake the snow globe. The flakes shimmy over the Big Ben.

"He's what?"

"Like changeable, moody. He can be kind of rough sometimes, you know, like yell and stuff. Then he can be really sweet, and treats me like a princess, buys me flowers. He gave me this." I show her the heart necklace he bought after our first fight. "He can be really romantic."

"He's an actor, they're kind of temperamental. They're always getting in trouble. I think that's just what they're like."

"Maybe. But he goes from one extreme to another. It's weird. I really think a therapist could help him, but what am I going to do—shove a gun in his back to get him there?"

"You could kidnap him. Put a bag over his head and pull it off when he gets onto the shrink's couch." She giggles.

"Riss, this is serious."

Her face falls. "You're right. Sorry."

"I just feel so bad for him. I mean, it's not his fault he had crap parents. He says I'm the best thing that ever happened to him."

"Maybe he'll come round to the idea."

"I hope so."

"Well, I have an idea that might cheer you up. How 'bout we have a sleepover at my house this weekend? With Jade and Morgan. We haven't done that in a looong time."

"That'd be awesome." The thought flashes across my mind—Kieran's not going to like this.

"Totally. So, I made one decision this summer. I want to go to college in a big city, somewhere exciting. I don't want to go to some small, boring place."

"Kieran took me to see NYU. It looked cool."

"I thought you didn't want to go to New York, it was too close."

"Yeah, but..."

"You'd be near Kieran, right?"

"Kind of, but I'd still love to go to California."

"Let's do it. Forget all these guy problems and go to California together."

"We could learn to surf."

"Hell yeah!" We high-five. Clarissa jumps up. "Let's go get brownies before my sister eats them all."

When Kieran texts that he's on his way to pick me up, Clarissa makes goo-goo eyes and smooching noises.

"Shut up." I smack her playfully on the arm. "You're just jealous." As soon as the words are out of my mouth, I realize I sound just like Kieran.

A horn beeps. "That's him." I run downstairs. If I don't come out quickly, he'll come to the door. I don't want him asking Clarissa what we talked about.

Clarissa runs after me. "You really can't wait to see him."

I turn to her, my hand on the doorknob. "Do me a favor. Don't mention anything to Kieran about the sleepover. Yet, I mean." She looks at me quizzically. "It's just ... I have to tell him first."

"Sure, but you can do whatever you want, you know. You don't have to let him control your life."

"We're just used to hanging out together all the time, that's all. I'll talk to you later." I dash to the truck, just as Kieran is getting out.

"I was going to say hi to Clarissa."

"That's okay. Her mom's on her case about going to bed early."

He buys it, and we climb in the truck. "How was it?" he asks.

"We had a good time."

"Go anywhere?"

"No, we hung out, ate barbecued chicken."

"Just you two or were there other people?"

"Just us. Why all the questions?"

"Curious. What did you talk about?"

“Oh school, camp, work, this guy Clarissa's got a crush on.”

“Nothing about us?”

“Just what we've been doing and stuff, nothing private. How was your class?” I have to get him off the subject of Clarissa.

He launches into a rant about Dorian, but I'm not really listening. How am I ever going to get him to agree to the sleepover?

Twelve

"Don't forget Tyler's coming home tonight," Mom says at breakfast at the end of the week. "Dad's picking him up. They'll be here by early evening."

"That's right. I did almost forget."

"I figured. I'm going to the store today to stock up."

Now she's going to the supermarket? "The fridge has been empty all summer. All of a sudden, you're stocking up for Tyler?"

She ignores me and goes to refill her coffee mug, but I know she heard. It feels good to state my feelings. It seems I'm always walking on eggshells these days, holding back what I'm really thinking and feeling and doing because I'm afraid of the reaction. It's like playing a never-ending game of chess, always measuring my moves against someone's response. It's exhausting, but I appear stuck on the board.

Now I'm faced with a major dilemma. I haven't told Kieran about Tyler's homecoming. He'll insist on meeting him and Dad, and I don't want to be embarrassed by Kieran hugging me to him and gushing about me. But I have to come up with an excuse not to hang out with him as usual. The sleepover is also coming up and I haven't told him about that, either. I toy with various excuses the whole day and finally settle on cramps.

I call Kieran mid-afternoon as I finish my story on vandalism at an elementary school.

"I went out to the scene to shoot video and stills. They really wrecked a couple classrooms—tossed the desks, threw eggs on the whiteboard."

"Kids with nothing better to do."

"That's what the cops basically said. Listen, I feel cramps coming on. Would you mind if I just go home tonight?"

"Why don't I come over and hang at your place? I can massage your back, make you tea."

"I just want to lie down with the heating pad and go to sleep early. I'm in a crabby mood."

He pauses, obviously weighing his decision. I hold my breath.

"All right, sweet pea. Call me later?"

I exhale. I hang up feeling a twinge of guilt then I remember the fibs he's told: the commercial audition, the flat tire on the way to NYU. *You do what you gotta do, sweet pea.* This is one of those occasions.

I finish my story and ask Marion if I can leave early since my brother and father are coming over. She says that's fine.

I feel strangely light as I drive home. I realize I'm looking forward to seeing Dad and Tyler and relieved at not being with Kieran.

An unfamiliar car is parked in the driveway. It must be Dad's rental. I rush into the kitchen. He and Tyler are sitting at the table with Mom.

There's an oddly somber air, which I attribute to Mom and Dad being in the same room. I refuse to let them dampen my mood. Dad gets up and kisses me on the cheek.

"How was camp, Ty?"

"Good," he says, not taking his eyes off the table.

"I see it didn't change your one-syllable responses." I notice Mom and Dad's faces remain grave. "What's up? Are we going to a funeral or something?"

"Tyler wants to go live with your father," Mom announces in a flat voice.

I glance at Tyler, who hasn't looked at me once. It's true, then.

"Tyler needs a male role model," Dad says. "And since he's going to a new school this fall anyway, this would be a good juncture to make a change."

I ease myself into the empty chair. The table feels crowded. All four chairs haven't been occupied in months. "You're going to live in New York City. What about school?"

"I've got a private school lined up," Dad says. "And you're welcome too, Chloe. I don't mean to exclude you, but I figured since you've only got one more year to go, you'd want to stay in Indian Valley."

"It's nice of you to leave me one of my children, Doug," Mom says.

"Bonnie, please. Tyler can come and visit whenever he wants. Chloe can come into the city. He's going to spend the week here, see his friends and pack. I'll be back to pick him up on Saturday."

Tyler fiddles with his hands. "I'm sorry, Mom," he blurts, finally looking up.

I feel the stinging invasion of tears. My family is literally disintegrating before my eyes.

Dad turns to me. "Why don't you come with us to the city on Saturday and see the apartment?"

I squeeze my eyes shut to hold the tears in and nod.

He clears his throat. "I better get going, then." He leaves. No one gets up.

We sit, listening to his car back down the driveway. When it's silent again, Mom pushes back her chair. "I'll get dinner on."

Tyler bolts upstairs. I follow him into his room. He's grown over the summer. He's now skinny as a blade of grass.

He's unpacking his duffel bag, stowing clothes pell-mell in the dresser. A mound of dirty laundry sits on the floor.

"Isn't that a waste of time?"

He turns, T-shirt in hand. "What?"

"Putting clothes away. You're just going to be packing them again."

He shrugs and turns back to his chore.

"Ty, why are you doing this?"

He strides across the room with socks dangling from a hand and shoves the door shut.

"I want to be with Dad."

"But you're breaking up the family." I sit on the bed.

"It's already broken up."

"Dad has a girlfriend, you know."

"I know, he told me."

"He's been cheating on Mom for a long time. Did he tell you that?"

"Chloe, stop trying to make me go against Dad. He's not a bad guy." He tosses his head to shake a shock of hazelnut hair out of his eyes.

"I'm just telling you the truth, that's all."

"The truth is, I don't like being around Mom the way she is now," he says.

"Me neither."

"See?"

"I guess I can't walk away from her the way you can. She needs me. She needs us. When did you plan all this?"

"He asked me if I wanted to live with him when he came up for parents' weekend. I said okay, then he said it depends if he can get me into a school. And he did."

It sounds so simple. I survey his room, the giant Lego spaceships and model cars that he built. "You going to take all this?"

"Nah, it's baby stuff. Well, maybe just a few things. You can come visit."

"Yeah, I know. Won't be the same though."

There doesn't seem much else to say. I leave him to his unpacking and go downstairs to find Mom studying the fridge magnets, phone in hand.

"I think I'll just order a pizza tonight. Is that all right?"

"You still have me, Mom."

"I know, Chloe, I know." We hug.

⁂

Friday rolls around and I have two conflicting plans for the next day—Clarissa's sleepover and the city trip with Dad and Tyler. My gut tells me that Kieran's more likely to favor the outing with Dad and Tyler. After all, he can't really object to me seeing my father and brother. I sit back in my chair and gnaw the pad of my thumb as the computer screen blurs in front of me.

"Earth to Chloe, do you read me?" I straighten with a start. "When you finish daydreaming, I need that calendar listing," Marion snaps.

My fingers leap to the keyboard. As I type in the listing, I have a brainstorm. I could tell Kieran I'm sleeping over at Dad's, go to New York for the afternoon, then come back and go to Clarissa's. That would avoid a fight and/or rage with Kieran, and I'd get to do both things. Perfect. My fingers speed up.

I drive to Kieran's after work. A thunderstorm is brewing, and the air is knitted with humidity. A crochet of black nimbus clouds rumbles across the sky, blanketing the sun. Fat raindrops splatter the windscreen as I turn down his street. Uncertainty pinches me. I hope he's in a good mood.

He's standing in the driveway, arms outstretched with palms up, face skyward.

"You look like a rain god," I call.

"I love thunderstorms," he says without budging. "Let's go watch it over the river from the house. Claudette's not here."

I wonder what happened with his rent situation, but I don't dare ask. We scurry in as raindrops gather speed. Kieran grabs the cushions off the living room couch and makes a little bed on the floor of the screened-in back porch. We huddle as the sky grows darker. It splits with a resounding crack and a flash from a jagged lightning bolt, which silhouettes the tree line beyond the river.

"Check that out!" Kieran says.

"It's like nature putting on a Shakespeare drama."

"Totally."

"This would be great to see from that ridge where we went on July Fourth," I say.

"That's a good idea. Let's do that next time."

The rain pummels the roof as thunder rolls and claps. Kieran seems calm so I tell him about Tyler moving in with Dad, and Dad inviting me to go into the city tomorrow and spend the night at his apartment.

"When did all this happen?"

"Just last night, late," I fib.

"How come you didn't tell me? This is major. I don't want you keeping things from me."

"I wasn't trying to keep anything from you. I'm telling you now."

"Don't be secretive, Chloe. What else aren't you telling me?"

Clarissa's sleepover. It's like he knows. "Nothing."

"I think it's pretty crappy of both your dad and Tyler. I don't think you should be rushing into the city for them. It's like rewarding them for breaking up the family."

"They're still my family. I haven't seen them all summer. What's so bad about that?"

"What about NYU? Who took you to NYU?"

"You did."

"And then you never heard boo from your dad until now, until it suits him, right?"

As another spear of lightning flashes, I see my perfect plan deflate before my eyes. I gather strength and push back. "But I still want to see them, Kieran."

"I have an audition coming up for a play and I'd really, really like you to help me rehearse on Saturday."

"You really have an audition?"

"You think I'd lie to you? It just came up today. It's for a lead role for a play at the Stagecoach Playhouse, Brick in 'Cat on a Hot Tin Roof.' Dorian says I stand a good chance of getting it. But you know what? If you don't want to help me, that's fine. I'll find someone else. You run along with your dad. There's a girl in my class who'll rehearse with me, the one who was at Joe's party. In fact, she'll help me more since she's an actor. She understands."

Anger flares in me. "One day I can't make it, and you run to some girl? When's the audition? Is it on Sunday?"

"It's okay, really. You have things that are important to you, and

I have things that are important to me."

"Prove you really have an audition."

He takes out his phone, types in a few words and shows me the screen—the Stagecoach Playhouse website.

Casting call: Cat on a Hot Tin Roof. All roles.

I bite my lip. I really don't want Kieran to call that girl to help him rehearse. That's my role. I'm the one he needs. I have a brainwave.

"How about this? I go into the city with Dad but skip the sleepover. I'll come back in the late afternoon and we can spend the night rehearsing."

He smiles and kisses my forehead, ruffling my hair. "That's my sweet pea. I knew you'd come through for me. I want to meet your dad and Tyler. I'll come over when he picks you up."

I fight the urge to scream. I don't want him to win, to get his way like he always does. "You know what? I won't go to the city at all. I'll spend the day rehearsing with you."

"You don't have to do that."

"The audition is more important."

"But I want to meet them."

"No, you're right. Dad just shows up when he feels like it. Why should he get to meet the people in my life when he clearly doesn't give a crap about my life? You can meet him another time."

He falls silent. I feel a ripple of triumph. For once, I foiled his plan.

When I get home, I text Clarissa that I can't make the sleepover because I'm going into the city with Dad and Tyler. Then I tell Tyler I won't be going into the city.

I sit on my bed. My victory over Kieran feels hollow. Yeah, I won, kind of, but I'm not doing either of things I wanted to. How did my perfect plan go so wrong?

After reading the whole play together and drilling the lines over and over, Kieran is actually pretty good at the role of Brick. He's got a real chance at landing the part. I tell myself that not hanging out with my friends and family will be worth it if he gets it.

Tonight is his acting class, which means I can hang with Clarissa, though this time I'm not telling Kieran.

He calls in the afternoon as I'm editing letters to the editor. "Can you pick me up some yogurt and fruit on your way over?"

"Way over where?"

"Here."

"Aren't you going to acting?"

"I'm behind on paying Dorian, and he says I can't come back until I pay him what I owe."

My stomach plummets.

"You didn't have anything planned, did you?"

"No," I lie.

After work, I run into the Pantry Market and buy nectarines, peaches and yogurt, and drive to Kieran's.

"Knock-knock," I call.

Kieran is sprawled on the bed. "You get the stuff I asked for?"

"Yep." I unpack the bag on the kitchen counter.

He ambles over and picks up a yogurt. "Why didn't you get the whipped style? You know I don't like the regular style."

"You didn't tell me what kind you wanted."

"I don't even like lime. Who eats lime?" He chucks the yogurt on the counter with a flick of his wrist. I catch it before it rolls onto the floor.

"You should have told me exactly what you wanted."

"You should know by now." He bites into a peach and grimaces. "This isn't even ripe." He throws it into the sink where it crashes on dirty plates.

"It'll ripen in a few days."

"I want to eat it now."

I lose it. "Then maybe you should have stopped on your way home and bought your own groceries."

"I've been working out in the sun all day. You've been sitting on your butt in an air-conditioned office. You could at least help me out."

"I did help you out. You could at least be grateful."

He says nothing and sinks into the bench at the table, head in his hands. He's obviously in a bad mood over the acting class.

"How about a spicy crunchy sandwich?" I say.

He grunts, which I take to mean "yes."

I fix the sandwiches and take the plates to the table. I should've got him the whipped yogurt, some ripe fruit he could've eaten right away. I should've put more thought into it instead of grabbing the first things I saw, then I could've avoided the fight.

I sit. "How was your day?" I ask as I take a bite of sandwich.

Kieran doesn't look up. "Crap."

"Because of Dorian?"

"Of course because of Dorian."

He picks up his sandwich. We eat in silence then I clean up. Kieran flops on the bed and switches on the TV.

I snuggle up beside him, resting my head on his chest. He drapes his arm around me, as usual, but something's off. My spidey sense tells me to leave.

"Know what? I think I'll go home. Mom's not feeling..."

"No." He tightens his embrace around me. "I want you to stay."

Fear grips me. I stay.

He's prickly all evening, demanding that I bring him a root beer, massage his shoulders, iron a shirt. I do everything he asks without protest.

If I don't, I know he's liable to explode. I just don't want to risk it. But all the while, I'm watching the clock. As soon as it's nine, I tell him I have to get going as I have to be up early. This time, thankfully, he doesn't object.

I get in my car and make as speedy a getaway as I can. I'm afraid he's going to appear in the driveway and force me to stay. Only when I turn onto the main road do I relax. I get home and plod up to my room. I feel like a wrung-out dish towel.

I'm writing a story about the closure of Our Lady of Sorrows School due to low enrollment when Clarissa calls.

"We're planning a bowling party Sunday night. Our summer grand finale so you've got to come since you couldn't make it to the sleepover. You, me, Jade, Morgan."

I hesitate. "Let me check with Kieran."

"Is he your keeper or something? You're your own person, Chloe."

"I know," I say in a mousy voice. "It's just ... you know."

"You're allowed to do something by yourself, even when you're in a relationship."

"I know, I'm sorry."

"Don't you ever get sick of him? It seems like he's on you day and night."

"He needs me."

"Your friends need you, too. I've barely seen you since I got back. You're always too busy to even talk. But whatever, do what you want."

"I want to come, Clarissa."

"Then come. Just tell him you're going and that's it."

I hang up, wondering how on earth I'm going to do that without Kieran flipping out on me.

Kieran texts me to bring a pizza. I call Valley Pizza, taking care to order extra pepperoni, his favorite.

When I bring it over, he opens the box and his face breaks into a smile.

"You remembered the extra pepperoni. I wanted to see if you remembered without me telling you, and you did."

Relief washes over me. I passed the test, did something right. He rewards with me with a kiss on my forehead. We sit on his bed to eat pizza and watch "Family Guy."

When we finish, Kieran leans back against the pillows, and I take out the box to the garbage.

"It's so much cooler outside," I say as I come back in. "Why don't we go down to the park or something?"

"Nah, I don't feel like it." Kieran chuckles at the TV and pats the bed beside him. I lie down.

"School's starting Monday." I say, realizing I'm actually looking forward to it.

"You're going to be around a lot of guys all day."

"That doesn't mean anything. I love you, Kieran." A weird feeling comes over me as I say those words. For the first time, they ring hollow.

He clutches my thigh. I seize the moment.

"Clarissa, Jade and Morgan want me to go bowling with them Sunday night, like a grand finale to the summer. I really haven't seen them much."

"We can do something in the afternoon, and then you can go on to your friends."

That was so easy, I'm taken aback. Maybe he's coming around. I hug him. "Thanks, I really mean that."

He grunts.

⁂

On the last day of my internship, Marion takes me to lunch at Soi Siam. After we order lemongrass chicken and red curry, she places one hand on top of the other on the table and looks at me.

"Chloe, I have to tell you that you're the best intern I've ever had. You've done a great job this summer. You've handled everything I've thrown at you."

Heat blooms in my cheeks. I know I'm blushing.

"I'd like you to stay on part-time, and I'd pay you a salary. What do you think?"

"That would be awesome!"

"I'd like to get you going on higher level reporting, such as covering council and school board meetings, and even helping me out doing some investigative stuff."

"I'd love that."

"You've really been a help to me this summer."

"I've loved working at the News. I know this is what I want to do with my life. It's going to be such a letdown going back to the school paper after this."

"This is just a weekly community newspaper. But if you learn the ropes here, you'll be way ahead of everyone else when you get to college," Marion says.

I barely touch my food, I'm so excited. I take the leftovers in a box and put them in the fridge at the office.

I'm on my way to Kieran's when he texts me.

I need pickles & peanut butter.

These shopping errands have become a regular thing. They're major pains in the butt, plus Kieran never pays me back.

Already on my way, no money on me, I reply.

You're still closer than me. Use debit card.

I feel a rise of anger. As usual, he didn't even say "please." We can eat the leftover Thai food. There's enough for two. I don't answer the last text.

I turn off toward the river then fear smacks me. If I show up without the peanut butter and pickles, he'll go into a rage. I've eaten plenty of his peanut butter and pickles over the summer. I guess I owe him. I swing a u-turn and plow back through rush-hour traffic to the Pantry Market.

Kieran's frame fills the doorway of the camper when I arrive. "What took you so long?"

"I had to turn around and go back in rush-hour traffic to the Pantry Market. I told you I was already on the way."

He takes the bag I hand him. "You sure you weren't meeting someone?"

"Give me a break."

I walk into the kitchen. Jars of peanut butter and pickles sit on the counter.

"Kieran, you have peanut butter and pickles. Why did you tell me to get them?"

"I'm almost out."

I check the jars. "There's enough for today. I could have gone tomorrow. You acted like it was a big emergency."

"I've gone out of my way for you tons of times. Like taking you to NYU, remember? I had to use a sick day."

How many times is he going to use the NYU trip to make me

feel obligated to him? I wish he'd never taken me.

"You offered. I didn't ask you."

"I still went out of my way."

"I don't want to fight with you."

"I don't want to fight either."

"The fact is I can't afford to keep buying this food every day. I'm not earning a salary. I just get paid a stipend, remember?"

"Know something, Chloe? You are the cheapest person I ever met." His eyes burn and he pokes his finger at me. Shit. He's going off.

Quickly, I raise my hands in the air like I'm surrendering, which I am—anything to avoid a flip-out.

"I'm cheap. You win." I remember my news, which now seems rather flat, but it's a good time to switch topics. "Guess what? Marion said I was one of the best interns she's ever had and offered me a part-time job as a reporter. I'm going to be covering council meetings and learning investigative journalism."

Kieran hugs me. "That's great, sweet pea. Didn't I tell you? You're going to be winning...what's that prize called?"

"The Pulitzer?"

"Yeah, and travelling the world for *The New York Times*, and you'll forget all about me."

"Don't be silly. I won't forget you."

"You will." His voice has a strange hurt undertone.

I change gears again. "I've got leftover Thai curry. Marion took me out to lunch."

Kieran dives for the bag. He takes the box and a fork to the table and digs in, not offering to share. I don't care. I managed to defuse an oncoming rage. That's all that matters. I make myself a peanut butter and pickle sandwich.

When I get home, Mom's lying on the couch reading. I twist my head to see the title, "Restarting Life after Divorce."

"Marion offered me a part-time job when school starts. With pay. She says I'm the best intern she's ever had."

"That's great, sweetie. I'm so proud of you." I sit on the sliver of couch space next to her. "When's school starting?"

"Monday."

Alarm springs on her face. "We should go shopping this weekend then."

"Don't worry. My clothes from last year still fit. I can use my old backpack. I'll need some new notebooks, but I can get them."

She pauses. "I've made a decision. I'm going to make this divorce a new beginning. I'm not going to let your father drag me down."

"That's great, Mom." I really don't want to hear the details. I stand. "I'm going to bed."

I plod upstairs, feeling the weight of my life on my shoulders.

Thirteen

$\mathcal{S}$unday afternoon has that lazy, draggy feel of a deep August heat wave. Kieran's lying shirtless on a towel in the front yard when I pull up. I give him a wolf-whistle.

He props himself up on his elbows and grins. "I've been waiting for you to get here. I have a place I want to show you down the river. We'll take Claudette's boat."

"I have to be back by six for the bowling party with my friends, remember?"

"I remember."

We head to the jetty and clamber in the boat. Kieran unmoors it and pushes us off with an oar.

"What's this place? I thought I'd seen all your special places," I say.

"I want to surprise you. You'll love it."

The sun toasts my face as Kieran rows. The houses hugging the riverbanks give way to woods. I trail my fingers in the water. The surface is bathtub warm while a few inches deeper is icy-cool. I let myself drift with the current. A dragonfly flits by. A bird coos. This must've been how the pioneers saw the land as they traveled into the unknown, I think.

Kieran docks the oars in the oar locks and stretches out in the stern of the boat, hands clasped behind his head.

"You've got be careful now with school starting, Chloe. Your friends are going to be really jealous of you."

My reverie is ruined. "The whole world is jealous, according to you."

"I mean it. You're working as a real reporter, got a real relationship. You're way above them now. You need friends who are on your level."

"I like my friends."

"I'm just saying."

Kieran rubs my toes with his. "I want to get you a ring, sweet pea."

"I don't want you to spend money on that," I say quickly. He'll just twist it to make it seem that I wanted the ring and then blame me for going broke over it.

"I want to get you a diamond."

"Kieran..."

"Something that shows guys at school that you're taken."

"Now you're the one who's jealous."

"I love you. Don't you love me?"

"Of course." I can't bring myself to say the words, though.

He sits up and grabs the oars, slicing them cleanly through the water in a steady rhythm. His shoulders glisten with perspiration as his muscles work. People float by in fat inner tubes, bantering and tossing beer cans. They have a cooler tied to one of the tubes. They wave at us. I wave back.

"We should do that sometime," Kieran says. "Looks like fun."

"How far have we gone? I don't want to go too far."

"We're almost there."

That can mean anything with Kieran. We're moving at a good clip down the river, propelled by his oar strokes and the current. He rows on.

"How much farther? I have to get back, remember?"

"Don't be a spoilsport, Chloe."

An uneasy feeling invades me, but I know better than to resist him. A little while later, he steers the boat toward the shore.

"This is it," he announces to my great relief. He hops into the shallow water. I get out, too, and he tugs the boat onto the sandy bank. "Now we walk."

Annoyance jabs me. "How far?"

"It's five minutes. It's totally worth it, believe me."

We plunge into the woods along a narrow trail. After walking Kieran's "five minutes," which is more like forever, we squeeze through a crevice between two massive boulders. A natural pool, surrounded by rock, lies in front of us.

Kieran beams. "See? Wasn't this worth it? Let's jump in." With a whoop that echoes off the rocks, he cannonballs into the water with a giant splash.

He surfaces, shaking his head. Water drops spray in an arc. "Come on in. Water's great!" He floats on his back, his body a googly, ghostly misshapen mass under the water.

I sit on the rock, hugging my knees. I don't want to go swimming. I want to go bowling. "I didn't bring clothes to change into."

Kieran swims over and splashes me. I crawl backwards. "Quit it. I don't want to get wet."

"Swim in your underwear. It'll dry off. No one's around."

"You should've told me to bring my bathing suit."

"So what? Don't be such a priss. That's one thing I don't like about you." Getting out, he cups water in his hands and throws it at me, laughing. He flops back into the pool. "Now you're wet."

"Let's go. We can come back another day when we have more time."

Ignoring me, he floats on his back and kicks his feet into a splash frenzy. I watch him, waiting until he's done. The light turns golden. It's getting late.

"Let's go already! I have to get back."

"Suit yourself." He heaves himself onto a rock. I stand, brushing the seat of my shorts.

"I have to take a leak. Wait here," he says.

Sighing, I fold my arms and lean against the boulder as he thuds down the trail. Time ticks by. A still silence reigns. I slap at gnats.

I wait.

And wait.

"What's taking you so long?" I call into the trees. No answer. "Kierannnn!"

I know something's up. I just know it. I speed like a bullet down the trail, stumbling over roots, branches and stones. When I get to the sandy cove, the boat's gone. I wade into the river and look upstream. Something flashes. The boat is rounding a distant bend.

"Kieran!" I scream. He disappears.

I check my phone, no reception. Panic stabs my gut. I force myself to think logically. I could walk back following the riverbank or swim, maybe? I look at the bank. There's no real trail. We've come too far to swim, especially upstream. I have no idea where I am. Maybe someone will come by on an inner tube or boat, and I can yell for help.

I sit on the sand, folding my arms on my jack-knifed knees. Resting my chin on them, I stare at the moving water. He did this on purpose. Because I wanted to spend one night with my friends, one measly night. I start to cry, but I wipe away the tears, shove them back inside me. Kieran can't hurt me if I don't feel hurt. I will not let him hurt me.

Daylight is fading when I finally hear the rhythm of oars in the water. My head whips around with a ray of hope. It's him. I wade out and climb in the boat before he can row off again.

"You didn't think I wouldn't come back for you, did you, sweet pea?" A note of victory sounds in his voice.

"I honestly didn't know what to think." I speak in a calm, measured voice. I will not give him the satisfaction of seeing how angry and hurt I am because that's exactly what he wants, and I will not let him win.

I sit facing him because I don't trust him with my back. He goes into a rant. I'm ungrateful for not appreciating his efforts, lazy for not helping him row. I'm two-timing him, that's why I don't want a ring. I'm using my friends as a cover to meet a guy.

I stay silent, letting his crazy words bounce off me like I'm made of granite. I refuse to engage with him, even look at him, and that gets him even angrier. Let him get mad. I feel nothing. I am completely numb.

Claudette's jetty finally comes into sight. Salvation. I fix my eyes on it. When we're close enough, I jump out and wade to shore as fast as I can, ignoring Kieran's shouts. I break into a run to my car as soon as my feet touch ground. I've never run so fast in my life. My heart hammering my chest, I peel out of his driveway.

I drive straight home, gallop upstairs and lock my bedroom door. Then, and only then, I allow myself to melt into sobs.

Lockers clang, bells buzz, kids yell. First day back at school. I'm dreading seeing my friends. After I recovered from my meltdown, I called Clarissa, but she didn't pick up. I tried Jade and Morgan, same thing. I can't blame them.

Clarissa's locker is in the same row as mine, so I know I'll see her first thing. I find her decorating the inside of her locker door with colorful stickers of flowers and hearts. I swallow.

"I'm so sorry, Riss. Please don't be mad at me."

She looks at me with a hard face. "We're not going to bother you anymore so you can hang with Kieran all you want. I don't know why you say you'll hang with us and then not show up. Not even let us know you're not coming."

"We went way down the river and there was no phone service ... and some things happened. I couldn't get back in time."

"I never thought you'd be one of those girls who makes a boyfriend her life and forgets her best friend. Boy, was I wrong."

"Don't be like that, please."

"You've changed, Chloe, and not for the better. In fact, I gotta say this, you look like shit lately."

"Rissa..."

"I gotta get to class. I have friends who really do want to see me." She grabs a notebook, slams her locker door and marches off.

I sink back against the lockers until someone asks me to move. I don't know how I'm going to make this right.

The bell rings, and I race to homeroom.

On the way to first period, I duck into the girls' room and study myself in the mirror. I do look like shit. My skin is splotchy. My eyes look vacant. My hair hangs limp and dull. How did I not see myself before? I know the answer. Because I'm always focusing on Kieran.

Through my morning classes of AP English, French and economics, I robotically answer "awesome" when people ask me how my summer was, tell them I did a newspaper internship, then ask about their summer and pretend to listen as they blab on. I couldn't care less. I'm just waiting for lunch when I'll have more time to explain everything to my friends.

When the bell for fourth period rings, I speed to the cafeteria. Jade and Morgan are already at our table with their trays.

"Hey guys, what's the lunch today?" I say.

"Are you blind now, too?" Morgan says in an acid tone. Turkey wraps are on their trays.

"I know you're mad at me, and you totally have every reason to be. We went on a boat trip and got lost down the river. There was no phone signal. It was night when we got back. I'll be there the next time, I promise."

"We decided last night that there won't be a next time," Jade says.

Clarissa arrives with her tray, shooting me a stony look. She addresses Jade and Morgan as if I'm not there. "I just saw Caleb, and he asked me how my summer went."

"Not this again," Jade says.

"I thought you were over him," Morgan says.

"I am, but you never know."

"Eww. Look at this." Morgan pulls a hair from her wrap.

"Totally gross," Clarissa says.

"Morgan, it's your hair," I say. "Look at the color."

"No way."

"Yes way," Jade says.

Morgan squints at it. "Oh yeah."

I smile. Things seem to be blowing over. "I'm going to get my lunch," I say, pushing back my chair.

I buy my wrap and return to the table. It's empty. They've

ditched me. I can feel people's eyes on me, so I sit quickly like I was expecting my friends not to be there and stuff the wrap in my mouth. It tastes like cardboard. I toss the rest of it and go to the library, the land of exile for kids with no friends.

After lunch, I have journalism and pre-calc followed by gym in the last period, which I have with Clarissa. I sit next to her on the bleachers and give it one more shot.

"I'm really, really sorry. There's stuff I need to tell you."

"Chloe, if Kieran was in school, you wouldn't even want to sit with us at lunchtime. You'd be with him. Since he's not here, you want to sit with us, so you won't look like a dork sitting by yourself. But when you have a choice, you always choose Kieran. That's not real friendship. You're just a hypocrite."

She gets up and moves to the other end of the bleachers as Mr. Reiss, the P.E. teacher, announces the three activities we can choose from for this marking period: badminton, social dancing and soccer.

I select soccer to avoid Clarissa because I know she hates it, even though I hate it, too.

At the end of the day, I'm walking to the student parking lot when I hear someone call my name.

"Chloe! Wait up!"

I'm surprised to see Trevor Papadopoulos jogging up to me. He's one of those super popular kids who always run for student government and win. Plus, he's captain of the fencing team, editor-in-chief of the yearbook, and cute, with black hair and sea-bright eyes.

"I saw your articles in the *Weekly News*. Are you working there?"

"I did a summer internship, now I'm working there part-time."

"Sweet. We're looking for an editor for the yearbook. Amanda Yaroslavsky is starting a Gay Straight Alliance chapter this year. We need someone who's really good at writing and editing. Would you be interested?"

"Sure." I feel a twinge of happiness, the first all day.

"Awesome. I'll let you know when we have our first meeting."

He trots off to get in a waiting car. I feel flattered that he thought of me and grateful that somebody wants me.

School settles into a flat routine as the first two weeks of the new year roll by. I avoid my friends since they made their feelings about me painfully obvious. I carry around textbooks, so I don't have to go to my locker and run into Clarissa. At lunch, I do homework in the library, except for the days the Yearbook Committee meets.

I haven't heard from Kieran. I know that's his m.o. after a fight, although this is the longest he's laid low. I hope that means he'll never call me again, but he still owes me a big apology.

The fact that my life has become one big irony strikes me one night as I'm lying in bed. I no longer have friends because I hung out too much with my boyfriend, and I no longer have a boyfriend because he didn't like my friends. I erupt into a bitter cackle. The more I think about the ridiculousness of it, the harder I laugh. Then I have a pang of self-pity over my loneliness and tears seep out of my eyes, but I'm still cracking up. I laugh-cry myself to sleep.

Labor Day is coming up this weekend. Marion asks me to work. "I need you to help me with some investigative reporting."

I'm glad to be busy. Last Labor Day, I went with my friends down the shore and had a great day flirting with guys, playing boardwalk games and just lying on the beach.

They're probably doing the same thing this year.

I come home to find Mom going through her clothes. I lean against her bedroom door, crunching into an apple as I wonder what's prompted this burst of energy.

"Guess what?" she says in a jubilant tone. "One of my college roommates called out of the blue, Suzanne Wheelton. She's organizing a reunion for the holiday weekend. She's been renting a house on Long Beach Island all summer. Her kids went back to school already, so she invited us all down."

"Cool."

"Would you mind staying with Dad? I emailed him and he said it'd be fine. He wants you to visit."

"Marion asked me to help her with some investigative reporting. I really want to do that, and I'd be making extra money."

Mom's face drops like a cement slab. "Oh. Well, I can't leave you here alone."

I feel totally guilty. I don't want her to miss her weekend. I can stay by myself, which is basically what I did all summer anyway.

"Don't worry. I can sleep over at Clarissa's." I never told Mom that Clarissa and I aren't friends anymore. I didn't tell her about Kieran either. She hasn't noticed anything amiss, of course.

"Thanks, sweetie. I'll let your father know you won't be coming. I'm going to have to get a new bathing suit. I can't wear this, right?" She holds up a faded, stretched-out, orange paisley one-piece.

"You definitely need a new one."

"That's what I thought. Maybe a new cover-up, too. And I can't find that evening purse I lent you for that party. Did you give it back to me?"

Shit. The one I ruined. "It must be in my room."

"Can you get it? I want to take it with me."

I slink into my room and get on my hands and knees to fish the bag out from under the bed. I blow off the dust and confirm my memory that it's beyond repair. I can't give it to her like this. I stick my head out the door.

"I can't find it right now. I'll look for it after I finish my homework."

I bury it in a shoe box on my closet shelf, hoping she'll forget about it.

Fourteen

Early Saturday morning, Mom loads her suitcase, which contains a new floral-print yellow bikini with matching cover-up, into the trunk of her car.

"What about that evening bag?"

Crap. "I forgot to look for it. Sorry. Do you really need it? I don't want you to be late."

"It's not a big deal."

After a quick hug, she gets in the car and lowers the window to wave.

"Have a good time. Don't worry about me." I wave back as she heads down the driveway.

I drive to the paper. Marion's there with a box of doughnuts. "Get a chair and your notebook, Chloe." I do as she asks and take a raspberry jelly doughnut, as well.

"I want you to do some court record searches on some names I'm going to give you." She types. "This is the Superior Court website. Criminal records are on this tab and civil on this one. That includes divorces, lawsuits, wills, bankruptcies. You can find out a lot of information in legal filings. People leave paper trails in their lives."

"What's the story?"

"I got a tip that three developers, who all have housing developments pending approval, have been paying off certain council members. We need to run the names of the council members and their spouses, as well as the developers, and see what we find on them. I also included a couple key town employees. They're probably in on it, too."

She hands me a long printout of names, and I scoot my chair back to my desk.

"What exactly should I look for?"

"Anything. Make a file for each person. Give a shout if something jumps out at you, like a criminal record."

"It seems a humongous task."

"That's why I need your help. I'm looking up business records and federal courts. This is how you investigate—start by plugging in the name, then follow all the avenues that lead from that. You keep overturning the stones, even ones that don't look likely. You never know what you'll find."

I type in names. I find three lawsuits for unethical practices filed by clients against a councilman who's a lawyer, a child custody dispute and a state complaint against a developer for illegal dumping. Seeing the trouble people get into is fascinating, but by the end of the day, my head is busting.

"We'll keep going tomorrow," Marion says. "If we nail this story, we'll be scooping up journalism prizes."

I go home, planning to chill and watch a movie. I'm staring into the freezer, tossing up between chicken nuggets or chili for dinner when the doorbell chimes. It must be some random knocker like Mormon missionaries or Girl Scout cookie sellers. I hesitate whether to answer. The bell chimes again, and I go to see who it is.

I swing open the door. Shock shudders through me. Kieran. Holding a bouquet of red and white roses. He smiles. It can't be more than five minutes after I arrived home.

I suddenly realize that even though I'm lonely without him, I don't want to be suffocated by him again. The apology that he's obviously about to deliver doesn't matter.

"What are you doing here?"

"I wanted to see you, sweet pea." He side-steps me to enter and thrusts the roses at me.

"I don't want roses."

"They're beautiful. They reminded me of you."

"Seriously, I don't want them."

"Just take them."

I toss them on the hall table. "Kieran, I can't go on like this."

"I know, sweet pea. I'm a scumbag. I came over to make it up to you."

"How can you make up what you did to me?" A mix of anger, bitterness and resentment overcomes me. My voice splinters. "You left me stranded alone in the woods for hours, just left me. The phone didn't even work."

"I was always going to come back for you. I lost it with your nagging to leave when I took you to a really nice place, did something for us. You would've gotten upset, too."

He's doing it again, twisting the truth. "How can I trust you when I never know when you're going to go ballistic?"

"I have a bad temper, but you know I don't mean it. I just take it out on you because you're the one closest to me. That's what they say—you always take things out on the people who are closest to you."

"I can't take it anymore. You go into rages over nothing. You say really horrible things to me. You do really horrible things. I'm done."

He tries to take me in his arms, but I step back to avoid him.

"Chloe, you don't want to throw this away, do you? You know I love you. I love you so much. I can't live without you. I know you love me. We're perfect for each other."

"Go."

"You don't really want me to go. I know you don't."

"Leave!"

He throws up his hands. "If you really want me to, I'll go."

I cross to the door and twist the knob. In a flash, he grabs my shoulders and twists me, forcing my back against the door. He pushes his lips against mine. I squirm, but he's too strong. He pulls back but leaves my arms pinned.

"If you want me to leave, I'll leave, but it'll be forever. You'll never find anyone else like me. You'll never have what we have again. This is it for us, Chloe. You don't want to give this up. You don't want to walk away from this. I know you don't. You don't really want to destroy everything we've built together, do you, sweet pea?"

He hits the kernel of truth. Deep down, I don't want to destroy it. I love Kieran, the good Kieran, not the crazy Kieran. But one comes with the other. His eyes search mine.

I shake my head from side to side to avoid his gaze because then he'll see in my eyes that he's right, but he follows my every movement. I squeeze my eyelids shut, and try to wriggle free, but it's useless. I'm trapped. Kieran always wins. I go limp and droop my head on his shoulder.

"I knew it, sweet pea. You don't want to give this up." He ropes his arms around me like a lasso and leads me to the living room where he sits me on the couch. My body quivers like half-set Jello.

He clutches fistfuls of my hair. "I need you so much. You just don't know what it's like being me, to have this pain inside. Do you think I want to be like this? I hate being me. You're the only one who's seen inside me. You're the closest I've ever let anyone come. I can't let you go."

I don't know what to say, think, do. I turn myself numb like I did in the boat. He smooths my hair.

"You're high strung, Chloe, too smart for your own good. That makes you unstable. That's how a lot of creative people are. But we'll get through this as long we stick together. I'll take care of you. I know what's best for you. I'm going to give you a spa treatment. You deserve it. We need candles."

"Kieran..."

He shushes me with his finger against my lips.

"Let me do this for you."

There's no point resisting. If I refuse to do what he wants, he'll go apeshit. I find candles and matches in a kitchen cabinet.

"Bring all of them." Kieran leads me upstairs.

"What are you...?"

"You'll see."

We enter the bathroom, and he turns on the bathtub faucets full blast. "Got any bubble bath?"

I give him a jar of blue bath beads from the linen closet. He upturns the whole jar into the bath and swishes the water around. Puffs of fragrance rise. When the tub's full, he turns off the faucets.

"In you get." I hesitate. "Water's going to get cold."

"Kieran..."

"This is your spa treatment." Kieran lights the candles and places them around the tub.

I undress and climb in the tub. The room glows with flickers like an old church as night descends outside the window.

Kieran pours steaming scented water over my back with the toothbrush cup. I gradually unwind. Kieran the monster has gone. My Kieran has returned.

"You're the best thing that ever happened to me, Chloe. I don't want to lose you, ever. You're like some type of angel. You're everything that I could want."

"I'm not an angel or even close. I'm just Chloe."

"You're an angel to me."

"It's like you put me up on a pedestal."

"I'm just so overjoyed at finding you, at being loved." He soaps my back.

"But you pull me off the pedestal then you put me up again, like I'm a yo-yo."

"I can't help it. It just comes out. I've made an asshole of myself so many times."

"Kieran, you've got to get help. You've got to call one of those places on the list I gave you or it'll keep happening. I can't keep going through this."

"It's not as easy as you think."

"Promise me you'll see a therapist, for real this time."

His lips curl into a sneer. "Promise me, promise me," he says in a mocking tone. "Nice try at brainwashing me, Chloe. You're such a nag, worse than my mother."

With one hand, he pushes my head under the water. I grab his arm with both hands, but it's like an iron clamp on my skull. I can't budge it. He keeps holding me. Holding and holding. My lungs are bursting. I'm going to die. I'm going to drown! He releases me. My head springs up. I draw huge breaths that scrape my throat. I drape myself over the side of the tub, clutching it. I'm afraid to let go or he'll shove my head under again.

He holds out a towel and smiles. "Ready to get out?"

I climb out and dry myself off. I can't trust him. The only thing I can do is go along with whatever he wants so he doesn't try to hurt me again.

We go to my bedroom. As I put on sweats, he studies my wall calendar. He's checking what I've been doing. There's nothing listed except yearbook meetings and homework due dates.

He turns back to me. "Wanna watch TV?"

Whatever he wants.

We go downstairs. He flips through the channels, settling on an action movie. I stare vacantly at the screen. I desperately wish Mom would come home. If only I could get a message to her. My phone. It's in the kitchen. With my car keys.

Kieran's voice startles me. "You're real quiet. You wouldn't happen to be planning a little escape from me, would you? That's the problem with quiet people, they're sneaky."

"I'm tired. I worked all day. Mom'll be home soon."

"I don't think so. She had a suitcase when she drove off this morning, and you called, 'Have a good time. Don't worry about me'."

I wheel my head at him, realizing he's been stalking me. I wonder for how long.

"I was keeping an eye on you, making sure you were okay."

I say nothing and turn back to the TV, trying to curb my growing sense of panic. I have to stay calm, clear-headed. The faint chirp of my phone sounds. I jump up.

"Where're you going?"

"My phone's ringing. It's in the kitchen."

He follows me. Before I can pick up the phone, he lunges for it and checks the screen. He hands it to me, narrowing his eyes.

"You're having a great time."

It's Mom. In a burst of hope, I press answer. Kieran hovers next to my ear so he can hear the conversation.

"How's it going, Mom?"

"We just got back for dinner now we're going for a walk on the beach. I just wanted to check in with you. How's Clarissa?"

A swell of emotion chokes me, and I can't speak. *Come back, Mom, please!* Kieran pinches my arm in a vise-hold. I suck in my lips to keep from crying out in pain.

"Chloe? You there?"

I clear my throat. "She's good. I'm having a great time."

Kieran slashes his finger across his neck in a sign to cut off the conversation. I desperately think of some way to send an SOS.

"I gotta get going and help clean up. The dog made a big mess," I blurt. Clarissa's deathly allergic to dogs. Mom knows that.

"The dog?"

"He's really out of control. Gotta go, love you."

I barely hang up when Kieran snatches the phone and tucks it in his pocket.

"Good. Got any ice cream?" He opens the freezer and takes out the tub of chocolate chip mint and places it next to the sink.

I get a dish and spoon and start scooping. A shove in my back rams my hip bone into the edge of the granite counter. Tears pierce my eyes from the shot of pain. I pivot only to recoil. Kieran's face is contorted. His eyes are bulging.

"Were you expecting your date to call, Chloe?"

"Why did you do that?"

"Who's that guy you walk with after school? Don't lie to me. I have people who tell me things."

"You mean Trevor Papadopoulos? He's yearbook editor. I'm on the Yearbook Committee."

"You told me you hated yearbooks, but now you don't? You had someone waiting in the wings. That's why you wanted to get rid of me. Girls always do that. They've always got someone waiting in the wings. You're not committed to me, Chloe. This is all a game for you. You were leading me on. Everyone told me that's what you were doing."

Scared of what he might do, I step to the side to get past him, but he seizes my wrist and raises it in the air.

"Let me go!" I wriggle my wrist, but his grip is a handcuff.

"You're not going anywhere! You're not running away from me again!"

He throws me. I stagger and fall, slamming my face on the edge of a wooden chair. Pain screams in my cheekbone. I thud to the floor. I lie dazed for half a second then see Kieran's sneakers in front of my face. He's going to kick me, trample me. I scramble to my feet, glancing at the back door. I dive for it, but Kieran leaps in front of me. I can't escape. I have to think my way out of this.

"I'm not leaving, Kieran, I'm not. You're scaring me, that's all. Stop scaring me, and I'll be okay. Let's chill out. Let's get ice cream and go watch TV."

Amazingly, he backs off, his face relaxing. I move slowly toward the counter and finish serving the ice cream. We return to the living room and sit on the couch. I feed him spoonfuls of ice cream. He seems to like that. When he finishes, he rests his head on my lap, and I hold him. My face throbs. My arm is stiff where he gripped me. My neck muscles are sore from straining to push my head against his hand in the bath. A tear splashes down my cheek. I let it fall.

Kieran obviously isn't going to leave or let me leave. I just have to keep things smooth, so he won't explode, until I figure something out. The night wears on in tense silence. Whenever I get up to go to the bathroom or kitchen, he follows me.

As "Saturday Night Live" comes on, Kieran yawns. Maybe he'll fall asleep. I know he's a deep sleeper so this could be my chance. He lies down, hooking me under his arm with my head on his chest. I'm wired with adrenaline and not tired at all. I wait.

His breathing gradually grows slow and steady. I test him by lowering the volume of the TV. Nothing. I extricate myself from his grasp. With little extra room on the couch, I have to slide myself out. If he wakes up, I'll say I'm going to the bathroom. I ease myself off him and bring myself to a sitting position at his feet.

I pause. He doesn't stir. I lift myself gently off the couch. He grunts, and I freeze, but he just rolls on his side. I tiptoe out. In the kitchen, I pat the counter in the darkness for my purse. It's not where I usually put it by the phone. Shit.

"Chloe! Where are you?"

My heart seizes. "Just getting water. Want some?" I try to make my voice sound as casual as possible.

The couch creaks in the living room. Shit. I guess I didn't succeed. Kieran's getting up. His footsteps thud. He's in the hallway. It's now or never. I dash for the back door, but I fumble with the lock, forgetting in my panic which way it turns to open.

"Chloe!" He's entering the kitchen. He's right behind me.

The tumbler clicks. I fling myself through the door and fly across the yard into the woods.

"Come back here! Chloe! What are you doing?" He crashes into the woods behind me. I up my pace. "You think you can run away from me? Don't bother coming back, ever. Hear me? I'm done with your shit!"

My legs pump. Branches slap my face. Twigs poke the soles of my bare feet. A stick slashes my calf.

"You're not getting away from me so easy, Chloe! I know everything about you, don't forget!"

Fear fuels me. I blunder wildly in the pitch black then a bare patch of ground shines in a lacy sliver of moonlight through the trees. The trail. I canter down the path. It comes to me suddenly. I know where I can hide. I come to the turnoff to a narrower path and veer down it. I hear Kieran thrashing through the trees behind me. I have the advantage of living next to these woods practically my whole life, but he's taller. His legs take longer strides.

My eyes adjust to the darkness. I spot the silhouette of the log I'm looking for a couple yards in from the path. I drop to my hands and knees next to it, scraping through the dead leaves frantically.

Kieran's footsteps are nearing. It has to be here. *Come on. Come on.* My hands detect the nylon tarp. *Thank god.* I yank it up, and feet first, I drop eight feet into the party pit, landing in a crouch that sends spears of pain up my legs.

Fifteen

The light of daybreak stirs me. I must've fallen asleep. Now I can see my surroundings. There's a rug and a couple of stolen milk crates that serve as tables with a wood plank over them. A bong and an overflowing ashtray are the source of the stink. Empty liquor bottles and cans clog a corner. This is where Tyler was hanging out.

Kieran. I suddenly remember my predicament. I have to get help, but I need my phone or car keys. Would Kieran still be at the house? If I were him, I'd have left, scared the neighbors would've heard the yelling and called the cops. But Kieran doesn't think like other people. My limbs aching, I climb the ladder resting against the wall, the normal way to get in and out of the pit. I raise the tarp a few inches and peer out.

Pale sunlight dapples the trees. Birds flutter, a squirrel scampers, a branch falls. I crawl out. Darting from tree to tree like I'm in a video game, I make my way home. I reach the tree line along the back yard and survey the house. Kieran's truck is not in the driveway. I race to the back door, but as I twist the knob, I hear a noise inside. He's there! He moved the truck to make me think he's gone. I dash back to the safety of the woods.

"Chloe, is that you?"

Mom! She stands in the doorway, her face aghast. I sprint back and hug her. I've never been so happy to see someone in all my life.

"What the hell is going on here?"

"Kieran, he…" A sob chokes me.

Mom's eyes widen. "Did he hit you? Is that where you got that bruise from?"

All of a sudden, my face hurts. "He shoved me, and I fell. I hit the chair."

"Oh my god." Mom ushers me inside and sits me down. "I woke up in the middle of the night, and I knew something was wrong. What you said about Clarissa and the dog didn't make sense," she says as she fills a plastic bag with ice.

"I called you, but your phone kept going straight to voicemail. I called Clarissa and woke her up. She said you weren't sleeping over there. In fact, you guys aren't even talking. I jumped in the car and got here fifteen minutes ago. I found the place a mess, the TV on, candles all over the bathroom, the tub full of water. I was just about to call the police. You better tell me everything."

As she presses the ice to my cheek, I tell her—Kieran's rages, the shoving, the name-calling, the stranding, the fight with my friends. It pours out of me in a torrent of pent-up words. Finally, I can stop pretending everything's all right.

"You should've told me," Mom says.

"I didn't want anyone to know. I was so embarrassed. Please don't tell anyone. Don't tell Dad."

"Chloe, I am so, so sorry. I should've seen this." A tear beads down her cheek. "I totally let you down."

"You didn't seem to care about me, Mom. I've been so worried about you."

"This whole thing with Dad just flattened me. I didn't see it coming. But let's forget about that now. We need to call the police and report this."

That's the last thing I want. "Mom, I don't want to make a big deal out of this."

"Chloe, he assaulted you. He could've killed you!" She crossed the kitchen to the landline.

"Mom, no!" I yelled as she picked up the receiver. "Don't call the cops!"

She put down the phone. "Sweetie, cops see this stuff all the time. There's no need to be ashamed."

"I don't want to get him in trouble, okay? He's had a really rough life. He used to get beaten by his stepdad. His real dad walked out on him and never came back. He's messed up. He loses control."

"I know you feel sorry for him but ..."

I cut her off. "He was just trying to get me back, that's all. He'll stay away from me now. I know him."

She frowns. "I still think we should call the police."

"I don't want him to have a criminal record and screw up his life. I don't want him to hate me forever. I just want to move on with my life and let him get on with his."

She studied me, then gave a big sigh. "If he shows up again, we're calling 911."

I nod. "I don't want a big fuss over this. It's done, it's over. I want to forget about it. Anyway, I'm supposed to work today."

"I'll call Marion and tell her you had an accident, and I'll call Clarissa to let her know everything's okay."

"Don't tell them, Mom, I really don't want anyone to know."

"Don't worry. I won't say anything. Let's make some tea and toast."

She feeds me and gives me a painkiller, the old Mom again. It's as if my falling to pieces is making her put her own pieces back together. I go up to my room and sleep.

I wake up mid-afternoon in a sweat of fear. My face feels weird. "Mom?" I yell.

She comes into my room right away. "I'm here, sweetie. I'm not leaving you alone. I'll make tea."

I get up and look in the mirror. My cheek blooms with puffy purple glory and half my eye has ballooned. The hurt of the bruise is nothing compared to the hurt inside me. I feel shattered, as if somebody took a baseball bat to a window pane, and all that's left is a frame.

I take a selfie of my banged-up face. I sit on the bed, staring at the picture. Is it really me? Violence happens to people on TV, in newspapers. Not to an A student, a reporter. But it did happen to me. I've become one of those people. How? How did that happen?

⊸⊶⸺⊷⊶

Over the rest of the weekend, Mom does her best to keep me busy. She drags me into the basement to sift through junk to give to charity.

"Do you want to invite Clarissa over, like a peace offering?" She examines a torn baseball mitt.

I shake my head. "She'll just think I'm calling her because Kieran and I broke up, that I'm using her again."

Mom tosses the mitt into the throw-out pile. "She'll get over it. Those things always happen with friends when boyfriends come along."

"I don't think so. I've lost my best friend forever."

I check my phone to see if Kieran has texted or called. Mom catches me. "Anything?"

I shake my head. "He usually leaves me alone for a while, then just when I think he's gone for good, he pops up."

"He waits for you to cool off, so the fight seems distant, and you start to miss him," Mom says. "Then he moves in again."

I'm amazed. "That's exactly it. And after every rage, he's waiting longer and longer."

"That's because he treats you worse each time, so he knows it's going to take longer for you to cool off."

"How do you know all this, Mom?"

"It's called getting old. Here, go through this box." She slides over a collection of old toys.

That night, I wake up in a sweat with Kieran's contorted face screaming at me in a nightmare. I don't want to go back to sleep so I power up the laptop to catch up on social media. Someone's posted a video of Kieran dancing in the bed of his truck with the girl from Joe Favola's party.

The caption reads, **Celebrating freedom with Monique!**

They bounce booties, high-five and holler like total idiots as passing cars honk their horns.

I feel kicked in the ribs. I'm hiding in my house, bruised and broken, while he's out partying with a girl who he had "waiting in the wings." I block him from my account. I pad into Mom's room and crawl into bed beside her.

In the morning, Mom calls me into the bathroom. She stands next to the toilet, her hands full of prescription pill bottles. "I want you to witness this."

She unscrews the cap off each bottle, dumps the contents into the toilet and with a flourish, presses the handle. Dozens of pills disappear in the splashy gurgle of the toilet flush.

I hug her. "Glad to have you back, Mom."

"Glad to be back."

"I have something to show you, too." I fetch the torn evening purse and hand it to her. "I was running away from Kieran after his rage at the party. The strap got caught in the truck door. I pulled it, and it ripped."

She turns it over in her hands. "I was wondering why you were so cagey about it."

"I'm sorry. I was scared you'd be mad."

"It's just a purse. Let's throw it away and forget about it."

"Mom, I don't want to go to school tomorrow. Everybody's going to stare and ask what happened."

"You fell. That's the truth. You don't have to give details."

"What if he shows up or something?"

"You go to a teacher or the office. If no one's around, call 911 then you call me."

I nod, but I still don't want to go.

The next morning, I cover the bruise with makeup as best I can, but it doesn't quite work. I also try a last-minute plea to Mom to stay home, that doesn't work either. I slink into school. Some people look away quickly, some people stare, and some people, including Clarissa, ask what happened.

In gym, she keeps glancing at me as we change into P.E. clothes. "Are you okay?" she says finally. "Your mom called the other night looking for you."

"I'm fine. I tripped and fell. Clumsy ol' me."

I slam my locker and hurry off. She only wants to talk to me now because I'm a gossip item.

It's hard to focus in class. Kieran haunts my mind. I'm afraid he's going to call or text or pop up in his Jack-in-the-box way or simply stalk me. When I walk to my car after school, I closely trail a group of kids as if I'm with them as my eyes hunt for his truck lurking. I don't see it.

I park as close to the door of the newspaper office as I can and run in. Marion does a double take when she sees my face.

"That was some accident."

"I tripped and said hello to the chair on my way to the floor."

"Were you drunk?"

"No! It was just a stupid accident." Fabulous. Now my boss thinks I'm an alcoholic.

"Just checking. You tripped in the parking lot over the summer, too. Maybe you need to get your equilibrium checked."

I'd forgotten about that lie. Another Kieran special. "I'll do that. What's going on today?" I nudge her onto a topic other than me.

"Police stuff from the weekend. They had a DWI checkpoint. There were some arrests. I'll shoot you the release."

"What about the court record searches?"

"If you have time. It's a long-term project."

I delve into my assignment. It's dark by the time I finish.

As I drive home, I check my rearview mirror for anyone following me. There's no one.

I pull into the garage, telling myself I'm crazy for being so paranoid. Kieran wouldn't dare show up again after what he did to me. Then again, he's not exactly predictable and he never seems ashamed of what he does.

Over the next couple weeks, the bruise turns a sickly, mottled shade of yellow, green, and brown then fades altogether. As that pain disappears, a new ache lodges inside me—I miss Kieran. It's crazy to miss somebody who treated me like crap, but I do.

I'm honestly glad he's leaving me alone, but at the same time I want to hear him call me sweet pea, crack up at his barking laugh, feel him wrap a shank of my hair around his fist, share our dreams as we curl up to watch TV in his camper.

I know there's no possibility of going back with him after what he did, but that also means I'll never have those moments again. The thought makes me incredibly sad and also makes me question my actions.

Should I have tried to help him more? Was I wrong to abandon him? What is he doing? Is he with that girl?

It's the last Sunday of September. I come downstairs and hear noises in Mom's studio. I look in. To my amazement, she's molding a huge block of clay on a table.

"I talked the gallery into taking a couple new pieces," she says.

"That's awesome. I thought you'd given it up forever."

"Just took a break, that's all. You could use some new clothes, Chloe. There's some money in my purse. Take it and go to the mall. I'd go with you, but I have to get moving on this."

"I don't really need anything."

"Buy yourself something nice. That's an order. You deserve it."

I kiss her on the cheek, catching her scent of soap and clay.

After breakfast, I head to the mall. I don't feel the least bit like shopping but maybe being in a crowd of people will take my mind off Kieran. Just the opposite happens. I see Kieran everywhere.

A guy browsing a window of lingerie. A guy eating a burger. A guy hugging his girlfriend. Something about each of them—height, hair, stance—reminds me of Kieran, and every time I think it's him, my heart clutches.

I wander into a gift store and out of all the hundreds of items there, a wooden peace sign pendant, like the one that hangs from Kieran's rearview mirror in his truck, jumps out at me. I leave the store then I go back and buy it.

In a music store, I look up all the old bands Kieran listens to. I buy the CD we always sang along to, "Earth, Wind & Fire's Greatest Hits." I go into a shoe store and walk out wearing the same brand of sneakers Kieran wears.

On the way home, I think I see Kieran's truck a dozen times, but they're just pickups of the same model or color. The driver in one looks like Kieran. I speed up alongside of it and peer in. He glances at me. It's not Kieran. I'm such an idiot. What would I have done if it were him?

That night, I wake up in the middle of the night. As I fumble for my phone to check the time, I can't help myself. I press the "photos" icon and scroll through the pictures of Kieran and me doing all our happy, silly "us" things.

I flick through them, fingering the half-heart necklace he gave me that for some reason, I'm still wearing. The picture show ends with the selfie of my bruised face. All the crazy bad things he did and said rush at me in a wave of shame. Why did I stay with him? Why did I let him do those things to me? Why do I miss him so much?

I have to focus on why I broke up with him. I poise my finger to erase the happy pictures, but for some reason I can't delete them. I put the phone down. My feelings are as tangled as a plate of spaghetti. I can't make sense out of them.

Maybe if I could talk to someone, find out how Kieran's doing, explain why I had to break up with him, how much this hurts me, too. Joe Favola. I could call him.

When I go into the newspaper later that day, I look up Joe's phone number on the database and call him when Marion goes to the bathroom. He doesn't pick up. I leave a voicemail, asking him to call me, and return to writing up the events calendar.

I lose myself in a daydream—Kieran's in a car accident and I drive by and rescue him. He realizes that I really do love him even though I can't be with him.

"Chloe, how's the calendar coming along?" Marion's voice brings me back to reality.

Dad calls as I'm going out the door. "How about coming into the city for dinner Saturday night? I want you to meet LuAnn, and Tyler's dying to see you."

I don't exactly have a full social calendar these days and I'm curious to see Dad's apartment. Mom's replacement, I could do without, but I'll have to meet her some time.

I tell Mom when I get home, leaving out the bit about the GF. She nods tersely.

"Have you started on college applications yet?"

"I'll do that this weekend."

I jog up to my room, realizing Joe never called back. I figure he's not going to and kick myself for calling him. I have college to think about, my family. I have to push forward not dwell in the past.

I get honked at practically every five minutes as I negotiate Manhattan's Upper West Side, waiting too long when the light changes to green, letting a pedestrian cross the street. A cab driver even leans out his window and yells, "Go back to Jersey!" But I make it to Dad's high-rise on Columbus Avenue and West Eighty-Fifth Street.

I take the elevator to the twentieth floor. The doorman let me into the garage and notified Dad of my arrival so he's at the door by the time I'm walking down the hall to his apartment.

"Chloe!" He hugs me and brings me inside. He seems glad to see me. That's something. "She's here!" he calls. "So, this is it, what do you think?"

The living room is walled with glass, making it seem as if we're surrounded by a forest of cement in the sky. I look down at the street. Vehicles glide like toy cars.

"Wow," is all I can say.

"Isn't the view spectacular? That's what sold me on the place," Dad says.

A shuffle of footsteps makes me turn. A woman with long crow-black hair stands with her hands clasped, smiling. She's thin, dressed in black leather boots, a black pencil skirt and a crimson turtleneck. LuAnn.

Dad introduces us. I flap my hand in some sort of greeting.

"Where's Tyler? Tyler, your sister's here," Dad bellows down the hallway. "He's always got those damn headphones on."

"Did you hit a lot of traffic coming in?" LuAnn asks.

"Not too bad. I got honked at a lot though."

"It's the Jersey plates." LuAnn rolls her eyes in sympathy.

"You want the nickel tour?" Dad says. He points to a coffee-colored leather couch. "The sofa pulls out into a bed, by the way, so, you're welcome any time."

"It's a comfortable sofa-bed," LuAnn interjects. "I made sure he got a good one."

I smile politely and follow Dad through a small, but gleaming kitchen of matching stainless-steel appliances. "The kitchen," he says uselessly. We go down the carpeted hall and stop at a doorway. "Guest bathroom." Everything is ultra-modern and shiny.

"Our room." It boasts a tidily made king-sized bed. My stomach turns to oatmeal. "And over here..." I do an about-face. I don't need to check out "our" bathroom and walk-in closet where his clothes hang next to LuAnn's. He catches up to me. "And Tyler's room."

The door's closed. Dad bangs on it. "Tyler!"

My brother opens, scowling as music buzzes loudly from headphones looped around his neck.

"Look who's here," Dad says.

Tyler's face clears when he sees me, and he smiles. I'm happy to see him too.

"Get your shoes on," Dad says, then turns to me. "We thought we'd go to a place called Sugar Reef. Ty thought you'd like it."

He joins LuAnn, who's waiting like a sentry at the end of the hall. I enter Tyler's room and sit on the bed as he pushes his feet into sneakers that need a wash. The room looks unlived in, like a hotel room. The only personal item is a poster of a babe with her butt cheeks oozing out of too-short shorts.

"Mom would never allow that," I say.

"Tight, huh?"

"I guess that's why you like living with Dad. How's school?"

He bends over to tie his shoelaces. "School's school."

"How's LuAnn?"

"I don't really pay attention to her."

"Tell me the truth. Did you just want to live with Dad to get back at Mom for sending you to soccer camp?"

He straightens and shrugs, which I take to mean "yes." "What's up with this guy Kieran?"

I'm startled. "What do you mean?"

"He called me."

"He called you?! When?"

"Like, I don't know, a few days ago. He wanted to know if you had another boyfriend."

"Oh my god! What did you say?"

"I said I wasn't up on your life. He said you were secretive and kept stuff from him. Are you cheating on him or something?"

"Of course not! We broke up. If he calls again, don't talk to him. He says really crazy stuff."

"He made me promise not to tell you he called, but I figured you should know."

"You should've called me right away."

"Why did you give him my number?"

"I didn't."

"So how did he get it?"

"Kids, let's go!" Dad calls.

We walk down the hall to the front door. Kieran must've gone through my phone.

There was that time at the newspaper on the Fourth of July when my phone wasn't on my desk where I'd left it. He'd probably watched me key in my password and checked it.

But I'm kidding myself if I think it was just that one time. He probably went through my phone numerous times over the summer when I went to the bathroom or left the room for some reason.

We file into the elevator, and then realization hits me. Who else's number did he harvest out of my contacts? I go hot and cold at the same time.

"Feel your ears pop?" Tyler says, smiling.

I nod absently.

We stroll two blocks to the restaurant. It's decorated like a Caribbean island with sand on the floor. Servers dressed in castaway-style cutoffs and straw hats serve drinks in coconut shells as tropical music blares. We get settled at a table and busy ourselves with ordering.

"How's school, Chloe?" Dad asks after the overfriendly waiter whisks off with our order.

"Good."

"Your dad tells me you want to study journalism," LuAnn says. "I wanted to be a journalist, too then I switched to marketing. It pays better." She smiles.

"Journalism is the only profession that's constitutionally protected so it's pretty important," I say. I don't care if I sound pompous.

"Chloe's always been a bookworm," Dad says. "Her mother would buy her a book when they went shopping. She'd sit on the floor of the store reading and by the time they got home, she'd finished it."

I chop the crushed ice in my water with the straw. Dad, who never bought me a book or took me to the library, doesn't have the right to tell cute stories about me being a kiddie-nerd. I feel a swell of anger.

"I joined this cool club at school. We build robots," Tyler says.

"That's really a growing field," LuAnn says.

"Dad used to kick our cat all the time," I blurt. "He was always yelling at me about something and making me cry."

Silence drops on the table like a wool blanket. Dad sighs and pinches the bridge of his nose.

"Dad built us that playhouse in the backyard, remember?" Tyler says. "And a go kart."

"Hip, hip hooray!" I sing.

Tyler shoots me a dirty look. LuAnn raises her eyebrows at Dad, who I'm satisfied to note, seems acutely uncomfortable. "I didn't know you had carpentry skills, Doug."

"Once upon a time," he says.

Ha. I know something about my father that she doesn't. Score one for Chloe.

"The appetizer's here," Dad says, clapping his hands and

rubbing them as the waiter delivers a plate of nachos.

I behave myself for the rest of the dinner. I order fish tacos, and they're actually pretty good.

"You want to watch a movie? We have a bunch of streaming channels," LuAnn says as we walk back to the apartment.

"I think I'll head home. I have to get started on college stuff tomorrow."

"You're leaving it a bit late, aren't you, Chloe?" Dad says.

The memory of Kieran taking me to NYU, not Dad, stabs me and I halt. My eyes brim. Dad puts his arm around my shoulders.

"You still have plenty of time."

He has no idea. We say goodbye in the garage.

"Next time, stay over, and we'll go out for pancakes in the morning." Dad inserts his arm around LuAnn's waist.

"Sure," I say, not sure at all. I get in the car. Tyler's already got his earbuds in. He waves.

Driving across the George Washington Bridge back to New Jersey, I figure Kieran called Tyler for the same reason I called Joe Favola. He's missing me like I'm missing him. We're seeking some kind of connection to each other through people who know us.

I also realize I'm not crazy for missing him in spite of all the bad stuff he did to me because Kieran isn't all bad. Just like Tyler pointed out that although Dad is far from the perfect father, he built a playhouse and a go-kart. It's Kieran's good side I miss, not the bad. But in the end, his bad side outweighs his good.

As the shopping malls along the highway give way to woods, the sky gets blacker and sugared with stars. I know it was okay to leave Kieran, and it was okay to miss him, too.

Sixteen

eaves turn gold and russet. A nip bites the air. Daylight grows watery and short. I replace T-shirts with sweaters in my dresser. The arrival of fall means college application deadlines loom. I throw myself into writing essays, gathering recommendations, taking practice SATs and then the test itself.

I hang with a bunch of kids from the Yearbook Committee at lunch. I see Clarissa, Jade and Morgan around the halls. I say hi and that's it. They're now in the past, another casualty of my relationship with Kieran like Mom's purse and my bruised self-esteem. I still think of him from time to time, but he's no longer front and center in my mind. Mom is right. He's fading. I'll get through this and I'm going to be okay.

A few days before Halloween, I come home from school and see Mom's jack-o'-lantern outside the front door. Every year she carves a pumpkin with an artistic face. I park the car and run up the walk to take a photo to post on social media. The screen door is ajar. Something's lodged there. I open the door. It's vase of blood-red rosebuds. I pull out the envelope tucked in the stems. It's addressed to "Chloe." Stomach lurching, I tear it open.

Chloe,
Please forgive me. I was cruel. I miss you so much, sweet pea. I adore you and will always love you.

**Please come back to me,
Kieran.**

All the feelings I've carefully balled up over the past two months unravel with the giant yank of his words. I pick up the vase and enter the house, my eyes blurring with tears. I fall into a kitchen chair, placing the flowers on the table.

Mom comes up from the basement. I dab my eyes. Her gaze falls on the roses.

"Don't tell me, Kieran?"

"They were at the front door."

"You don't want them, do you?"

"I guess not," I say, but the truth is, I do want them.

"Put them straight in the garbage. That's the best thing."

Heartstrings tugging, I get up and toss the vase in the bin outside the back door, but I hold on to the card, his admission of cruelty, the validation that he was at fault, that I was right to break up with him. It's what I've been waiting for all this time.

I read the card again. I actually don't feel like this is a triumph. It's another fake apology. He was never truly sorry for what he did because he did it again.

He only apologized to manipulate my feelings and reel me back in. I throw the card into the bin, close the lid firmly and return to the kitchen.

Mom's cooking pork chops at the stove when I re-enter. "There's an open position at the community college to teach sculpture next semester. I'm going to apply."

"That's great, Mom." I hardly sound enthusiastic.

"How about peeling some potatoes?"

She's keeping me busy, so I don't think about Kieran. I pick up the peeler and a spud, but it's too late. He's right there in my head again, and I miss him.

He calls around ten-thirty as I'm reading in bed. I hesitate for an instant then I answer.

"Hey, sweet pea." His tone is marshmallow soft. "Did you get the roses?"

"Yes." I make my tone stiff and cold. I don't want to seem friendly, but honestly, it feels good to hear his voice.

"I miss you, a lot. Do you miss me? Just a little?"

"Yes," I whisper.

"Chloe, is there someone else?" His voice cracks, and I totally melt.

"No, why would you even think that?"

"You cut me off so suddenly. There must be someone."

"Kieran, you held me hostage in my own home. You held my head under water. You threw me. You shoved me, called me names. I had a huge bruise on my face." I choke up.

"I'm sorry. I know we have our problems. We could go to couple's counseling, work things out."

Our problems? *Couple's* counseling?

"Chloe, you knew what you were getting into from the get-go. You stayed with me all this time."

His crazy, upside-down logic broadsides me yet again. "Wait. You're blaming *me* for staying with you? In other words, you know you're impossible to have a relationship with."

"Let's go for pizza. We can be friends at least."

"No."

"Why not? We'll just talk. I have no one to talk to."

At that moment, I see everything is about what he wants. Whenever he did something for me, there was something in it for him, like checking out NYU for student film auditions, tagging along on July Fourth so he could meet the mayor.

"No, Kieran. I have to go."

"Who have you been talking to? Who's putting stuff in your head?"

"No one. It's just over. I can't see you anymore."

"Okay, if that's the way you want it." He hangs up.

I fall back against the pillow. Why did I talk to him? Why? He's doing it again—waiting until the sting wears off and then swooping in with an apology and flowers. I'm an idiot.

The phone chimes with a text.

I'll always love you no matter what.

I switch off the phone and toss it under the bed.

I'm taking a test on "Candide" in French three days later when my phone buzzes. And buzzes and buzzes.

"If I hear that phone again, it'll be confiscated until the end of the year," snipes Mademoiselle Berteau.

A couple kids turn and look at me. I worm my hand into my purse, hoping she doesn't see it's my phone, and power it off. As soon as I'm in the hallway after class, I check it. Seven missed calls from Kieran.

He keeps calling during economics, then through the yearbook lunch meeting. I know he's trying to get me to talk to him again. Everybody stares at me, wondering why I don't pick up the call. I say nothing. Finally, I turn off the phone.

I figure that by the end of the day, he's gotten the message that I'm not going to pick up.

But the next day, the calls start again. This time, he leaves a rambling voicemail.

"You're a cold and evil witch. You saw your chance with me and reeled me in. You think you're better than me. You'll see."

Then another one, this time he's syrupy sweet. "Just pick up, Chloe. I don't understand why you won't talk to me. I need you, sweet pea."

I power off the phone again. As I walk to the student parking lot after the last class, I check it. No more calls. I feel a gush of relief. Then the phone vibrates. A text.

Pick up the damn phone!

I wheel around, frightened he's watching me, but I don't see him. I hurry to my car and drive to the newspaper.

The texts continue at work. Marion gets annoyed. "That buzzing noise is driving me insane. Can you tell your friends you're working?"

My mistake was to pick up his call that one time. He thinks I'll answer if he persists enough.

When he texts again as I'm driving home, I seize the phone, planning to call him back and scream at him, but then I realize that's just what he wants. I drop the phone.

Later that night, Mom and I are watching a detective drama on TV and eating ice cream. My phone rings in the kitchen. I make no move to answer it. It rings again.

"Aren't you going to get that?" Mom says.

"It's probably Kieran."

Her spoon clatters in the bowl. "Has he been calling you?"

"Actually, he hasn't stopped for two days."

"We have to change your number immediately."

"Mo-om. That's such a hassle."

"Just notify people you have a new number. People do it all the time."

She calls the phone company and in six minutes, I have a new number.

"You'd better block him on your email account, too," Mom says. "He'll quit bothering you when he doesn't get results. I'm glad you didn't answer."

I power up my laptop and delete five emails from him. As I figure out how to do the block, an instant message box pops up.

Hey sweet pea! How are you?

I jump as if someone had stuck my butt with a pitchfork. This is a real live version of Whac-A-Mole. I block him on the instant messenger and email.

The next day, peace is restored. When I join the yearbook gang at our lunch table, Trevor Papadopoulos leans over to me.

"Good to see you smiling. You looked like you had the weight of the world on your shoulders the last couple days."

My face boils with embarrassment. "Yeah, just...stuff, you know. It's over."

"I'm glad you got whatever it was figured out. If you ever need anything, I'm here. I mean, whatever I can do." His cheeks color slightly.

"That's really nice of you. Thanks."

He turns to talks to someone else. Why couldn't I have fallen in love with someone like Trevor?

Marion assigns me to cover the town council, which means attending a lot of long night meetings about super exciting things like pothole repair and bicycle lanes. I'd rather do crime news, but Marion says covering local government is how reporters start their careers. So, off I go.

I'm at a meeting where the night's endless debate is over which streets to include in a sewer project. My temples are pounding when the meeting is finally adjourned. I'm hurrying across the parking lot when a voice slashes through the darkness.

"Chloe, does it have to be like this?" Kieran steps from the shadows, holding up a hand like he's saying "how."

The shock of his ambush stops me dead and immediately twists my stomach into a pretzel. I resume walking.

"Does it have to be like this?" he repeats.

The splinter in his voice pierces my resolve to ignore him. I turn. "Kieran, I don't want it to be like this, but you make it like this. You won't leave me alone."

"Remember all the fun times we had? I miss that so much. We can get through this and get that back. I don't understand why you won't work on this with me. I'm really trying here. You know I am. Why don't you try, too? We're perfect for each other."

I'm not trying because...? I struggle to regain my mental footing. He's spinning my mind, like always. "I tried already. It just doesn't work. Please leave me alone." My voice rises an octave.

Kieran looks around. People are exiting town hall. "Shhh."

"It's okay for you to yell when you want to, but it's not okay when other people yell, is it?" I say.

"You're bitter and resentful. You have an anger problem."

"I'm not bitter or resentful, and I'm allowed to be angry. Everybody gets angry."

"So, I'm allowed to get angry, too."

I want to jam my fingers into his eyes.

"But you fly into rages over stupid stuff, over nothing!"

"I think this is stupid, but you're the one raging now. You need anger management."

"Aggghhhh!" I yell. I pivot toward my car.

He steps forward. "Chloe, did you ever love me?"

In the spill of light from a lamp post, his eyes are shining ponds. My heart aches.

"How can you even ask? Of course, I loved you."

"Do you still love me?"

"I have to go."

"One day everything's fine. The next it's not."

"I tried to talk to you. You promised to get help but you didn't. In fact, you got worse. You treated me like shit, you know you did."

"Chloe, I've given you enough time." That razor edge is now in his voice.

He's given me time? "Kieran, it's over. Leave me alone. Stop stalking me."

"Do you know what happened to me after Labor Day? I was puking my guts out!" Kieran's voice twists like a corkscrew. "You poisoned the ice cream you gave me! I'm going to go to the cops and report for you for attempted murder!"

In that instant, I know Kieran is truly insane and dangerous.

He continues his tirade. "Everything's turning around for me now that I got rid of you! You were holding me back. I've got three auditions lined up next week. So, stay out of my life!"

He marches back into the shadows. I jog to my car, cursing myself. Why did I talk to him, allow him to do that to me again? I take a deep breath. But maybe it's for the better. I delivered the message, loud and clear, that I wasn't going back to him.

After school the next day, I see bits of paper scattered over the hood of my car as I'm crossing the parking lot. I think it's regular litter by some jerk who didn't want to walk all of ten yards to dispose of his trash in the garbage can until I get closer.

The shreds of paper are actually photos. I pick up a handful of them. My legs tremble as I recognize them.

They're Kieran's face, my face. They're the photos from

Kieran's book, "The Chronicle of Us." He's literally ripped me into pieces.

I jerk my head around, afraid he's watching me. Clarissa gazes at me curiously from a distance. I scoop up the shreds and throw them in the trash.

I can never speak to Kieran again. I have to bring down an iron curtain against him and hold it with all my might. It's the only way.

Seventeen

We're rotating sports in gym, and this time I get my second choice: volleyball. I want to sink under the bleachers when Clarissa's name is called for volleyball, too, but there's nothing I can do. Luckily, we're assigned to different teams, but Clarissa's team is our first opponent. Fantabulous.

Janice Rickenbacher is first up to serve for my team. She's in the stoner crowd that gets high in the woods behind school during lunchtime and always reeks of pot and cigarette smoke. I've never been friends with her.

I stand ready at the net, knees bent, hands clasped to punch the ball, when a massive blow crashes the back of my head. I stagger forward, gasping, vision blurring.

"Soooorrry!" Janice calls.

I put my hands on my knees until my head stops zinging.

"Are you all right?" Melody, the girl beside me, asks.

I take a deep breath and straighten. "Yeah."

The game starts again. Janice's next serve smacks me in the back of the legs, buckling my knees. I almost fall, but I manage to take a big enough step to brace myself. I pivot.

"What are you doing?"

Janice shrugs. "Jeez, my aim is really off today. Sorry." The half-smile on her face tells me her aim is right on—at me. What did I ever do to her?

I switch places with Melody so I'm not in Janice's firing line. The next serve sails over the net, to my relief, but a few plays later, the ball socks me in the back. I twist around.

"Will you quit it, Janice?"

"It was an accident, sorry."

"You did it on purpose." Clarissa is ducking under the net. "I've been watching you. You're aiming right at Chloe."

"Who appointed you class cop?" Janice sneers.

Everybody gathers around. Mr. Reiss jogs over blowing his whistle. "What's going on, girls?"

Clarissa points to Janice. "She's hitting Chloe with the ball on purpose—three times already."

"It was an accident, Mr. Reiss," Janice says.

"It was not," Clarissa retorts.

"Are you all right?" Mr. Reiss asks me. I nod, embarrassed at the fuss. "Janice, switch out with a player on that team." He points to a court on the far side of the gym. "If there's any more trouble, the whole class is doing push-ups for the rest of the week."

Janice shuffles off in a sulk.

"Play ball!" Mr. Reiss blasts his whistle.

I smile at Clarissa. She smiles back and resumes her game position.

After class, I hurry to the locker room, grab my clothes and head to my car without changing. I don't want to bump into Janice. I'm throwing my book bag into the back seat when Clarissa's blond head bobs across the parking lot.

"Clarissa, wait up." She stops and I trot over. "Thanks for today. It really meant a lot to me. You don't know how much." My voice quavers and my eyes well up. I bite my lip to keep the tears in.

"She was being a real asshole. What's up with you and her?"

"Nothing. I have no idea why she was doing that to me. I guess she just felt like picking on someone."

"You might have bruises. It was pretty nasty what she did."

I hike my shoulders. I'm used to bruises.

Clarissa shifts her feet. "What's happened to you lately, Chloe?

I mean, I know we're not talking, but you don't even look like your old self. You walk all hunched in. You have dark circles under your eyes."

"You told me I look like shit, remember?"

"I'm sorry. That was mean. I shouldn't have said it."

"Why not? It's true."

I can no longer contain my tears, which seem to lie just under the surface of my skin these days. Embarrassed, I dig the heel of my hands into my eyes.

"Is it Kieran?"

I nod, not bothering to try to stop crying now. It seems an impossible task.

"He called me."

"When?"

"Like a month ago. I wanted to tell you, but you were avoiding me like crazy."

"What did he say?"

"He said he was having problems with you, and he thought you were unstable and needed help. He said he was trying to take care of you, but you were very stubborn and 'high strung.' He asked if I had problems with you. He also said not to tell you he called."

"He called Tyler, too. What did you tell him?"

"I said I didn't know what was up with you, and we weren't friends anymore."

"I can't believe this. Clarissa, all this stuff has happened."

"He also said you told him that I was spoiled and stuck up, and you were only friends with me because you didn't have anyone else to hang with."

"That's a total lie! I never said any of those things. Don't believe anything he says!"

"I know it's a lie. We've been friends since middle school. I figured the rest was a lie, too. He didn't know you told me about his problems. There was also that weird call from your mother looking for you on Labor Day weekend and then you showed up at school with a massive bruise on your face. What the hell is going on?"

I slump against the trunk of her car. "I broke up with him. It's been a nightmare—you have no idea."

"Want to come over?"

"Yes. Yes, I do."

I call Marion and say I don't feel well, which is actually the truth, and drive behind Clarissa to her place.

Sitting on the floor in her bedroom, I tell her the whole story in one giant tsunami of words. Clarissa listens with wide eyes, uttering "oh my gods." Her hand flies to her mouth when I get to the whole Labor Day weekend catastrophe.

When I finish, she leans back against the footboard of her bed. Ashamed, I can't look at her, so I pick up a snow globe and shake it. The flakes float down on the miniature Eiffel Tower and Arc de Triomphe.

"I am so incredibly glad you dumped his ass, Chloe. There's something seriously wrong with that dude. I can't believe you didn't tell me any of this."

"I felt so humiliated. I thought you would think there was something wrong with me for staying with him, and you wouldn't want to be my friend anymore."

"I did want to be your friend. I thought you didn't want to be my friend because you had Kieran. I didn't know he was turning you against us."

"I didn't know what to do. Whenever I tried to resist him, he'd do something to punish me."

"I had no idea."

Clarissa hugs me. I hug her back, hard.

"Come sit with us tomorrow at lunch?" she says.

"What about Jade and Morgan?"

"Do you want me to tell them?" she says.

I consider, then I nod. "But I don't want anyone else to know, okay?"

"I'll tell them to keep it just between us. So, what's the deal with Trevor Papadopoulos? I've seen you with him. He's cute."

I smile.

As I drive home, I feel a shift, like jigsaw puzzle pieces finally snapping into place to create a normal picture.

Mom's working on her laptop in the living room. I flop on the couch. "I'm friends with Clarissa again."

I tell her what happened in gym.

"Clarissa's a true friend," she says.

"Yeah, she is." I get up. "I have to write an essay for English. It's due tomorrow, and I haven't even started."

I go upstairs and power up my computer. The assignment is to explore the themes of T.S. Eliot's "The Lovesong of J. Alfred Prufrock" or write our own poem. I open a blank page intending to blather on about "Prufrock," but feelings flow out of me instead. I end up writing three poems about Kieran. I finish at midnight.

As I brush my teeth looking in the mirror, I see Kieran's gold heart necklace around my neck, his makeup gift after his first rage.

Despite everything, I haven't been able to take it off. I thought it was a symbol of his love for me, but now I see it for what it really was, just one more manipulation. I unclasp it and drop it into my garbage can. It sinks into the nest of used floss and tissues. Then I cross to my bed and pick up the white teddy bear with the red heart, which has lain against my pillow since the night Kieran won it for me at the carnival. I take the Yamamoto's baseball cap that he gave me off the bed post and grab the garbage can containing the necklace. I go downstairs and deposit everything in the trash bin.

It's as if writing the poems released me from Kieran for good. They were my goodbye to him and my permission to myself to move on.

In English the next morning, Ms. Margolis asks for the assignments. I freak. I can't hand in these raw, personal poems. But it's too late now. I place my paper on the pile on her desk.

At lunch, I buy my hamburger and approach the table where Clarissa, Jade and Morgan are sitting. I hesitate, afraid I'll get the cold shoulder again. I'm thinking of turning around when Morgan beckons me over. "Chloe!"

Clarissa smiles at me. "I told them, not everything but most of it."

Jade and Morgan smile, too. "We're glad you got rid of him," Jade says.

"He was baaad news," Morgan says.

"I'm sorry, I really am," I say.

"We're sorry, too," Jade says. "But it's over. Let's put it behind us."

"What are we going to do this weekend?" Clarissa says.

"How about bowling?" Jade suggests.

"Bo-ring," Morgan says. "I'll see if there's a party somewhere."

On an impulse, I grab the fork off my tray and hold it to my mouth like a microphone. "Breaking news. I'm here in the cafeteria of Indian Valley High School for an important announcement," I say in a news anchor voice. "Jade, the champion of gutter balls, wants to go bowling this weekend, and Morgan wants to party hearty. What do you think of these surprising developments, Ms. Coluccio?"

I thrust my fork at Clarissa. "I think hanging out at the video arcade and playing pool and foosball is a much better idea," she says.

"And why would that be?" I ask.

Jade grabs my "microphone." "Two words..." She and Morgan yell in unison, "Mike McGuinness!"

Everyone turns to stare at us, including Mike McGuinness, who happens to be sitting a couple tables away.

"Oh my god, I can't believe you did that!" Clarissa slides down in her chair until she's practically under the table.

We crack up. It's the first time I've laughed in months.

Eighteen

The aroma of cinnamon and nutmeg greets me as I enter the kitchen. It's the day before Thanksgiving. Tyler's peeling Granny Smith apples for pie. Mom's rolling out the dough for the crust on the counter, flour dusting her hair. I feel a little sparkle of happiness at being a family again, as close as we're going to get anyway.

"Ty! I didn't think you'd make it."

"No kisses or hugs." He holds up crossed index fingers.

"Who would want to kiss or hug you?"

"Wouldn't you like to know?" He wiggles his eyebrows.

"Did Dad bring you?"

"Nope. School let out at noon, and I didn't want to wait for him to get off work, so I got the bus from Port Authority."

"Going to the game tomorrow?"

"Yep, you?"

"Yep." Every Thanksgiving, Indian Valley plays a football game against our archrival, Lake High. The whole school goes.

Tyler slices the peeled apples. I snatch a piece and crunch into it. "Going with your old buddy Skyler?"

"Yep."

"Sky and Ty, together again."

He chucks a peeling at me. "Look at the abuse I get when I come home. Forced labor and harassment."

"You missed it and you know it." I grin. "What can I do, Mom?"

"You can make the cranberry sauce."

"Are we going to have pumpkin pie as well as apple?" I ask.

"Of course." The phone rings. She looks at the caller ID. "It's Grandma." Wiping her hands on her apron, she moves into the dining room to talk.

"I'm going to change, then I'll cran the berries." I snatch another apple slice.

Tyler smacks my hand. "Leave some apples for the pie."

"Yes, Mom!" I sing.

I'm in my room pulling on sweatpants when the doorbell rings. "Chloe, someone's here for you," Tyler calls.

I trot downstairs. A man and a woman in dark suits stand at the front door. Something tells me they're not here to borrow pumpkin pie spice.

"Chloe Ann Quinn?" the woman says.

"Yes."

She holds up an ID in a wallet. "I'm Detective Goldsmith from the Indian Valley Police Department. This is Detective Bridges."

The man displays his ID. I barely glance at it. My mind is whirring for any possible reason the cops might be here. Did I write something they didn't like?

"Are your parents home?"

"Mo-om!" Tyler yells.

Mom enters the foyer. "What is it?" She looks puzzled at the detectives. "What's going on?"

"We're investigating a harassment complaint filed by Kieran Dubrowski against your daughter," Goldsmith says. "We'd like her to come down to the station and answer a few questions."

When I was seven years old, a soccer ball barreled into my stomach and knocked the air completely out of me. I couldn't breathe for a second, and I thought I was going to die. That's how I feel now. Air finally whooshes into me. My legs quake, and I lean on Mom for support. She wraps her arm around my shoulders like a cape.

"This is absurd. *He*'s harassed her. She's not going anywhere until I contact my lawyer," Mom says.

Goldsmith hands her a business card. "We'd appreciate it if she could come down as soon as possible. Your lawyer can call and make an appointment."

"In the meantime, we'd advise you not to have any contact with Mr. Dubrowski," Bridges says.

I can't speak. They turn to go back to their car, and Tyler closes the front door. "So that's what real-life detectives look like," he says.

"Mom, what has he done?" My voice snaps like a piece of bone china. Tears spill down my cheeks.

She leads me into the kitchen and sits me down. "This is just another of his harassments." Mom crosses to the phone. "Don't worry. I hope I can catch Carol before she leaves for the day."

"Who's Carol?" Tyler asks.

"Lawyer," Mom answers over her shoulder.

I lower my face into my hands. Kieran has won. He's found a way to ruin my life. I feel my back being rubbed. It's Tyler, worry etched on his face.

I hear the rumble of Mom's voice, then she returns.

"Carol's going to call that detective on Monday and find out what it's all about. She said we'll have to go in and answer their questions, but we did the right thing. We shouldn't say anything unless she's there." She blows a piece of stray hair out of her eyes.

A vision of myself handcuffed in a jail cell flashes through my mind. "Am I going to be arrested?"

"If they were going to arrest you, they would've done it. Carol said cops see a lot of frivolous complaints, but they're obligated to check them all out. There's nothing we can do about this now. Let's try and forget about it til Monday."

"How can I forget about this?"

"Carol said just live our lives." She hands me an apron. "We've got cranberry sauce to make."

I put it on like an automaton. Mom hands me the bag of

cranberries, which I pour into a saucepan with water. I add sugar and stir as my head swirls. I can't think. Everything seems to be moving in slow motion.

After dinner, I head up to my room and call Clarissa.

"Oh my god, Chloe! This is crazy, I mean for real crazy, like mentally ill."

"How am I going to prove that I didn't harass him? How am I going to ever defend myself?"

"You've got a lawyer. She'll figure it out. Everything will be all right, it will."

"I wish I could believe that." There's a knock on my door, Mom's head appears. "My mom's here. I better go."

"I'll see you at the game tomorrow. Hang in there, Chlo."

Mom sits on my bed. "So, are you coming to say it?" I say.

"Say what?"

"It's all my fault for getting involved with Kieran in the first place, and that I should've reported him to the police."

"No, I was coming to say I'm really sorry this happened to you and not to worry. We're going to take care of it." She rubs my knee.

"Just when everything is going so well in my life, when I finally feel I've really got past everything. It's like he knows that, and he's trying to pull me back."

"That's exactly what he's doing."

"What if Kieran gets me thrown in jail?"

"Don't drive yourself crazy with what-ifs. You have the truth on your side and me as a witness."

"Mom, you didn't even ask me if it's true that I harassed him."

"I know my own daughter. Whatever he's saying is a pack of lies."

"I can't believe he would do something like this just to get back at me for breaking up with him. If he hadn't been so abusive, I would never have broken up with him. Why can't he see that?"

"He's a very troubled young man, Chloe. He doesn't see the world like the rest of us."

"I tried to get him help, but he wouldn't do it."

"People have to help themselves. There's nothing you can do.

You have to protect yourself from dangerous people, and sometimes that means walking away." Mom pats my leg. "Come and watch TV. Don't stew here by yourself."

She leaves, and I look at my phone in my hand. I open the photos, and flip through the snapshots of Kieran and me, so happy. I had no clue back then what lay in store. The pictures, those memories, are meaningless now. I erase the photos, one by one, until I get to the final photo, the selfie with my bruised face. I keep that one. I put the phone aside and go downstairs.

The next morning, I'm hung over with lack of sleep. I can't face going to the football game. I call Clarissa and tell her.

"It won't be the same without you," she says.

"I just don't feel like seeing anyone, tell you the truth."

Instead, I help Mom chop bread and celery for the stuffing while Tyler goes to the game with his buddy. I do my best to put on a smiley face at Thanksgiving dinner, but my performance is hardly going to win an Oscar. I barely eat.

"Why don't we go see a movie?" Mom suggests after pie and ice cream.

"There's a bunch of good ones opening today," Tyler says. "I'll check online."

"Look for a comedy, no romance," Mom calls.

"You think I'm going to pick a romance?" he says.

We see a college frat house comedy, "Frat Fry." It works. It gets my mind off Kieran for a couple hours.

I go to see three more movies over the weekend with my friends and with Mom and Ty. It's the only thing that distracts me from the lump that's back inside me bigger than ever, a tumor of shame and guilt, anger and sadness, fear and regret. I'm never going to beat this.

I haul myself to school on Monday. Mom texts me around eleven.

We're going with Carol to see the detectives at four-thirty. We'll meet her at her office beforehand and go over the case.

I can't eat at lunch, but my friends practically force rice pudding down my throat.

"You have to eat something," Morgan says.

"If I don't eat, I get faint," Clarissa says.

"You'll need your strength to answer the detectives' questions," Jade says.

I eat a couple spoonfuls just to shut them up.

It's the longest school day of my life. When the final bell rings, Clarissa and I race to the parking lot.

"Good luck, Chloe." She gives me a thumbs up.

I'm going to need it.

Carol Snyder is small and thin as a sparrow, but her manner isn't birdlike. She's no-nonsense, take-charge. "I got a copy of Kieran's complaint from the police this morning." She rifles through a pile of papers on her desk.

Trying to calm my nerves, I look around the office and make a mental list of what I see—cherry wood paneling with plush, hunter-green carpet, shelves full of law books lining a wall, small oil paintings with little lights on the gilt frames.

She finds the document and puts on her glasses. I feel nervous again. "He's really going all out. He's alleging stalking, harassing telephone calls and physical abuse," she says.

I start to weep. Mom's hand squeezes mine.

"We can't have crying," Carol says in a firm voice. It works. My tears dry right up. "Here's his statement:

My ex-girlfriend has been harassing me ever since I broke up with her several months ago. She won't leave me alone.

She's been harassing my new girlfriends with hang up calls. She hacked into my social media accounts and posted crap about me. She called my invalid mother, telling lies about me and asking if I had a new girlfriend. She called my friend about me. She stalked me at my job and embarrassed me in front of my boss.

She's been calling everyone to prevent me from getting acting jobs. She is unstable and from a broken, dysfunctional family.

Her mother is a drug addict. I am afraid of her because she has been violent toward me in the past, scratching my face and shoving me in jealous fits. I think she's going to harm me.

"He's twisting everything around," I say.

"Chloe's right. He did all that to her," Mom says.

Carol questions me about the relationship, scribbling on a yellow legal pad as I tell her. She shows no reaction, which I'm grateful for. Finally, she looks up.

"Let's go to the police station."

We sit on a bench in the lobby to wait for Detective Goldsmith. I hope I don't see Lt. Villamil, the media relations officer I know. How would I explain that Chloe Quinn, reporter, was now Chloe Quinn, criminal suspect? A panicked thought leaps into my head: Could Marion fire me over this?

A door opens and Detective Goldsmith walks in. Mom and I stand.

"Mrs. Quinn, I'll need you to wait here. It'll be just Chloe and her attorney."

"But she's a minor," Mom says.

"It's all right, Bonnie. I'll be there, and you're a potential witness," Carol says.

Carol and I follow the detective down a non-descript corridor and into a small, windowless room identified on the door as "Interview Room 1." We sit on one side of a wooden table, which has a metal ring sticking out of it. I finger it, wondering what it is.

"That's to handcuff people to the table," Carol explains. I immediately place my hands in my lap. Have murderers and rapists sat in the very chair I'm sitting in?

Goldsmith sits on the other side of the table then Bridges enters and takes the chair next to her.

"We're in the initial stages of our investigation of the complaint," Goldsmith says.

"It's our position that this is really a domestic violence case," Carol says. "He's trying to get revenge over her breakup with him."

The detectives ask me about the relationship. Goldsmith asks most of the questions. Bridges chimes in now and then.

"Everything he says I did to him, he actually did to me," I finish.

"Did you ever go to the police to report Kieran's incidents of violence or seek a restraining order?" Bridges asks.

"I never thought about that. I was too embarrassed, and he promised to stop and get help."

"How about after the breakup? Did you ever report this stalking and harassment?"

"No, I...I didn't want to cause him any more trouble. I didn't want to hurt him more than I had by breaking up with him. I just wanted him to go away."

Goldsmith takes some papers out of her folder, scans them and looks up. "Do you know a Zoe Kovac?"

I frown. "No."

"How about Janice Rickenbacher?"

My stomach drops. "She goes to Indian Valley. She's in my gym class."

"Joseph Favola Junior?"

"He's a friend of Kieran's."

"We have statements from them supporting Kieran's allegations." She places the papers on the table.

"They're lying!" I cry. Carol's hand grips my arm, a signal to calm down.

"Why weren't these given to me earlier today?" Carol asks.

"We just received them this afternoon."

"I'll need copies of these." Carol gathers the documents and skims them. "He's a little too eager with a ready-made case, don't you think?"

"We'd like to ask Chloe about them while she's here. Saves time," Goldsmith says.

Carol nods. Goldsmith reads the first statement:

I worked with Kieran Dubrowski at Yamamoto's Nursery. In September, I noticed his face had scratch marks. I asked him what happened, who done that to him. He didn't want to tell me, but I pressed him. He told me it was his girlfriend, Chloe.

She got insanely jealous and went crazy. He told me she has

emotional problems, and he was trying to help her. He told me he was afraid she would harm him or herself, but he had to break up with her because she was so violent.

Since then, I seen other scratches two other times. Kieran said she took the breakup bad and won't leave him alone. I seen her hanging around the parking lot, stalking him several times. I was with him several times when he got phone calls from her. She wouldn't stop calling him.

Sworn under the penalty of perjury,

Zoe Y. Kovac.

I gulp at the boldface lies and look at Carol, shaking my head. She leans over to me, and I whisper in her ear.

"I never scratched him. I've never hung around the parking lot at his job. I never called him. That's a total lie."

"Say that exactly like that to them," Carol says. So, I do.

Goldsmith reads the next page.

Chloe Quinn is in my gym class at Indian Valley High School. She pretends to be real quiet and nice, but that's not really her. She accused me of deliberately throwing the ball in volleyball class at her. She has a real bad temper. I told Kieran to stay away from her, but he wouldn't listen to me.

Sworn under penalty of perjury,

Janice Rickenbacher

"I didn't..." I start to say but Carol holds up a hand to stop me.

"That statement says absolutely nothing relevant to the complaint," she states.

Goldsmith picks up the final page.

I am a friend of Kieran Dubrowski's. I met his ex-girlfriend at a party at my house. Kieran told me that since the breakup, Chloe will not leave him alone. He said she has called him repeatedly, called his girlfriends at all hours and hung up, and stalked him at his job, house and online.

She also called his acting teacher and the Stagecoach Playhouse to stop him from getting a role in a play there. He said she has called his sick, elderly mother and harassed her, wanting to know information about Kieran.

She has also called me. I don't know how she got my number. Kieran has been very, very upset. It has ruined his life over the past few months.

Sworn under penalty of perjury,
Joseph Favola Jr.

I lean into Carol. "I did call Joe once and left a voicemail. He never called back. The rest is a lie."

Carol gestures that it's okay to tell the police that. I wipe my clammy hands on my thighs and repeat what I just said.

Bridges leans forward and glares at me. "These are very serious allegations, Chloe. We need you to tell the truth. If you're lying to us, it'll be worse for you in the end. You understand that?"

"I'm not lying," I say firmly.

"My client has been through enough today." Carol stands.

Goldsmith follows suit. "We'll be in touch as the investigation progresses."

When we reach the lobby, I rush into Mom's arms, wailing. "Kieran got people to lie for him. I'm going to go to jail!"

Carol nudges us outside.

"What's the next step, Carol?" Mom says as we walk to our cars.

"We have to wait, but it shouldn't take too long. The cops don't have the manpower or time to invest in minor cases like these. We gave our response. I also noted that these alleged witness statements seem a little too pat. Chloe handled herself very well. One of the cops got a little tough with her at the end and shook her up." She turns to me.

"I have a suggestion to make. I've had a number of clients involved in domestic and dating violence cases. Many women get help from a support group at a women's shelter called Journeys. I've volunteered at its legal clinic." She takes a card from her briefcase and hands it to me. "You might want to give them a call."

Domestic violence? I drop the card in my purse. We say goodbye and get in our car.

"Mom, what if Carol loses the case?"

"Carol's a good lawyer. She'll make sure that doesn't happen," Mom says.

I don't really believe her. I feel as if the world is crushing me like a vise.

Nineteen

I stare at the Boston University application on the website when I come home from school a couple days later. What's the use of filling it out? I'm probably going to jail or even if I don't, I'll have a record, a black mark against my name forever.

What college is going to accept me with that? How can I have a career as a journalist? I can't even blame Kieran. It's my fault. Why didn't I break up with him after his first rage?

I look out my bedroom window. The neighbors are stringing up icicle lights from their roof and inflating cheesy reindeer and snowmen figures in the front yard. Ho-ho-ho. Meanwhile, my future hangs on the actions of a deranged individual. So much for goodwill to all men.

"Let's go buy the Christmas tree," Mom calls up the stairs.

"I really don't feel like it."

"Might cheer you up?"

"I have homework, Mom."

I hear the garage door open and close. I pick up Walt Whitman's "Leaves of Grass" and try to focus. The phone rings.

"Hi Dad."

"Want to come in and see the Christmas displays this weekend? We can check out the windows on Fifth Avenue, go ice skating at

Rockefeller Center. Maybe you could stay over to catch a matinee on Broadway on Sunday."

"I'm not really into the whole jolly-and-merry thing this year, to tell the truth."

"Why not? What's wrong?"

I'm too embarrassed to tell him about the police complaint, and I made Tyler swear not to tell him. What does Dad care anyway? He's living the life he wanted, which doesn't include me. I have to get off the phone as emotion catches in my throat.

"Nothing. I have homework to do. I'll talk to you later."

I hang up as he squawks, "Chloe, wait."

A short while later, I hear banging and rustling downstairs. I go down and see Mom hauling in a six-foot Douglas fir through the front door. I give her a hand, and we set up the tree in the living room.

"I'll get the ornament boxes." Mom dusts the pine needles off her hands.

"Maybe later, Mom. I don't feel like decorating."

"Okay. I have to finish the inventory anyway."

"What inventory?"

"Of everything in the house. For the divorce."

She picks up a pad and pen and goes into the dining room, where she opens the glass doors of the large cabinet where the good china and silver is displayed.

"Your father wants everything. I'm going to propose dividing the china and crystal so we each have four place settings. They were wedding presents. He can have the silver since he bought it." She scribbles on the pad.

I envision rooms with dents in the carpet where chairs and tables have sat for years, dustless spots on shelves where knick-knacks and books now live, walls with empty squares instead of the paintings I know like old friends. My family's fallen apart and now the things that formed the landscape of my life are disappearing, too.

I can't watch this collapse of my home. I put on my coat and gloves and head out the back door into the woods. My feet crunch on the carpet of dead leaves. My breath frosts in the cold air. The washed out sky filters a grey light between the stark branches of trees. The scene blends with my mood.

It's the first time I've been in the woods since that fateful Labor Day weekend. I find myself returning to the party pit, where I halt and stare at the tarp. I no longer feel any sentimental sympathy or nostalgia for Kieran. All that time, I was justifying his actions. *He doesn't mean to harm me. He wouldn't really hurt me. He just doesn't want to lose me because he loves me so much.* But for Kieran, love *is* the reason to hurt someone. And that's not love.

I wander in the woods until it's almost dark. The cold air is crisp and pure. I take deep, cleansing breaths that push all my anxiety into the atmosphere, where they dissolve.

Mom has a slightly guilty look on her face when I come in. "Dad's worried about you."

"Why?" I hang up my coat, my frozen cheeks burning in the warmth.

"He called me just now. I had to tell him what was going on."

"Mo-om!"

"It's okay, Chloe, really."

"I can't believe you told him."

"He should know."

"He doesn't deserve to know."

I stomp up to my room. Why does Dad get to know about my private life when he kept his private life a big secret?

Clarissa drags me to the mall to go Christmas shopping. I know exactly what to buy Mom, a new bathrobe. I find a plush teal velour one on sale. I hold it up for Clarissa's opinion.

"Get it. She'll love it."

"I can't wait to toss that crappy old one in the garbage. I'm going to do it right on Christmas Day," I say as I pay the cashier.

"I could really go for a cinnamon roll," Clarissa says. "Shopping is making me hungry."

We head to the food court and buy our rolls, taking them to a table.

"Have you seen that foreign exchange student from Spain?" Clarissa says. "He's in my digital design class. His name is Claudio.

He says it 'Clowdeeo'."

"And you think he's cute."

"I do. What do you think?"

I nod as my mouth is full.

"I was thinking, should I offer to like show him around or something?"

I swallow. "He'd probably like that. You could go to the Statue of Liberty, Empire State building, that type of stuff."

"That's a great idea. Think I should text him? I have his number. We're on the same project team."

If she doesn't, she'll be hemming and hawing about it all day. "Go ahead."

She taps away on her mobile. I rummage in my purse for my phone, so I have something to do while she's occupied. Something sharp digs into the bed of my fingernail. It's the card Carol gave me from the domestic violence place.

Clarissa's phone whooshes with the sent text. She looks over at the card in my hand. "What's that?"

I give it to her as I suck my punctured fingertip. "The lawyer suggested I go to this support group for domestic violence victims." I smush my face in a can-you-believe-it expression.

She studies the card. "I think you should go."

"You do?"

"Why not? It might help you."

"Domestic violence?"

"All I'm saying is, you're super down about all this, and I don't blame you at all, but the support group could be good. You could just check it out. If you don't like it..." She hoists her shoulders.

Her phone chimes. She scans the incoming text. "He said yes!"

For the rest of the shopping trip, she frets over where they should go, what she should wear. I reply automatically, but I'm mulling over what she said.

Maybe I should check out this group, just once.

When I get home, I call the twenty-four-hour hotline number on the card to find out when the support groups are.

"I'd like to attend the support group."

"Do you have or had an abusive partner?"

I swallow. "Yes."

"We have several meetings a week." She gives me the schedule and address. "We don't have a sign or a street number to make it more difficult for abusers to locate. They come here, tracking down the women. If you see any men hanging around the gate or sitting in a car outside, let someone know immediately."

My fingers tighten around the phone. That's Kieran exactly. I know then that I absolutely have to go to this support group.

I go on Saturday morning. After driving around the block a couple times, I figure the nondescript, boxy building has to be Journeys. I'm buzzed through a locked gate under the eye of a security camera and knock on the unmarked door the voice on the intercom directed me to. The door cracks open. Someone checks me out, and I'm let in. It all seems very cloak-and-dagger, but I remember how Kieran stalked and ambushed me. They're right to do this, I think.

"Is this the support group?" I ask.

"It is. Is this your first time here?" The woman's face looks young, but she has long, grey hair. I nod. "Welcome. Take a seat and sign in." She smiles and gives me a paper and pen as I slide into a chair at a conference table where eight women sit. There's a box of tissues in front of me. I notice they're around the table. I jot down my name and age and look around.

Paperbacks and toys fill several bookcases. A handwritten sign says, "Shelter donations accepted here." An easel displays a poster board: "Wheel of Domestic Violence" with arrows pointing around the circle: "Build Up," "Explosion," "Make Up."

The woman speaks. "Let's get started. My name is Casey. I'm the facilitator for this evening's session. You can share if you want to, or just listen. We go in order of arrival.

"I remind everyone to refrain from commenting while each person is sharing. Let's see—Sandra, you're first. Would you like to share?"

She looks at a slightly chubby woman sitting next to me. Her jaw is a scary shade of purple and blue, just like my cheek was.

"Jeez, where do I begin? I guess with this." Sandra points to her face. "I was cooking rice the other night for dinner, and I tested some to see if it was done. I tapped the fork against the side of the pot, you know, to shake the water off it. Vinny, that's my boyfriend, we live together, got mad and told me to stop the noise, so I did. But then I dropped the fork in the sink, and he yelled at me to stop making so much noise, that it bothered him.

"I told him you can't make dinner without making noise. He got up from the table and shoved me. I went flying across the kitchen and fell against the handle of the fridge. So now I have this black-and-blue. I feel so embarrassed to go outside. Makeup barely covers it. I love Vinny, but not when he's like this. I got him to leave this time, but now he wants to come back. The thing is I miss him. I know I can't let him do this to me, but it's hard, it's really hard to keep him away when I miss him so much. I just wish he wouldn't do this stuff, but he does."

Change a few details and it's my story. I can hardly believe it.

"Sandra, would you like feedback?" Casey asks. Sandra nods. "Coralee?"

A woman wearing glasses speaks. "You gotta stay strong, girl. You can't let him back in or he do the same shit to you over and over. They never stop. And yeah, it's hard when you miss 'em, but eventually there's nothing good left to miss because the abuse just gets worse and worse. That's what you gotta think of anytime you feel yourself getting weak."

"Ronit?"

"It's great you got him to leave," says a plain-faced woman with a scarf covering her hair. "He's going to beg and beg you to come back, but you have to think of what he did to you."

"Li Mai?"

"How can you live with someone who doesn't like kitchen noise? He's just crazy," a petite woman says. "If you let him back in, you'll be scared all the time."

"Anyone else?" Casey looks around. No one raises a hand so she continues. "Vinny's in the makeup phase after the explosion." She points to the Wheel of Domestic Violence poster. "He's promising to change, saying it'll never happen again, giving you gifts and flowers. That phase can last quite a long time sometimes, but things will inevitably build up inside him and lead to another explosion of violence. The question is, do you want to expose yourself to that violence again?

"Don't feel guilty for missing him. Of course, you're going to miss him. You fell in love with him for a reason. Batterers don't show that side of themselves at first. Once they have you emotionally hooked, they start the abuse. If you stay, they feel licensed to abuse you more and more."

I'm stunned. She just described my relationship with Kieran perfectly.

"Thank you," Sandra whispers, looking round the table at everyone.

"Coralee, would you like to share?"

Coralee pushes her glasses up her nose. "I'm going to court next week. You know why? I spit at my husband after he took away my car keys. He called the cops and filed against me for battery, says I need to be taught a lesson. *I* need to be taught a lesson! I never filed a charge on him even though the cops came to our house many times, called by the neighbors because of him yelling and breaking things.

"The other night he smashed my porcelain collection because I was late coming home after picking up our daughter." Coralee lowers her voice and picks her cuticles, which are raw and red. "I'm afraid to leave because he's says he'll get me declared an unfit mother and get custody of our daughter. He says he'll never let me see her."

As each woman speaks, I recognize something in her story that happened to me.

Brenda's ex-husband blames her because he can't get a job after she called the cops on him and now he has a criminal record, just like Kieran blamed me for being broke when he spent the money.

Li Mai's ex-boyfriend was wildly jealous and insisted on having sex with her before she went to work every morning so she wouldn't be tempted by men at her office. That was as crazy as me having sex with Joe Favola in his bathroom at the party.

Griselda's boyfriend stalked her after she broke up with him and posted nude photos and obscene things about her on social media. "I got some of it off, but there's still some stuff on the internet," she says. "I don't think I'll ever get it all off. I feel so humiliated."

Kieran followed me, posted that video, called Clarissa and Tyler. And I feel humiliated.

The other women and Casey offer support and advice. "Domestic abuse is all about control," Casey says. "Abusers seek complete control of their partners through fear and intimidation. The most dangerous time is when the partner leaves the abuser. That prospect of losing control can provoke the abuser into an extreme rage. They'll do just about anything to reassert their control, including kill."

Labor Day weekend rushes to my mind.

It's my turn. "This is my first time here, and I'm just ... I'm really amazed. I'm hearing my own story over and over again. Everything that happened to everyone here has happened to me, and I didn't even want to come here tonight. I can't believe I'm a victim of domestic violence."

The words detonate inside me. I disintegrate into huge chest-wracking sobs that I can't stop. Someone slides the tissue box in front of me. I pluck a couple and try to gather myself. Everybody silently waits. I feel waves of sympathy and compassion coming from them. "I'm sorry. I guess it just got to me."

I tell them my story, twisting the wet tissues in my fingers. By the time I get to the police complaint, I've made a mole hill of shreds on the table. "I feel like such a fool. At the beginning, I thought he was like an angel sent to me from heaven. I really thought that."

"Would you like feedback, Chloe?" Casey says. I nod.

"These guys are real smart," Li Mai says. "They find your vulnerability and exploit it. The problem is we're not trained to look for the signs of an abuser so sometimes we can't see those red flags.

"My boyfriend just wouldn't leave me alone at first. I thought it was because he was so in love with me, that's what he told me anyway. What I didn't see was that he was trying to control me, but how was I to know? Nobody taught me anything about this."

"I can see you're a really strong woman," Sandra says. "You're also very compassionate to try to help Kieran. Some people can't be helped. It's sad, but it's true. You've just got to look at this as a learning experience for the future, so you don't make the same mistake."

Griselda speaks up. "One of the best things about this place is that nobody judges you because we've all gone through it. You see you're not alone in this. Other women have gone through the same thing."

"Chloe, I'm so glad you came," Casey says. "It's not easy to come here. It takes courage, and you have plenty of that. This type of legal abuse is not uncommon. Instead of you filing a complaint or getting a restraining order against the batterer, he files against you to make you look like the crazy abuser. He has projected onto you all his own actions. What you described is textbook abuser harassment."

Fresh tears prick my eyes, but now they're tears of relief. I want to hug Casey.

"It's only natural that you miss him. Don't feel bad about that. You're grieving the loss of a relationship, of someone who was a big part of your life. It's like a mourning process, but you're strong. You will get through this. Domestic violence happens to women of all social classes, races, religions, ages, professions and educational levels. It can happen to anyone, believe me."

I am overcome by their words. No questions, no judgment. They know exactly what I've been through.

We go around the table and say "affirmations," sayings like "I am strong," "I have the right not to be abused by my partner," "I am worthy." The meeting ends.

I wish I'd found Journeys months ago. It's precisely where I belong.

Twenty

The support group makes me feel a whole lot better, but I still have this police investigation hanging over me like a giant dumbbell waiting to drop. Mom keeps telling me it'll be over soon, but it's taking forever.

I can barely concentrate in school and at work. What else is Kieran making up about me? Who else is he getting to tell lies? I feel like a wreck. Now I know why Mom took those pills. I secretly wish she hadn't flushed all of them away.

I arrive home from the paper one day when Mom comes in the kitchen, her face grave. "The detectives finally interviewed me today. About time. It's been two weeks since the complaint. They told me they're short-staffed."

Alarm ripples through me. "What did you tell them?"

"The truth."

"Do they believe me or Kieran?"

"They didn't say. They just said they should be wrapping up the investigation soon."

Typical cop speak. A stone of dread forms in the pit of my stomach. "They'll believe him. I know they will."

Mom hugs me. "Have faith," she says.

"You don't know Kieran, Mom. He always finds a way to get

what he wants. He always wins."

At lunch the next day, Clarissa, Jade and Morgan babble on while all I can think about is how the detectives are going to believe Kieran over me. Why wouldn't they? He was the one who made the complaint, after all. My defense—that he's twisting around the things he did to me—seems a weak, knee-jerk response. I'm simply pointing the finger back because someone's pointing at me, like a little kid saying, "She pulled my hair first."

During my interview, Detective Bridges even implied that he didn't believe me when he asked why I didn't report Kieran if he did all those things that I said he did. I just never thought of it, that's why. Who thinks of going to the cops? The answer to my own question glares at me: Kieran, that's who. But where did he get the idea?

My attention reluctantly turns to the conversation. "Claudio wants to go ice skating on a pond. He's never done that before," Clarissa is saying.

"Never?" Jade says.

"They don't have a lot of frozen ponds in the south of Spain where he's from."

I tune out. Ice skating dates are trivial compared to the prospect of my life destructing.

I suddenly remember Kieran mentioning neighbors calling cops on his parents when he was a kid. That must be how he got familiar with police and witness statements. That's one mystery solved, but a bigger one remains.

Where did he dig up this Zoe Kovac, who swears she saw scratches on Kieran's face—his only "evidence" against me of "violence"? The bell rings. I gather up my books and shuffle off to class.

At work, Marion has some names for me to run court searches on. She's still trying to nail down the developer bribe story. I'm glad to work silently at the computer and not talk to anyone. I'm also glad to be scrutinizing someone else's life and not my own for a while.

When I get home, Mom's sculpting in her studio, so I grab a

box of cheese crackers from the kitchen and flop on my bed as I stuff them in my mouth.

Zoe Kovac invades my head again. Who is she? Is she Kieran's new girlfriend? Or maybe Janice Rickenbacher is. Why would Zoe lie about me when she doesn't even know me? Wait. My hand freezes as I go to grab a handful of crackers. Of course, I can find out who she is. Investigating people is exactly what I've been doing for Marion at the newspaper.

Tossing the box aside, I jump up and switch on the laptop on my desk. Facebook is the logical place to start. I key in her name. Amazingly, three "Zoe Kovacs" pop up in Quebec, New Orleans and Indian Valley, New Jersey. Bingo! I click on that Zoe, and luckily, her page is public.

Her photo shows a plain face with dirty blond hair that skirts her shoulders. She's twenty-six years old, no employment listed. Doesn't she work at Yamamoto's? She just joined Facebook in October and has only twenty-three friends. I scroll through the list and see a name that almost knocks me off my seat.

Janice Rickenbacher. Could she be the connection between Kieran and Zoe? It sounds logical, but I didn't even know Kieran knew Janice. Since I blocked Kieran, I can't see if he's Zoe's "friend," or Janice's "friend." It doesn't matter.

I google Zoe Kovac, but there are no results. I sit back and gnaw the pad of my thumb. I can search court records, but I don't know what that's going to prove. I hear Marion's voice: *You never know what you'll find or what you can use, so look up everything.*

I call up the New Jersey Superior Court webpage and plug in the name in the "criminal" search field. The screen states, Loading, loading. I know from my searches at work, it means there's something on her. My palms sprout sweat.

Her name appears followed by a list. I scroll down, hardly believing what I'm reading.

Shoplifting-guilty,
Prostitution-guilty
Drug possession-guilty

Probation violation-guilty
False representation to a law enforcement officer-guilty
Burglary-dismissed
Theft-dismissed
Possession of a false driver's license-dismissed
Forgery-guilty
Issuing check on insufficient funds-guilty

Zoe Kovac is a criminal!

Wait, is it the same Zoe Kovac? The court page lists her birth date. I check her Facebook page. The same date is listed as her birthday. It's her. Triumph zooms through me, followed almost instantly by a crash. So what? How does this affect my case?

I put that quandary aside for a minute. I should run the names of the other "witnesses," too. Like Marion says, check all links.

I type in "Joseph Favola Jr." He comes right up.

Drug possession. Guilty. 2 yrs probation, $5,000 fine.

So, what Kieran told me is true, but Kieran also said Joe is still using meth. It occurs to me that Joe may have written the statement because Kieran threatened to report him to the cops or his parents. It sounds like something Kieran would do.

I check Janice Rickenbacher. Nothing.

I pause. I know I have to search for the person who I probably should've looked up months ago. My stomach clenches, and I mistype **Kieran Dubrowski** and his birth date twice before I enter it correctly. I hold my breath.

Nothing comes up under criminal. Under civil, a filing is listed from six weeks ago.

Eviction. Claudette Stein, landlord, vs. Kieran Dubrowski.

Claudette kicked him out of the camper. I guess that's no surprise.

My head is whirling. I've discovered a lot, but nothing that really proves anything for my case. I return to the mysterious Zoe Kovac. I can't believe Kieran could be involved with such a person. I slowly read through the details of her offenses and realize she was in prison for her last five crimes.

Disposition of case: 2 years, 3 months, custody of the state Department of Corrections.

Something seems off. I calculate the dates—she should have been in prison until October, but she said she saw Kieran's scratches in September. Prisoners sometimes get time off for good behavior. Maybe she got out early.

Or maybe she lied.

I have to find out when she was released from prison, but how? I sit back.

Think, Chloe.

Mom calls me for dinner.

My head is aching, and I decide to take a break. Maybe something will come to me.

Over shepherd's pie, I tell Mom what I found. "But I'm missing the key information. Without her release date, I don't have much."

"You could ask Detective Goldsmith. Police must be able to find that out."

I shrug dejectedly.

"I don't know if she'd really do it. It seems like she believes Kieran."

"Hang on. Zoe was convicted of false representation to a police officer—that means she lied to police. She's a convicted liar," Mom says.

"Is that what that means?"

"That should count for something. I'll call Carol in the morning. See what she suggests."

I trudge up to my bedroom and sit at the computer again. I google How to find out prison release date? Nothing comes up. I groan. I can't believe I got this far only to be stymied. After a few more attempts at searches, I give up. I'm more depressed than ever.

Kieran is going to win.

⋙———⋘

My eyes open, but it's still dark. I check the time. Four forty-three. I lie back but the case re-enters my mind. I know I'm not going to fall back to sleep, so I get up. On my way to the bathroom, I pass my laptop and idly punch a key. Zoe's court record displays on the screen where I left it:

Custody of the state Department of Corrections.

I lean on the chair back and study it. The state Department of Corrections. It has a website. I hear Marion's voice again, *Leave no stone unturned.* I'd left a stone. I sit and call up the web page.

The tabs say, Visit Restrictions, Offender Statistics, Frequently Asked Questions and Offender Search.

I feel a spark of hope. That's what I need.

A search form for current and former inmates pops up. There are fields for name, sex, hair color, eye color, race, county of commitment, date of birth.

Thanks to Zoe Kovac's Facebook photo and court record, I have all that information. I fill it out and press submit.

I can't take my eyes off the screen as the website processes the data. *Come on, come on.* Three seconds later, the name **Zoe Yvonne Kovac** appears with her list of crimes.

Status: Released.

I pound my desk. No date!

Her inmate number is boldfaced, indicating there's another link. I click it.

The screen fills with her mugshot and **Incarceration History**.

I scan the page. At the end, it says,

Date out of custody: October 23.

Oh my god, that's it! I reel. She was in prison at the time when she swore she saw Kieran's scratched face! I now have proof she's lying.

"Mo-om!" I race into her bedroom. "Mom, wake up. You have to see this! Kieran lied! I can prove that he lied!"

She stirs groggily. "What?"

I thrust the laptop at her. "Look what I found."

I explain my search, and she snaps out of her haze. "You just flushed his case down the toilet."

"I've got to get over to the police station now."

"It's five in the morning. They're not going to be there yet."

"But they told you they're finishing up the investigation soon. I need to get this to them before they close the case."

Mom throws off her covers. "I'll get coffee on."

I print out all the court records I found, shower and dress, and fly out the back door.

"Wait, I'll come with you," Mom calls.

"I can't wait."

I pull into the visitor's parking at the police station and rush in. Breathlessly, I ask for Detective Goldsmith or Bridges at the front desk. The officer makes a phone call.

"They're due in at seven," he says.

"I'll wait." It's six-twenty. I sit on the bench and take out my phone to call Mom. I remember I have that photo of me all bruised up in my phone. I can show the detectives that, too. Why didn't I think of that before? I'm such an idiot. I take out my notebook and make a list of things I have to tell the police.

"Chloe? You wanted to see me?" I look up. Detective Goldsmith is approaching, holding a coffee cup. Her hair is still damp.

"I have evidence that Kieran and his witness lied."

"What've you got?"

I hand her the printouts. "Zoe Kovac was actually in prison when she said she saw scratches on Kieran's face. Here's her court record and her prison history. She was released October 23, but she said she saw the scratches in September. And she's a convicted liar. Look, guilty of false representation to a police officer."

Goldsmith scrutinizes the papers. "We know about her record, but prison commitment and release dates aren't in our database. I'll have to verify this date with Corrections."

I hand her Joe's court record. "And Joe Favola? He's on probation for meth, but Kieran said he's still using. I think he threatened Joe with reporting him if he didn't say what Kieran wanted him to."

She sips her coffee. "We're aware of his probation. If he's using again, that could certainly be a problem."

"And I have a photo of myself after Labor Day, when I told you he shoved me, and I fell." I show her the picture and the date it was taken.

"Why didn't you show me this before?"

"I guess I wasn't thinking clearly. Besides, it's not something I was trying to remember."

"Can you email me that photo now?"

"Are you going to check this out?"

"We will. Thanks for bringing it in, Chloe."

I email her the photo as she disappears behind the door into the interior of the police station. I can't help but feel crestfallen as I walk out. I hoped she'd say something like, "Case dismissed. We'll throw Kieran in jail for what he did to you."

All I can do now is wait. Again.

Twenty-One

Two weeks pass and there's no news about the investigation. I grow gloomier.

"I know what I found isn't going to count. It was all an epic waste of time. I shouldn't have even tried," I say at lunch one day.

"The detective said she'd check it out and that's what she's doing. It takes time to do all that investigation stuff," Clarissa says as I stare at my club sandwich lying like a corpse on my tray.

"It didn't take me that much time."

"She probably has rapes and murders to solve. I'm sure they're the priority," Morgan says.

"And drug busts," Jade adds.

"But this is my life!"

"She's probably embarrassed she didn't think to check prison records," Morgan says.

"She should hire you, Chloe," Jade says. "Maybe you should be a detective instead of a reporter."

"They're going to believe Kieran. I just know it."

"I bet they won't," Clarissa says.

"Three more days until winter break," Jade says.

"Can't wait," Morgan says. "Ski slopes here I come. The cutest guys are skiers."

The bell rings. There's a massive scraping of chairs in the cafeteria as everyone heads out. I join the exodus.

When I arrive home, a car with New York plates sits in the driveway. Dad? Another car is parked at the curb. I hurry in.

Mom's in the kitchen. "Chloe, the detectives are here to talk to you about the case. Dad's here, too."

"Are they going to arrest me?"

"I don't think so."

"Why is Dad here?"

"I called him when the detectives phoned."

"And you didn't call me?"

"I didn't want you to panic. I wanted you to finish the school day."

We enter the living room. I squeeze between Mom and Dad on the couch. The detectives sit in the armchairs across from us.

The Christmas tree is still naked in the corner. I haven't felt like decorating it despite Mom bugging me.

Detective Goldsmith looks me in the eye.

"Chloe, you gave us crucial information. I admit our progress on this investigation was slow because of our manpower shortage. We've got a huge case backlog at the moment and a lot of major crimes to investigate so smaller cases sometimes get put on the back burner. It's not fair, I know, but sometimes that's how it is. So, your research was a big help in pointing us in the right direction." She takes a breath.

"I confirmed Zoe Kovac's prison sentence with the state Department of Corrections. She was, in fact, incarcerated when she claimed to have seen scratches on Kieran's face."

My heart leaps. Mom grips my arm, and Dad gives me a one-armed side hug.

"We confronted Ms. Kovac with the discrepancy. She said she was confused about the dates. We pressed her on details of what she saw, and we did not find her version of events to be credible."

"She also told us," Bridges adds, "that Kieran is obsessed with revenge over the breakup, and said he wanted to ruin you."

I gulp.

"He did almost ruin her," Mom says. "She's just starting out in life. She has her whole future in front of her, and this sick guy…" Her voice catches.

"Bonnie, it's okay," Dad says.

"It's all very well for you to say, you weren't even here, Doug." Mom wipes her eyes.

Goldsmith continues. "We also spoke to Joseph Favola. We pressed him, using the fact that he's on probation and is therefore obligated to cooperate with any police investigation. He admitted to signing a statement that Kieran wrote for him but denied using any illicit substance. However, we notified his probation officer of that possibility."

"What about Janice Rickenbacher? Why did she sign?" I ask.

"Her parents are bringing her into the station tomorrow," Bridges says. "Like Favola, she didn't specifically lie about witnessing violence, but we're going to give her a severe warning about going along with schemes to harm people and wasting police time."

I ask the biggest question of all. "What did Kieran say?"

"He stuck to his story and insisted it was all true, that Kovac got the dates wrong and so on," Goldsmith said.

"We found numerous discrepancies in his story, as well," Bridges said.

"The upshot is we're dropping the case," Goldsmith says.

Elation fills me to bursting. I hug Mom.

"What's going to happen to Kieran?" Dad asks.

"We're charging him with filing a false police report," Goldsmith says. "We don't take this stuff lightly. This is a significant drain on our already strained resources."

"Will he go to jail?" I ask.

"He'll probably get probation. He has no criminal record," Bridges says.

"We'll also recommend that he participate in a program for domestic batterers," Goldsmith adds.

"He could use that," Mom says.

Goldsmith's eyes bore into mine. "Chloe, if anyone is abusive to you in any way, whether it's a shove or stalking, go to the police immediately. File a report, start a paper trail on them. Don't feel sorry for them or embarrassed. It's important that you protect yourself so if something serious happens, you have evidence to back you up and we can move on them."

"We've had cases where women have been killed by abusive boyfriends," Bridges says.

I nod, feeling small.

"We won't take any more of your time." Goldsmith stands. "Chloe, you did impressive work."

"You should be a detective," Bridges says.

"She's going to be a journalist," Dad says.

"She'll be a good one," Goldsmith adds.

We walk to the front door and say goodbye. Sadness suddenly overwhelms me.

"You don't seem that happy," Dad says as he shuts the door.

"I am, but I feel sad that this whole thing happened in the first place."

"Hopefully, Kieran will get the help he needs now," Mom says. "Maybe some good will come of this."

Dad draws me into an embrace. "I am so incredibly proud that you're my daughter."

I hug him back, inhaling the slightly spicy aroma of aftershave, the dry-cleaning scent of his suit, the faint tang of his body odor—the smell of my father.

I text the news to Clarissa, Jade and Morgan. Forty-five minutes later, the doorbell rings. It's them, holding a cake box.

"Congratulations Chloe!" they chorus.

We ignore my parents, who are arguing over china and crystal in the dining room, and go into the kitchen.

Clarissa opens the box with a flourish. "Cupcakes from the Cupcakerie—vanilla filled with strawberries and cream. The best."

"Tell us everything, Chloe," Jade says.

We sit at the kitchen table and demolish the cupcakes as I tell them what the detectives said.

"This is better than a TV show," Morgan says.

"Kieran is such a moron," Clarissa says. "He totally underestimated you and overestimated himself."

"A total asshole is more like it," Morgan says. "I hope he goes to jail. And that Zoe whatever her name is. You have the last cupcake, Chloe."

A brainwave hits me as I bite into it. "I'm going to ask Marion about writing a story on Indian Valley detectives not having money to investigate cases."

They all laugh.

Ms. Margolis hands back our poetry assignments the day before winter break. I hold my breath. A big "A+ Please see me" is penned in red across the top of mine. What's up with that?

I nervously shuffle to her desk at the end of class. She looks up and smiles. I relax.

"I'd like to publish your poems in ValleyScape, the school literary magazine. They're really brave and impactful. Merry Christmas, Chloe."

My face prickles with heat. I actually skip down the hall to my next class.

On Christmas Eve, I go to a support group at Journeys and share about my victory.

"When one woman stands up to an abuser, it's like all of us are doing it," Brenda says.

"We know how hard it was for you to do that," Sandra says.

"You got guts, girl," Coralee says.

After the meeting, the women gather round me, asking me how they can look up their boyfriends' court records.

I go to the paper for a few hours to help Marion finalize the holiday edition then head home. Dad's rental car is in the drive. Tyler's sitting in the kitchen, feet propped on the table, shoving gummy bears into his mouth from a bag in his hand.

A large suitcase and several bags are next to him. The sound of fierce parental voices come from upstairs.

"What's up, Ty?"

"I'm moving back."

"How come?"

"New York's lame."

"What about Dad?"

He shrugs. "I like it here better."

"And the poster of the babe?"

"Whatever."

"Cool."

I hold out my cupped hand, and he pours candy into it. I shove the lot into my mouth and chew.

"Why haven't you decorated the tree yet?" he asks.

"Waiting for you, dumbo." I pick up his feet and drop them on the floor.

We drag the boxes of Christmas ornaments up from the basement and dig into them. I hang a little elf from a branch.

"Remember this?" Tyler dangles a goofy clay Santa I made in fourth grade.

"You broke it because you were jealous when Mom put it on the tree."

"And you threw a wobbly til Mom glued it back together."

The tree fills up with ornaments. As we hang them, we exchange memories and stories of each trinket and good-naturedly argue over details that we remember differently. The last piece is the golden-haired angel I fix to the top. Then, we drape the branches with silver tinsel. Tyler plugs in the lights. Sparkles dance on the tree.

"What do you want for Christmas?" Tyler asks.

I sit on my legs tucked under me. "I think I already got everything I want."

Twenty-Two

MAY

beauty is in the eye

i bought silvered sneakers so my feet would
look like yours
nylon wrapped and pointy-toed
i play 'september' so loud
my ears hurt with the memory
of speeding down the highway
in a tangle of hair and falsetto laughter
our first date
you leaned back on your elbow
and drank me with your smile
beauty is in the eye
you said
i buried the tip of my nose
in the pockets of your cheeks
to inhale your skin
i tucked
shanks of hair behind your ears
just how i like it

but i had to leave
before i saw you swim
before i ate an egg
from the hollow in your breastbone
before we waltzed in the surf
all i can do now
is pass the park
where we played
baseball caps backwards
sweatshirts tied around waists
and look down at my feet

The noise in the cafeteria fades into a dull seashell roar as I read my poem in the literary review. I experience an odd out-of-body sensation for a moment. Did I really write that?

"It's amazing," Clarissa says.

"Totally romantic," agrees Jade.

"I would love someone to write a poem about me like that," Morgan says.

"You know this may sound really, really weird," Clarissa says, "but after reading that, I understand why you were with Kieran, why you stayed with him. You had an awesome love, like the real deal, before it turned bad, I mean."

"You were so totally into each other," Jade says.

"Truth is I don't know if I can date anyone ever again," I say.

"You will," Morgan says.

"I wonder what Kieran would think of it," Clarissa says.

"It's online, so who knows, he might see it one day," I say.

"Maybe it's better he doesn't see it," Jade says. "He might use it as an excuse to pop up again."

"God forbid," Clarissa says with a dramatic shudder.

"When I wrote the poem, I kind of wanted Kieran to see it. I wanted him to know how hard our breakup was on me, that I was as shattered by it as he was. But now I don't care. I wrote it for me, not him."

"Have you seen him around?" Jade asks.

"Nope, but I don't exactly go looking for him."

"Burger-O-Rama's out of bounds and forget even driving past Yamamoto's," Clarissa says. "The other day, I was with Chloe and we were going to drive by there and suddenly she turns off. I'm like, 'What the…?' Then I figured it out." Her eyes are warm as she looks at me and I know she's not saying it to be a jerk.

"It's just too painful to go by places I went with him, plus I don't want to run into him," I say. "

"Like the time when we came out of the movies and he was standing next to your car in the parking lot," Morgan says. "We hid in the coffee place until he left. You went all shaky and had to sit down."

"Don't remind me," I say.

"It's hard, Indian Valley being so small," Jade says.

"But you'll be off to Boston University soon," Clarissa sings.

"Incoming," Morgan mutters. "Stage right."

Trevor Papadopoulos approaches our table, lunch tray in hand. "Nice poem, Chloe."

"Thanks." I twitch an embarrassed smile.

"Coming to the yearbook end-of-year party?"

"Wouldn't miss it."

He flashes a row of white teeth in a smile and goes to sit with a bunch of senior boys.

Jade elbows me. "He likes you."

"He does not. We're just on yearbook together."

Clarissa twists her mouth. "He does, Chloe. You should go out with him."

"Or throw him my way. He's too cute to waste," Morgan says.

"You have to get over Kieran some time," Clarissa says.

"But who's going to want me now? I'm like … damaged goods or something. I mean, if I tell a guy about this, what are they going to think of me?"

"They're going to think you're brave and smart because you got yourself out of it and beat his stupid complaint," Clarissa says.

That evening, I decide to go to the support group. I haven't been for a little while, but the poem and the conversation at lunch stirred up the dust of settled feelings.

"I feel like I'm stained with some kind of black mark that I'm going to carry on me forever," I share. "What if there's something wrong with me, and I make a bad choice again and I end up with another Kieran?"

"Anybody who knows you, knows it was all lies," Casey says. "Your family or friends didn't believe it for a second, did they?" I shake my head. "And now you've learned to look for the red flags, and second, you have us. Whenever you have any kind of fear or doubt, we're here for you. We're not going anywhere."

She's right. As I drive home, I think that maybe I'll never fully get over Kieran. You go through an emotional earthquake like that, and it's going to stay with you. But you have to stop being afraid of it.

Gripping the steering wheel, I drive past my turnoff and into downtown. I force myself to continue down Indian Valley Road. Then I see the sign, "Yamamoto's Garden Center," and the weirdest thing happens—all my nerves, fear and anxiety, my embarrassment and humiliation, vanish. A calmness wraps around me like angel wings.

As the sign disappears in the rearview mirror, I know that's where it's staying.

I call Clarissa. "Let's meet for a burger."

"Where do you want to go?"

"Burger-O-Rama."

"Seriously?"

"Seriously."

As I pull into the parking lot, I steel myself for the knife of memory, but the only thing that happens is a text from Trevor Papadopoulos as I wait for Clarissa.

I know this is really late notice, but would you go to prom with me?

I smile and type, Yes.

⸻

I look in the mirror and gaze at the full-cheeked girl staring back at me. She stands tall in a strapless apricot satin gown, nails glossy in a matching color, hair swept in an updo, a smile not on her face but in her face.

Is that me, for real?

I pick up my phone and scroll through the photos until I find that other girl—the one sad and lost with a fat eye and a black bruise. I press "delete" and she's gone.

I look in the mirror—that girl is me. Then I walk downstairs into the sunlight.

Acknowledgments

This novel was inspired by my own experience. The incidents in the book are fictional although some bear close resemblance to actual events. The dialogue is also close to real conversations.

Although this experience happened to me as an adult, I was moved to write about it for a teenage audience because no one teaches young people about the red flags of abuse, such as pressure for a quick involvement, isolation and jealousy. Once you know these signs, they are clearly spotted, and it is much easier to get away from an abuser early on. But when you don't know the signs, they can be misread as the Hollywood version of romance, which is what happened to Chloe.

I also wanted to write about the aftermath of the breakup of an abusive relationship, where I found most books about the subject end. If only it were so easy. Survivors know this stage is often the most difficult and dangerous part of the journey.

My undying thanks goes to Sojourn, whose pro bono legal clinic and support group provided me with succor and courage in my time of crisis. More than a decade later, I volunteered as a trained facilitator at those same support groups to offer strength and hope as others did for me.

If you know someone in an abusive relationship, offer help not judgment. It will be much appreciated. If you are in such a relationship, know that you are not alone. You can get out, but please seek help first. Call a hotline, confide in a trusted friend or family member and form a plan to exit safely.

About the Author

Christina Hoag is a former journalist who has had her laptop searched by Colombian guerrillas, phone tapped in Venezuela, was suspected of drug trafficking in Guyana, hid under a car to evade Guatemalan soldiers, and posed as a nun to get inside a Caracas jail. She has interviewed gang members, bank robbers, thieves and thugs in prisons, shantytowns and slums, not to forget billionaires and presidents, some of whom fall into the previous categories. Now she writes about such characters in her fiction.

She lives in Southern California, where she has taught creative writing at a prison and to at-risk teen girls and has facilitated a support group for survivors of domestic violence. For more about her, see ChristinaHoag.com.

If you liked this book, please help spread the word and leave a review or rating on Amazon and other book review sites.

The author is available for speaking engagements. Please get in touch via her website, ChristinaHoag.com.

Girl on the Brink is also available on Audible
and in Spanish, *Chica al borde.*

www.ingramcontent.com/pod-product-compliance
Lightning Source LLC
Chambersburg PA
CBHW061247310726
48971CB00007B/2258